［匈］威利·波加尼（Willy Pogán）所作《鲁拜集》插图（1930）选之一

[匈] 威利·波加尼 (Willy Pogán) 所作《鲁拜集》插图 (1930) 选之二

［匈］威利·波加尼（Willy Pogán）所作《鲁拜集》插图（1930）选之三

［匈］威利·波加尼（Willy Pogán）所作《鲁拜集》插图（1930）选之四

[匈]威利·波加尼（Willy Pogán）所作《鲁拜集》插图（1930）选之五

[匈]威利·波加尼（Willy Pogán）所作《鲁拜集》插图（1930）选之六

［匈］威利·波加尼（Willy Pogán）所作《鲁拜集》插图（1930）选之七

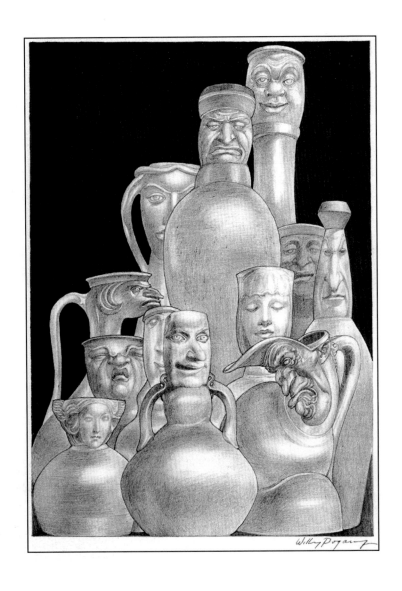

[匈]威利·波加尼（Willy Pogán）所作《鲁拜集》插图（1930）选之八

莪默絕句集譯箋

[古波斯]莪默·伽亞謨◎原撰
[英]菲茨傑拉德 溫菲爾德◎英譯
眭謙◎漢譯及箋

華東師範大學出版社

自題 _1

自序 _1

甲集 _1

 其一 _3

 其二 _3

 其三 _4

 其四 _4

 其五 _5

 其六 _6

 其七 _7

 其八 _8

 其九 _8

 其十 _9

 其十一 _10

 其十二 _11

 其十三 _11

 其十四 _12

 其十五 _13

 其十六 _13

 其十七 _14

 其十八 _15

 其十九 _15

 其二十 _16

 其二十一 _17

 其二十二 _18

 其二十三 _18

 其二十四 _19

 其二十五 _19

 其二十六 _20

 其二十七 _20

 其二十八 _21

 其二十九 _22

 其三十 _23

 其三十一 _23

 其三十二 _24

 其三十三 _24

 其三十四 _25

 其三十五 _25

 其三十六 _26

 其三十七 _26

 其三十八 _27

 其三十九 _28

其四十 _28
其四十一 _29
其四十二 _30
其四十三 _30
其四十四 _31
其四十五 _31
其四十六 _32
其四十七 _32
其四十八 _33
其四十九 _33
其五十 _34
其五十一 _34
其五十二 _35
其五十三 _36
其五十四 _36
其五十五 _37
其五十六 _37
其五十七 _38
其五十八 _38
其五十九 _39
其六十 _40
其六十一 _40
其六十二 _41
其六十三 _41
其六十四 _42
其六十五 _42
其六十六 _43

其六十七 _43
其六十八 _44
其六十九 _44
其七十 _45
其七十一 _46
其七十二 _46
其七十三 _47
其七十四 _47
其七十五 _48
其七十六 _49
其七十七 _49
其七十八 _50
其七十九 _50
其八十 _51
其八十一 _51
其八十二 _52
其八十三 _53
其八十四 _53
其八十五 _54
其八十六 _54
其八十七 _55
其八十八 _55
其八十九 _56
其九十 _56
其九十一 _57
其九十二 _58
其九十三 _58

其九十四 _59

其九十五 _59

其九十六 _60

其九十七 _60

其九十八 _61

其九十九 _61

其一百 _62

其一百零一 _62

外編

一、見於菲氏譯介諸篇 _64

二、見於注釋諸篇 _65

三、僅見首版諸篇 _66

四、僅見第二版諸篇 _67

五、異譯諸篇 _71

菲茨傑拉德傳 _80

乙集 _87

其一 _89

其二 _89

其三 _89

其四 _90

其五 _90

其六 _91

其七 _91

其八 _92

其九 _92

其十 _92

其十一 _93

其十二 _94

其十三 _94

其十四 _94

其十五 _95

其十六 _95

其十七 _96

其十八 _96

其十九 _97

其二十 _97

其二十一 _98

其二十二 _98

其二十三 _98

其二十四 _99

其二十五 _99

其二十六 _100

其二十七 _100

其二十八 _101

其二十九 _101

其三十 _102

其三十一 _102

其三十二 _102

其三十三 _103

其三十四 _103

其三十五 _104

其三十六 _104

其三十七 _105	其六十四 _117
其三十八 _105	其六十五 _118
其三十九 _106	其六十六 _118
其四十 _106	其六十七 _118
其四十一 _107	其六十八 _119
其四十二 _107	其六十九 _119
其四十三 _108	其七十 _120
其四十四 _108	其七十一 _120
其四十五 _109	其七十二 _120
其四十六 _109	其七十三 _121
其四十七 _110	其七十四 _121
其四十八 _110	其七十五 _122
其四十九 _110	其七十六 _122
其五十 _111	其七十七 _122
其五十一 _111	其七十八 _123
其五十二 _112	其七十九 _123
其五十三 _112	其八十 _123
其五十四 _113	其八十一 _124
其五十五 _113	其八十二 _124
其五十六 _114	其八十三 _124
其五十七 _114	其八十四 _125
其五十八 _114	其八十五 _125
其五十九 _115	其八十六 _126
其六十 _115	其八十七 _126
其六十一 _116	其八十八 _126
其六十二 _116	其八十九 _127
其六十三 _117	其九十 _127

其九十一 _128

其九十二 _128

其九十三 _128

其九十四 _129

其九十五 _129

其九十六 _130

其九十七 _130

其九十八 _130

其九十九 _131

其一百 _131

其一百零一 _131

其一百零二 _132

其一百零三 _132

其一百零四 _133

其一百零五 _133

其一百零六 _133

其一百零七 _134

其一百零八 _134

其一百零九 _135

其一百一十 _135

第一百一十一 _136

其一百一十二 _136

其一百一十三 _136

其一百一十四 _137

其一百一十五 _137

其一百一十六 _138

其一百一十七 _138

其一百一十八 _138

其一百一十九 _139

其一百二十 _139

其一百二十一 _140

其一百二十二 _141

其一百二十三 _141

其一百二十四 _142

其一百二十五 _142

其一百二十六 _142

其一百二十七 _143

其一百二十八 _143

其一百二十九 _143

其一百三十 _144

其一百三十一 _144

其一百三十二 _145

其一百三十三 _145

其一百三十四 _146

其一百三十五 _146

其一百三十六 _147

其一百三十七 _147

其一百三十八 _147

其一百三十九 _148

其一百四十 _148

其一百四十一 _149

其一百四十二 _149

其一百四十三 _149

其一百四十四 _150

其一百四十五 _150
其一百四十六 _151
其一百四十七 _151
其一百四十八 _152
其一百四十九 _152
其一百五十 _152
其一百五十一 _153
其一百五十二 _153
其一百五十三 _154
其一百五十四 _154
其一百五十五 _154
其一百五十六 _155
其一百五十七 _155
其一百五十八 _156
其一百五十九 _156
其一百六十 _157
其一百六十一 _157
其一百六十二 _157
其一百六十三 _158
其一百六十四 _158
其一百六十五 _158
其一百六十六 _159
其一百六十七 _159
其一百六十八 _159
其一百六十九 _160
其一百七十 _160
其一百七十一 _161

其一百七十二 _161
其一百七十三 _161
其一百七十四 _162
其一百七十五 _162
其一百七十六 _162
其一百七十七 _163
其一百七十八 _163
其一百七十九 _164
其一百八十 _164
其一百八十一 _165
其一百八十二 _165
其一百八十三 _165
其一百八十四 _166
其一百八十五 _166
其一百八十六 _167
其一百八十七 _167
其一百八十八 _167
其一百八十九 _168
其一百九十 _168
其一百九十一 _169
其一百九十二 _169
其一百九十三 _170
其一百九十四 _170
其一百九十五 _170
其一百九十六 _171
其一百九十七 _171
其一百九十八 _172

其一百九十九 _172
其二百 _173
其二百零一 _173
其二百零二 _174
其二百零三 _174
其二百零四 _175
其二百零五 _175
其二百零六 _176
其二百零七 _176
其二百零八 _177
其二百零九 _177
其二百一十 _178
其二百一十一 _178
其二百一十二 _179
其二百一十三 _179
其二百一十四 _179
其二百一十五 _180
其二百一十六 _180
其二百一十七 _181
其二百一十八 _181
其二百一十九 _182
其二百二十 _182
其二百二十一 _183
其二百二十二 _184
其二百二十三 _185
其二百二十四 _186
其二百二十五 _186

其二百二十六 _187
其二百二十七 _187
其二百二十八 _188
其二百二十九 _189
其二百三十 _189
其二百三十一 _190
其二百三十二 _190
其二百三十三 _191
其二百三十四 _192
其二百三十五 _192
其二百三十六 _193
其二百三十七 _193
其二百三十八 _194
其二百三十九 _194
其二百四十 _195
其二百四十一 _195
其二百四十二 _196
其二百四十三 _196
其二百四十四 _197
其二百四十五 _198
其二百四十六 _198
其二百四十七 _198
其二百四十八 _199
其二百四十九 _199
其二百五十 _200
其二百五十一 _200
其二百五十二 _201

其二百五十三 _201
其二百五十四 _202
其二百五十五 _202
其二百五十六 _203
其二百五十七 _203
其二百五十八 _204
其二百五十九 _204
其二百六十 _205
其二百六十一 _206
其二百六十二 _206
其二百六十三 _207
其二百六十四 _207
其二百六十五 _208
其二百六十六 _208
其二百六十七 _208
其二百六十八 _209
其二百六十九 _209
其二百七十 _210
其二百七十一 _210
其二百七十二 _211
其二百七十三 _211
其二百七十四 _212
其二百七十五 _212
其二百七十六 _213
其二百七十七 _213
其二百七十八 _214
其二百七十九 _214

其二百八十 _215
其二百八十一 _215
其二百八十二 _215
其二百八十三 _216
其二百八十四 _216
其二百八十五 _217
其二百八十六 _217
其二百八十七 _218
其二百八十八 _218
其二百八十九 _219
其二百九十 _219
其二百九十一 _220
其二百九十二 _220
其二百九十三 _220
其二百九十四 _221
其二百九十五 _221
其二百九十六 _222
其二百九十七 _222
其二百九十八 _223
其二百九十九 _223
其三百 _223
其三百零一 _224
其三百零二 _224
其三百零三 _225
其三百零四 _226
其三百零五 _226
其三百零六 _227

其三百零七 _227
其三百零八 _228
其三百零九 _228
其三百一十 _228
其三百一十一 _229
其三百一十二 _229
其三百一十三 _230
其三百一十四 _230
其三百一十五 _231
其三百一十六 _231
其三百一十七 _232
其三百一十八 _232
其三百一十九 _232
其三百二十 _233
其三百二十一 _233
其三百二十二 _234
其三百二十三 _234
其三百二十四 _234
其三百二十五 _235
其三百二十六 _235
其三百二十七 _236
其三百二十八 _236
其三百二十九 _236
其三百三十 _237
其三百三十一 _237
其三百三十二 _238
其三百三十三 _238

其三百三十四 _238
其三百三十五 _239
其三百三十六 _240
其三百三十七 _240
其三百三十八 _240
其三百三十九 _241
其三百四十 _241
其三百四十一 _242
其三百四十二 _242
其三百四十三 _243
其三百四十四 _243
其三百四十五 _244
其三百四十六 _245
其三百四十七 _245
其三百四十八 _246
其三百四十九 _246
其三百五十 _247
其三百五十一 _247
其三百五十二 _248
其三百五十三 _248
其三百五十四 _249
其三百五十五 _249
其三百五十六 _250
其三百五十七 _250
其三百五十八 _251
其三百五十九 _251
其三百六十 _251

其三百六十一 _252
其三百六十二 _252
其三百六十三 _253
其三百六十四 _253
其三百六十五 _253
其三百六十六 _254
其三百六十七 _254
其三百六十八 _255
其三百六十九 _255
其三百七十 _256
其三百七十一 _256
其三百七十二 _257
其三百七十三 _257
其三百七十四 _257
其三百七十五 _258
其三百七十六 _258
其三百七十七 _259
其三百七十八 _259
其三百七十九 _260
其三百八十 _260
其三百八十一 _261
其三百八十二 _261
其三百八十三 _262
其三百八十四 _262
其三百八十五 _263
其三百八十六 _263
其三百八十七 _263

其三百八十八 _264
其三百八十九 _264
其三百九十 _265
其三百九十一 _265
其三百九十二 _266
其三百九十三 _266
其三百九十四 _267
其三百九十五 _267
其三百九十六 _268
其三百九十七 _268
其三百九十八 _269
其三百九十九 _269
其四百 _270
其四百零一 _271
其四百零二 _271
其四百零三 _271
其四百零四 _272
其四百零五 _272
其四百零六 _273
其四百零七 _273
其四百零八 _273
其四百零九 _274
其四百一十 _274
其四百一十一 _275
其四百一十二 _275
其四百一十三 _275
其四百一十四 _276

其四百一十五 _276
其四百一十六 _276
其四百一十七 _277
其四百一十八 _277
其四百一十九 _277
其四百二十 _278
其四百二十一 _278
其四百二十二 _279
其四百二十三 _279
其四百二十四 _279
其四百二十五 _280
其四百二十六 _280
其四百二十七 _281
其四百二十八 _281
其四百二十九 _281
其四百三十 _282
其四百三十一 _282
其四百三十二 _283
其四百三十三 _283
其四百三十四 _283
其四百三十五 _284
其四百三十六 _284
其四百三十七 _285
其四百三十八 _285
其四百三十九 _285
其四百四十 _286
其四百四十一 _286

其四百四十二 _287
其四百四十三 _287
其四百四十四 _287
其四百四十五 _288
其四百四十六 _288
其四百四十七 _289
其四百四十八 _289
其四百四十九 _289
其四百五十 _290
其四百五十一 _290
其四百五十二 _290
其四百五十三 _291
其四百五十四 _291
其四百五十五 _292
其四百五十六 _293
其四百五十七 _293
其四百五十八 _293
其四百五十九 _294
其四百六十 _294
其四百六十一 _294
其四百六十二 _295
其四百六十三 _295
其四百六十四 _295
其四百六十五 _296
其四百六十六 _296
其四百六十七 _297
其四百六十八 _297

其四百六十九 _298
其四百七十 _298
其四百七十一 _298
其四百七十二 _299
其四百七十三 _299
其四百七十四 _300
其四百七十五 _300
其四百七十六 _301
其四百七十七 _301
其四百七十八 _301
其四百七十九 _302
其四百八十 _302
其四百八十一 _302
其四百八十二 _303
其四百八十三 _303
其四百八十四 _304

其四百八十五 _304
其四百八十六 _304
其四百八十七 _305
其四百八十八 _305
其四百八十九 _306
其四百九十 _306
其四百九十一 _306
其四百九十二 _307
其四百九十三 _307
其四百九十四 _308
其四百九十五 _308
其四百九十六 _308
其四百九十七 _309
其四百九十八 _309
其四百九十九 _310
其五百 _310

步黃克孫韻題

其一
西風古調瑣窗深,隔葉黃鸝送妙音。
唱至薔薇零落後,始知四海一同心。

其二
緇帷疊疊隱幽情,獨賞荒原天外聲。
佳夕渾忘寄塵日,萬花影下自觀經。

其三
生涯草草對樽壺,門外寒楊道不孤。
借問清魂北邙上,洛陽宮闕尚看無。

自序

　　譯詩殊難，論者甚夥。修辭立其誠，得義忘其言，貴其篤實，期在妙會，譯藝之要，庶其在茲。至若刪繁不爲義短，踵飾不爲蕪累，欲仁至仁，則近乎道矣。既臻秘境，遑顧來蹊，登涘棄舟，不亦可乎。詩海者，神淵也，默存之際，涵泳之間，湌霞飲瀣，偶吐馨淬，譬之譯事，誰曰不然。初，余援覽莪默之篇，驚謂其殆非魏晉名士而游于西海者耶！何探玄覓蹟、耽花湎酒、憂生樂死若斯之甚耶！遂冥搜旁求，殫其所撰，吟哦積年，似有冥期，考槃深趣驟得，唔歌幽思迺生。乃潛運靈宅，尋付譯筆。操吾華之舟楫，亂外方之芳流。萃暇樂之餘物，睎郢悦之高明。

　　莪默者，古波斯之疇人也。論其宗信，清真玄士，夷言謂蘇非也。所賦妙解人天，旨歸玄道，詞麗以則，義微而隱。其體曰魯拜，而其律與吾國絕句幾等匹，疑或出一源，余嘗有論。其詩播芬泰西，蓋得英倫紳士菲茨傑拉德之翼助也。晚近復流韻中土，亦大率以菲譯爲津梁。洎今華譯凡四十餘家，前惟黄克孫氏百一篇（題曰《魯拜集》）以絕句衍譯，贍麗雅絕，允爲翹楚，今則有鍾錦氏亦以近體述譯（題曰《波斯短歌行》），雅澹含弘，清質高拔，它俱貌合，未爲中節。然莪默玄歌，隱淪蓋多，數非止此，第英譯即有溫菲爾德氏五百章，而其迻譯今尚闕如。余好之如醒，欷其不淑，乃不揣譾陋，悉加象寄。驢背詩囊，纂匯成編。復爲筆識，不避猥雜。雖皆麟爪，可鑒繹思。惟貫鉉抗鼎，恐有覆餗之懼。災梨禍棗，尚祈方家之原。

　　乙未孟夏識於由栨齋

根據愛德華・菲茨傑拉德《納霞堡莪默・伽亞謨魯拜集》
(Rubáiyát Of Omar Khayyám Of Naishápúr)第五版轉譯

其一

覺起東君掃夜還，紛紜列宿逝冥闕。赫戲萬丈光如箭，正射君王宮闕間。

譯箋：東君，洪興祖《楚辭補注》："《博雅》曰：朱名耀靈。東君，日也。《漢書·郊祀志》有東君。"○赫戲，《楚辭·屈原〈離騷〉》："陟陞皇之赫戲兮。"王逸章句："赫戲，光明貌。"《文選·張衡〈西京賦〉》："叛赫戲以煇煌。"李善注："赫戲，炎盛也。戲，音羲。"○闕，《說文解字》："闕，門觀也。"徐鍇《說文解字繫傳》："蓋爲二臺於門外，人君作樓觀於上，上圓下方。以其闕然爲道，謂之闕。以其上可遠觀，謂之觀。以其縣法，謂之象魏。"○參看附錄首版其一及溫譯其二百三十三。

I

Wake! For the Sun, who scatter'd into flight
The Stars before him from the Field of Night,
    Drives Night along with them from Heav'n, and strikes
The Sultán's Turret with a Shaft of Light.

其二

酒肆昏昏拂曙天，忽聞棒喝意茫然。神宮設醮皆齊具，香客何猶闑外眠。

譯箋：棒喝，禪宗十一傳至南嶽系鎮州臨濟義玄慧照禪師以喝叱爲機鋒，開示於人。○《文選·宋玉〈高唐賦〉》："醮諸神。"李善注："醮，祭也。"○闑，門檻。漢揚雄《甘泉賦》："天閫決兮地垠開。"○參看溫譯其一。

II

Before the phantom of False morning died,
Methought a Voice within the Tavern cried,
　　"When all the Temple is prepared within,
"Why nods the drowsy Worshipper outside?"

其三

雞聲茅店忽聞喧，啓戶迎賓暫駐軒。他日歸鴻江海去，悠悠不復返斯垣。

譯箋：唐溫庭筠《商山早行》詩："晨起動征鐸，客行悲故鄉。雞聲茅店月，人跡板橋霜。"同以羈旅起興。○是篇意與唐李白《春夜宴桃李園序》起首頗類，其云："夫天地者，萬物之逆旅；光陰者，百代之過客。"大抵皆人生如寄之意。○參看溫譯其四百八十三。

III

And, as the Cock crew, those who stood before
The Tavern shouted —"Open then the Door!
　　You know how little while we have to stay,
And, once departed, may return no more."

其四

宿願新春又蘖芽，魂思夢慮隱孤笳。但看淑氣神州徧，素手新裁万樹花。

譯箋：晉陸機《思歸賦序》："懼兵革未息，宿願有違。"○素手，英譯原謂摩西之素手。典出《舊約‧出埃及記》第四章："（耶和華）又曰，置手於懷，遂置於懷。出之，手乃生癩，其白如雪。又曰，再置手於懷，遂置於懷。出之，手復原，同乎體。"詩中借指一種波斯花，菲氏以爲類於山楂花。○淑氣，英譯原作耶穌之嘆息，據菲注耶穌治愈之力在其呼吸之中。○參看溫譯其一百一十六與二百零一。

IV

Now the New Year reviving old Desires,

The thoughtful Soul to Solitude retires,

　　Where the White Hand Of Moses on the Bough

Puts out, and Jesus from the Ground suspires.

其五

翳林湮滅葬薔薇，照世御杯何所歸。惟覩蒲桃赤瓊灼，千園繞水滿芳菲。

譯箋：翳林，據菲注波斯古園名，湮於阿拉伯沙漠之中。○照世御杯，英譯原作賈姆什德之七環杯。據元文琪譯祆教古經《阿維斯塔》之《亞斯納》篇，賈姆什德乃人間始皇，在位期間"既沒有嚴寒和酷暑，也沒有衰老和死亡，更沒有魔鬼製造的忌妒"，"他使動物和人類長生不老，使江河奔流不息，草木永不枯槁，使食物豐盛，取之不盡，用之不竭"。《扎姆亞德亞什特》篇又云："一旦（賈姆什德）出言不遜，説了假話，靈光隨即化作飛鳥，離他而去。擁有良畜的賈姆什德眼看靈光離去，心中懊悔，茫然若失；面對（衆妖魔）的猖獗，他一籌莫展，只得潛藏地下，銷聲匿跡。"失去靈光庇佑，賈姆什德終爲其兄弟斯皮圖爾鋸殺。菲爾多西《列王紀》則列賈姆什德爲神話中丕什達德王朝第四位國君，爲阿拉伯族扎哈克所殺。傳賈姆什德有一杯，斟酒後可覩世界各地，故《明史》稱之爲照世之杯。《明史·列傳西域四》："（洪武）二十七年八月帖木兒貢馬二百。其表云："……欽仰聖心，如照世之杯，使臣心中豁然光明……"照世杯者，其國舊傳有杯光明洞徹，照之可知世事，故云。"名之七環杯者，蓋古波斯人以爲世界七分，西、東、東南、西南、西北、東北、中央各立其一，波斯居中。○據張鴻年《波斯文學史》注，波德林圖書館藏莪默絕句抄本校訂者赫榮-愛倫謂，菲譯一百零一首譯本中，四十九首類似原文，四十四首糅合數首而作，數首則係他人作品，三首乃菲氏自作。此首乃菲氏雜撷諸篇而成，非任何一首全部或主要部分之翻譯。

V

Iram indeed is gone with all his Rose,
And Jamshyd's Sev'n-ring'd Cup where no one knows;
　　But still a Ruby kindles in the Vine,
And many a Garden by the Water blows.

其六

韓娥已絕繞梁音，淒豔長聽莺嘯吟。佶屈殷勤恭喚酒，萎花病頰暈霞侵。

譯箋：韓娥，英譯原作大衛。傳大衛能歌善詩，《舊約》之《詩篇》多爲其所撰。韓娥，亦善歌哭者。《列子·湯問》："昔韓娥東之齊，匱糧，過雍門，鬻歌假食。既去而餘音繞梁欐，三日不絕，左右以其人弗去。過逆旅，逆旅人辱之。韓娥因曼聲哀哭，一里老幼悲愁，垂涕相對，三日不食。遽而追之。娥還，復爲曼聲長歌，一里老幼喜躍抃舞，弗能自禁，忘向之悲也。乃厚賂發之。故雍門之人至今善歌哭，放娥之遺聲。"○嘯，《說文解字》："嘯，吹聲也。"《詩經·召南·江有汜》："其嘯也歌。"鄭玄箋："嘯，蹙口而出聲。"○佶屈，唐韓愈《進學解》："周誥殷盤，佶屈聱牙。"馬其昶注："佶屈聱牙，皆艱澀貌。"原詩作巴列維語，乃三至七世紀古代波斯所流行之國語，故以佶屈一詞傳其古奧之義。○參看溫譯其一百七十四。

VI

And David's lips are lockt; but in divine
High-piping Pehleví, with "Wine! Wine! Wine!
　　　Red Wine!" — the Nightingale cries to the Rose
That sallow cheek of hers to'incarnadine.

其七

春暖邀君酌羽觴，尤裘悔襺盡除將。韶光振翮無多路，跂翼時禽欲遠揚。

譯箋：酌羽觴，《漢書‧孝成班倢伃傳》："酌羽觴兮銷憂。"顏師古注引孟康曰："羽觴，爵也，作生爵（雀）形，有頭尾羽翼也。"○《論語‧爲政》："言寡尤，行寡悔，祿在其中矣。"重襺，《説文解字》："襺，袍衣也。以絮曰襺。"《爾雅‧釋言》："袍，襺也。"郭璞注："《左傳》曰：'重襺衣裘。'"今本《春秋左傳‧襄公二十一年》作"重繭衣裘"。○跂翼，《詩經‧小雅‧斯干》："如跂斯翼。"毛傳："如人之跂竦翼爾。"《爾雅‧釋詁》："翼……敬也。"馬瑞辰《毛詩傳箋通釋》："《傳》云竦翼者，正以竦釋翼，以狀跂立之貌，有似翼然起敬也。"揚，《詩經‧大雅‧大明》："維師尚父，時維鷹揚。"毛傳："鷹揚，如鷹之飛揚也。"○赫榮-愛倫云此首爲雜擷數篇而成，參看溫譯其四百二十五。

VII

Come, fill the Cup, and in the fire of Spring
Your Winter-garment of Repentance fling;

> The Bird of Time has but a little way
> To flutter — and the Bird is on the Wing.

其八

往復二京安立身，樽中甘苦與誰論。命如茜酒滲將盡，枯櫱永飛歸故根。

譯箋：往復，《周易·泰卦》："無平不陂，無往不復。"《象》曰："無往不復，天地際也。"二京，原詩本作納霞堡（又譯内沙浦爾）與巴比倫。納霞堡，莪默生地，於今伊朗東部呼羅珊省，時爲國之大都會。巴比倫，古巴比倫王國之都城，位於今伊拉克境内，借指阿拉伯帝國阿拔斯朝首都巴格達。○茜酒，《春秋左氏傳·僖公四年》："爾貢苞茅不入，王祭不供，無以茜酒。"《說文解字》："茜，《禮》祭束茅加於裸圭而灌鬯酒，是爲茜，像神飲之也。"段玉裁注："茜讀爲縮，束茅立之，祭前沃酒其上，酒滲下去，若神飲之，故謂之縮。"○參看溫譯其一百三十四與其三百零九。

VIII

> Whether at Naishápúr or Babylon,
> Whether the Cup with sweet or bitter run,
>   The Wine of Life keeps oozing drop by drop,
> The Leaves of Life keep falling one by one.

其九

朝花日日開千樹，昨夕薔薇無拾處。孟夏纔將衆豔來，復攜古帝逍遥去。

譯箋：古帝，英譯原作 Jamshyd and Kaikobád，即賈姆什德與凱古巴德。賈姆什德，參看菲譯其五拙箋。凱古巴德爲神話中凱揚王朝首任君王，據菲爾多西《列王紀》，凱古巴德乃丕什達德王朝第六任君王法里東後裔。○赫榮-愛倫云此首爲雜撮而成，參看溫譯其四百一十四、其四百四十四與其四百八十四。

IX

Each Morn a thousand Roses brings, you say:
Yes, but where leaves the Rose of Yesterday?
　　And this first Summer month that brings the Rose
Shall take Jamshyd and Kaikobád away.

其十
祖孫帝業底干卿，父子稱雄一轉睛。據水斷橋皆往矣，誰聽門下鋏歌鳴。

譯箋：祖孫，原詩作 Kaikobád the Great, or Kaikhosrú（凱古巴德大帝與凱霍斯魯）。凱古巴德見菲譯其九拙箋。據菲爾多西《列王紀》，凱古巴德死後傳位長子凱卡烏斯。凱卡烏斯子西亞沃什避難土蘭部，入贅駙馬，與土蘭公主法蘭吉斯生一子，即凱霍斯魯。凱霍斯魯後回國承繼祖父凱卡烏斯之王位。凱爲巴列維語尊稱，義爲首領或統治者，凱揚則是凱之複數。後凱揚演變爲世間爲王者之代稱。波斯史中凱揚靈光即指世間人君所享有之神恩與福佑，與中國所謂真命天子義等。底，何也。馬令《南唐書・馮延巳傳》："延巳有'風乍起，吹皺一池春水'之句，元宗嘗戲延巳曰：'吹皺一池春水，干卿何事？'"○父子，原詩作 Zál and Rustum 扎爾與魯斯塔姆。父子皆爲凱揚王朝之勇夫，事跡俱見菲爾多西《列王紀》。○《三國志・蜀書・張飛傳》："表卒，曹公入荊州，先主本江南。曹公追之，一日一夜，及於當陽之長坂。先主聞曹公卒至，棄妻子走，使飛將二十騎拒後。飛據水斷橋，瞋目橫矛曰：'身是張益德也，可來共決死!'敵皆無敢近者,故遂得免。"〇英譯 Hátim 哈蒂姆乃阿拉伯貴族,以慷慨聞。舊時阿拉伯部族俗尚豪俠,哈蒂姆,蓋有古之餘風者。《戰國策·齊策四》:"(馮諼)居有頃,倚柱彈其劍,歌曰:'長鋏歸來乎!食無魚。'左右以告。孟嘗君曰:'食之,比門下之客。'"〇參看溫譯其六十四與其四百五十五。

X

Well, let it take them! What have we to do
With Kaikobád the Great, or Kaikhosrú?
　　Let Zál and Rustum bluster as they will,
Or Hátim call to Supper — heed not you.

其十一

田園荒磧隔漫漫,芳甸橫陳一帶寬。臣主假名渾不記,無愁天子倚金鑾。

譯箋:假名,佛教以為,諸法為因緣和合而成,無真實之體,故不可自差別,假名僅有差別之諸法,離名則無差別之諸法,故指諸法為假名。鳩摩羅什注《維摩經》:"緣會無實,但假空名耳。"《法華經·方便品》:"但以假名字,引導於眾生。"〇無愁天子,《隋書·音樂志中》:"(北齊)後主亦自能度曲,親執樂器,悦玩無倦。倚絃而歌,別採新聲為《無愁曲》……樂往哀來,竟以亡國。"《北齊書·幼主紀》:"(後主)乃益驕縱,盛為《無愁》之曲,人間謂之無愁天子。"天子,英譯原作 Mahmúd 瑪赫穆德,乃波斯伽茲尼王朝最顯赫之統治者(公元九九八至一零三零年在位),雖為突厥種,亦能以波斯語作詩。臣主者,或係指蘇丹瑪赫穆德與其寵臣、將軍埃亞茲,埃氏本為奴隸。

XI

With me along the strip of Herbage strown
That just divides the desert from the sown,
　　Where name of Slave and Sultan is forgot —
And Peace to Mahmúd on his golden Throne!

其十二

一片乾餱一卷詩，一壺美酒傍疏枝。荒原有汝歌清發，爰得樂郊無盡時。

譯箋：《詩經・小雅・伐木》："民之失德，乾餱以愆。"《説文解字》："餱，乾食也。"《廣雅・釋器》："餱，糒也。"○《詩經・魏風・碩鼠》："樂土樂土，爰得我所。"又："樂郊樂郊，誰之永號。"○赫榮-愛倫云上二首宜合觀。並參看溫譯其四百七十九與其四百五十二。

XII

A Book of Verses underneath the Bough,
A Jug of Wine, a Loaf of Bread — and Thou
　　Beside me singing in the Wilderness —
Oh, Wilderness were Paradise enow!

其十三

或戀榮華此世希，或求遐舉望瑤池。花開堪折直須折，遠鼓鼉鳴那復知。

譯箋：瑤池，英譯原作 the Prophet's Paradise（先知之樂園）。先知，指穆罕默德。《穆天子傳》卷三："乙丑，天子觴西王母於瑤池之上。"○唐杜秋娘《金縷衣》詩："勸君莫惜金縷衣，勸君惜取少年時。花開堪折直須折，莫待無花空折枝。"○陸佃《埤雅・釋魚》引晉安《海物記》："鼉宵鳴如桴鼓，亦或謂之鼉更；更則以其聲逢逢然如鼓，而又善夜鳴，其數應更故也。"秦李斯《諫逐客書》："樹靈鼉之鼓。"菲注謂鼓指王宮外之鼓。據納忠《阿拉伯通史》云，阿拔斯朝哈里發宮門外設鼓樂，每日五次禮拜時皆鳴之。蘇非重內心修煉而非外在禮儀，則朝覲無須拘泥形式。主摒棄一切慾念，則俗世榮華與來世福祚皆非宜有，惟萬念寂滅，始可見主，或即此章之義。○參看溫譯其一百零八、其一百八十四與其九十四。

XIII

Some for the Glories of This World; and some

Sigh for the Prophet's Paradise to come;

　　Ah, take the Cash, and let the Credit go,

Nor heed the rumble of a distant Drum!

其十四

轉眄四際盡薔薇，鬧罷紅塵笑語歸。旦暮看其繡囊裂，奇珍園囿散霏霏。

譯箋：《詩經・小雅・采薇》："今我來思，雨雪霏霏。"毛傳："霏霏，甚也。"○菲注謂後二句狀薔薇之金色花蕊。可參看溫譯其一百二十二。

XIV

Look to the blowing Rose about us — "Lo,

Laughing," she says, "into the world I blow,

　　At once the silken tassel of my Purse

Tear, and its Treasure on the Garden throw."

其十五
或持金粟惜如珠，或任風拋雨委輪。死化丹砂同不得，封塋誰復掘其污。

譯箋：丹砂，英譯原作 aureate Earth（金色之土）。《周易參同契》："丹砂木精，得金乃並。金水合處，木火爲侶。"晉干寶《搜神記》："臨汜縣有廖氏，世老壽。後移居，子孫輒殘折。他人居其故宅，復累世壽。乃知是宅所爲，不知何故。疑井水赤，乃掘井左右，得古人埋丹砂數十斛。丹汁入井，是以飲水而得壽。"○參看溫譯其一百七十五。

XV
And those who husbanded the Golden grain,
And those who flung it to the winds like Rain,
    Alike to no such aureate Earth are turn'd
As, buried once, Men want dug up again.

其十六
心牽塵慮世間情，旋滅死灰旋復生。如鬭玉龍沙磧雪，須臾熠燿即巡行。

譯箋：《史記·韓長孺列傳》："死灰獨不復然乎！"○《詩經·豳風·東山》："町畽鹿場，熠燿宵行。"毛傳："熠燿，燐也。燐，螢火也。"《説文解字》："熠，盛光也。""燿，照也。"

XVI

The Worldly Hope men set their Hearts upon

Turns Ashes — or it prospers; and anon,

    Like Snow upon the Desert's dusty Face,

Lighting a little hour or two — is gone.

其十七

逆旅千年想弊穿，陰陽遞轉戶樞圜。列王隆貴今安在，時命相追鶴馭煙。

譯箋：文理本《舊約·利未記》第二十五章："田畝屬我，汝乃賓旅，不得永鬻於人。"《歷代志上》第二十九章："我儕在爾前，為遠人，為羈旅，同於列祖，在世之日如影，無永存之希望。"吳經熊譯《新經全集·聖伯鐸祿書一》二章："親愛之同道乎！人生在世，猶如作客他鄉，務望自愛，切弗縱情恣慾，以戕賊心靈。"唐李白《春夜宴桃李園序》："夫天地者，萬物之逆旅；光陰者，百代之過客。"其義與此章同。諸如 Tavern, Caravanserai 皆我默習用之意象。○陰陽，英譯原作晝夜，然其義當非限於日夜一科，故易以陰陽。圜轉，《漢書·梅福傳》："從諫若轉圜。"顏師古注："轉圜，言其順易也。"戶樞，《呂氏春秋·盡數》："流水不腐，戶樞不螻，動也。"○隆貴，英譯原作壯觀。《史記·叔孫通列傳》："於是高帝曰：'吾迺今日知為皇帝之貴也。'"○鶴馭煙，唐吳融《和皮博士赴上京觀中修靈齋》詩："鶴馭已從煙際下。"鶴馭，死之諱稱。○參看溫譯其七十。

XVII

Think, in this batter'd Caravanserai

Whose Portals are alternate Night and Day,

    How Sultán after Sultán with his Pomp

Abode his destined Hour, and went his way.

其十八

野驢馳踐羿王元，猶夢黃粱伏草宛。荒殿人皇曾醉臥，長蛇封豕守無言。

譯箋：羿王，《說文解字》："羿，羽之开風。亦古諸侯也。一曰射師。"拙譯取射師之義。英譯原作 Bahrám, that great Hunter，偉大獵手巴赫拉姆，指古波斯薩珊王朝第十任君主巴赫拉姆五世，公元二七三至二七六年在位，以勇力稱，熱衷狩獵。見菲爾多西《列王紀》。或云其喜獵野驢，而於策馬逐驢之際落井而亡。波斯語野驢與墳墓同音古爾，故其名又作巴赫拉姆·古爾。元，《孟子·滕文公下》："勇士不忘喪其元。"趙岐注："元，首也。"《春秋左氏傳·僖公三十三年》："狄人歸其元，面如生。"杜預注："元，首。"○黃粱，見唐沈既濟《枕中記》。宛，音冤。《說文解字》："宛，屈艸自覆也。"○人皇，英譯原作 Jamshyd 賈姆什德，參見其五與其九。長蛇封豕，原作獅與蜥蜴。○參看溫譯其七十二。

XVIII

They say the Lion and the Lizard keep
The Courts where Jamshyd gloried and drank deep;
　　And Bahrám, that great Hunter — the Wild Ass
Stamps o'er his Head, but cannot break his Sleep.

其十九

薔薇何處最紅妍，愷撒王陵喋血殷。風信飄園如落帽，自誰蓁首墮華鬘。

譯箋：愷撒，謂蓋烏斯·尤利烏斯·愷撒，古羅馬政治家，公元前四十四年爲元老院成員刺殺。○風信子，花名，希臘神話謂美少年雅辛托斯死後由其血所化。落帽，《晉書‧孟嘉傳》："九月九日，（桓）溫燕龍山，僚佐畢集。時佐吏並著戎服，有風至，吹嘉帽墮落，嘉不之覺。"○螓首，《詩經‧衛風‧碩人》："螓首蛾眉。"毛傳："螓首，顙廣而方。"鄭玄箋："螓，謂蜻蜓也。"《爾雅‧釋蟲》："蚻，蜻蜻。"郭璞注："如蟬而小，《方言》云：'有文者謂之螓。'"華鬘，印度風俗男女多以花結貫飾首或身，謂之俱蘇摩摩羅 Kusumamala，因而以爲莊嚴佛前之具。《西域記二》曰："首冠華鬘，身佩瓔珞。"《守護國界經》曰："以種種寶，用作華鬘，而爲莊嚴。"○參看溫譯其一百零四。

XIX

I sometimes think that never blows so red
The Rose as where some buried Cæsar bled
    That every Hyacinth the Garden wears
Dropt in her Lap from some once lovely Head.

其二十
輕臥河滸覆碧茸，甡生芳甸正芃芃。麝香暗吐誰家女，教惜櫻脣一點紅。

譯箋：河滸，《詩經‧魏風‧伐檀》："寘之河之滸兮。"《説文解字》："滸，水厓也。"茸，草初生柔細貌。《説文解字》："茸，艸茸茸皃。"○芃，《説文解字》："芃，艸盛皃。"《詩經‧鄘風‧載馳》："我行其野，芃芃其麥。"毛傳："願行衛之野，麥芃芃然方盛長。"《詩經‧曹風‧下泉》："芃芃黍苗，陰雨膏之。"毛傳："芃芃，美貌。"○借用宋蘇軾《蝶戀花》詞："帳底吹笙香吐麝。"《文選‧王延壽〈魯靈光殿賦〉》："發秀吐榮。"○參看溫譯其六十二。

XX

And this reviving Herb whose tender Green

Fledges the River-lip on which we lean —

　　Ah, lean upon it lightly! for who knows

From what once lovely Lip it springs unseen!

其二十一

命酌同心盡此朝，後憂前悔泯然消。悠悠明日身何在，當化池灰作劫燒。

譯箋：酌，《說文解字》："酌，盛酒行觴也。"同心，《周易·繫辭上》："君子之道，或出或處，或默或語。二人同心，其利斷金。同心之言，其臭如蘭。"○宋王安石《傷仲永》："泯然眾人。"○《高僧傳·竺法蘭》："昔漢武穿昆明池底，得黑灰，以問東方朔。朔云：'不知，可問西域胡人。'後法蘭既至，眾人追以問之。蘭云：'世界終盡，劫火洞燒，此灰是也。'"劫，爲梵語劫波之音略。譯言分別時節，謂年月日時不能算之遠大時節也，故又譯大時。原詩作昨日之七千歲，蓋古波斯以爲世界之壽爲七千歲。菲注謂每一星各司一千歲。○參看温譯其三百一十二。

XXI

Ah, my Beloved, fill the Cup that clears

TO-DAY of past Regrets and future Fears:

　　To-morrow! — Why, To-morrow I may be

Myself with Yesterday's Sev'n thousand Years.

其二十二

江山歷代有才人，醇釀能醅幾日新。換盞推杯數巡後，山阿託體藉橫陳。

譯箋：清趙翼《論詩絕句》："李杜詩篇萬口傳，至今已覺不新鮮。江山代有才人出，各領風騷數百年。"趙詩末二句言人才代有，以明潮流無常之意，而莪默則言歷史舞臺之上才人但如過客，終歸寂滅。二者用意不同。○原詩本言世人所愛之一干才人，皆如從所穫蒲桃中軋出之精髓，喻皆爲時代所造就也。○晉陶淵明《擬挽歌辭》其三："死去何所道，託體同山阿。"○參看溫譯其二百一十九。

XXII

For some we loved, the loveliest and the best
That from his Vintage rolling Time hath prest,
　　Have drunk their Cup a Round or two before,
And one by one crept silently to rest.

其二十三

椒房金屋樂無垠，夏日穠芳衣著新。終託吾身泉下土，吾身上又託何人。

譯箋：椒房，漢班固《西都賦》："後宮則有掖庭后妃之室。"金屋，《漢武故事》："若得阿嬌作婦，當作金屋貯之也。"○《春秋左氏傳‧隱公元年》："不及黃泉，無相見也。"杜預注："地中之泉，故曰黃泉。"○參看溫譯其三百六十六、其七十三與其三百九十。

XXIII

And we, that now make merry in the Room

They left, and Summer dresses in new bloom,

　　Ourselves must we beneath the Couch of Earth

Descend — ourselves to make a Couch — for whom?

其二十四

極慾窮奢君莫遲，一歸塵土復誰知。塵來塵去塵中臥，無酒無歌無曉期。

譯箋：《文選·陸機〈挽歌詩三首〉》其二："廣宵何寥廓，大暮安可晨。"李善注引張奐遺令："地底冥冥，長無曉期。"○參看溫譯其一百零七。

XXIV

Ah, make the most of what we yet may spend,

Before we too into the Dust descend;

　　Dust into Dust, and under Dust to lie,

Sans Wine, sans Song, sans Singer, and — sans End.

其二十五

今世辛勞終是空，寄瞻來世亦歸同。司辰幽閣呼羣妄，玄道休尋二者中。

譯箋：幽閣，清真寺內多建一塔或一樓閣，有宣禮者守之，以時召喚信徒禮拜。然菲譯我默用幽閣喻死亡。吳經熊譯《新經全集·福音若望傳》一章："太初有道，與天主偕。道即天主，自始與偕。微道無物，物因道生。天地萬有，資道以成。斯道之內，蘊有生命。生命即光，生靈所稟。光照冥冥，冥冥不領。"光即生命，暗即死亡。

司辰，原作穆安津，即宣禮者。〇真道，原作報償。赫榮-愛倫謂加爾各答抄本作道路，指玄道，即蘇非所追求之神秘主義拯救之道。〇參看溫譯其三百七十六。

XXV

Alike for those who for TO-DAY prepare,
And those that after some TO-MORROW stare,
　　A Muezzin from the Tower of Darkness cries,
"Fools! Your Reward is neither Here nor There."

其二十六

二世羣賢論別裁，流同術士亦愚哉。猥辭瑣語隨塵散，佞口簧言靜積埃。

譯箋：二世即前章之今世與來世。《說文解字》："佞，巧諂高材也。"簧言，《詩經·小雅·巧言》："巧言如簧。"〇參看溫譯其四百二十八與其一百四十七。

XXVI

Why, all the Saints and Sages who discuss'd
Of the Two Worlds so wisely — they are thrust
　　Like foolish Prophets forth; their Words to scorn
Are scatter'd, and their Mouths are stopt with Dust.

其二十七

俊賢捫蝨坐談論，壯歲求知切問存。闊論炎炎雖滿耳，終兮還出入時門。

譯箋：捫蝨，《晉書·王猛傳》："桓溫入關，猛被褐詣之，一面談當世之事，捫蝨而言，旁若無人。"〇《説文解字》："存，恤問也。"〇《莊子·齊物論》："大言炎炎，小言詹詹。"〇魯米詩云："空無所得亦空還，洞悉高玄感大患。携手終由一門去，何緣爭競忍斯間。"（Inside the Great Mystery that is, we don't really own anything. What is this competition we feel then, before we go, one at a time, through the same gate?）與我默此章皆以門為喻，門謂生命出入世間之門。與《老子·第六章》"谷神不死，是謂玄牝。玄牝之門，是謂天地根"可合參。惟波斯人謂生命復當由此門而歸，老子若無斯義。

XXVII

Myself when young did eagerly frequent

Doctor and Saint, and heard great argument

    About it and about: but evermore

Came out by the same door where in I went.

其二十八

齊培慧種共耕躬，長育拮据勤苦功。問我於茲何所獲，來隨流水逝隨風。

譯箋：耕躬，《説文解字》："躬，身也。"三國蜀諸葛亮《出師表》："臣本布衣，躬耕於南陽。"〇長育，《春秋左氏傳·昭公二十五年》："爲温慈、惠和，以效天之生殖長育。"拮据，《詩經·豳風·鴟鴞》："予手拮据。"陸德明《經典釋文》引《韓詩》云："口足爲事曰拮据。"《説文解字》："拮，手口並有所作也。"〇傳我默與尼查木、哈桑同就學於哲人莫瓦伐，相約苟富貴毋相忘。後尼查木爲大塞爾柱王朝宰相，舊友來訪。哈桑喜爲官，我默喜爲學，皆各遂所願。然哈桑因謀反而遭貶黜，復立伊斯蘭別教易司馬儀派，養刺客，謀行刺。蓋哈桑所立係屬什葉派別支，尼查木則持正統遜尼派。哈桑於一零九零年佔據裏海南岸山中之阿剌模忒城，十字軍稱之爲山老，即山王之誤稱也。事見《馬可波羅遊記》之《山老》等三章。稍晚山老滅於蒙古旭烈兀汗，其教又稱阿薩辛派，即今西語"刺客"一詞之來源。尼查木後亦爲哈桑刺殺。詩人阿塔爾曾記述："於瀕死之際尼查木曰：'嗟夫！真主，吾將逝於此風之手兮。'"菲氏謂即用此章詩義。○赫榮-愛倫謂前二首宜合參。參看溫譯其三百五十三、其二百六十四與其一百九十。

XXVIII

With them the seed of Wisdom did I sow,
And with mine own hand wrought to make it grow;
　　And this was all the Harvest that I reap'd —
"I came like Water, and like Wind I go."

其二十九

不知何日亦何由，天地玄黃水自流。橐籥出風何處去，無心蕩蕩過荒疇。

譯箋：玄黃，天地之二色也。○《老子》："天地之間，其猶橐籥。虛而不屈，動而愈出。"○吳經熊譯《福音若望傳》三章："天風翛然而作，爾聞其聲，而不知其何自何往，生於神者，亦復如是。"○參看溫譯其一百四十五與其二十六。

XXIX

Into this Universe, and Why not knowing
Nor *Whence*, like Water willy-nilly flowing;
　　And out of it, as Wind along the Waste,

I know not *Whither*, willy-nilly blowing.

其三十

莫問何來疾若風，焉知此去又何從。平生柱屈無窮憶，盡在杯杯禁酒中。

譯箋：參看溫譯其一百一十與其四百九十。

XXX

What, without asking, hither hurried *Whence*?
And, without asking, *Whither* hurried hence!
　　Oh, many a Cup of this forbidden Wine
Must drown the memory of that insolence!

其三十一

遐升帝闕七重門，安坐填星致極尊。中道漫漫頻破惑，獨餘性命惑猶存。

譯箋：古波斯以爲天有七重，而七重天由土星主之。○填星，土星也。○據張鴻年《波斯文學史》云，福州郊外一伊朗人墓碑上鐫有此作。亦參看溫譯其三百零三。

XXXI

Up from Earth's Centre through the Seventh Gate
I rose, and on the Throne of Saturn sate,
　　And many a Knot unravel'd by the Road;
But not the Master-knot of Human Fate.

其三十二

孤門扃鐍固難開，深閉緇帷瞀目哀。卿我閒言方偶及，便隨風逝滅塵垓。

譯箋：《莊子·胠篋》："固扃鐍。"《說文解字》："扃，外閉之關也。"○緇帷，英譯原作帷幕，波斯文學中借喻真主奧祕之隱蔽莫測。《莊子·漁父》："孔子遊乎緇帷之林。"成玄英疏："緇，黑也。尼父遊行天下，讀講《詩》《書》，時於江濱，休息林籟，其林鬱茂，蔽日陰沉，布葉垂條，又如帷幕，故謂之緇帷之林也。"○據菲氏原注，我、卿分指個體與整體。案末句似就寂滅合一而言。○《說文解字》："垓，兼該八極地也。"《國語·鄭語》："故王者居九畡之田，收經入以食兆民。"畡，同垓。○參看温譯其三百八十九、其四十七與其一百九十二。

XXXII

There was the Door to which I found no Key;

There was the Veil through which I might not see:

　　Some little talk awhile of ME and THEE

There was — and then no more of THEE and ME.

其三十三

陸不言兮海泣號，紫波失眷競相逃。星躔隱現陰陽界，默運璿璣天意韜。

譯箋：英譯 all his Signs 指黃道十二宮。揚雄《方言》："日運爲躔。"○璿璣，《尚書·堯典》："在璿璣玉衡，以齊七政。"《史記·天官書》引作"旋璣玉衡"，司馬貞索隱："《尚書》'旋'作'璿'，馬融云：'璿，美玉也。'璣，渾天儀，可轉旋，故曰旋璣。"

XXXIII

Earth could not answer; nor the seas that mourn
In flowing Purple, of their Lord forlorn;
　　Nor rolling Heaven, with all his Signs reveal'd
And hidden by the sleeve of Night and Morn.

其三十四

卿動緇帷藏我內，教予覓燭探幽晦。忽聞心外喝聲來，我在卿中乃瞽昧。

譯箋：緇帷，參看其三十二譯箋。首句言卿在我內，乃謂我所分有之真主神性。末句則反言之。瞽昧者，謂神性難測也，猶西塞羅言命運乃瞽者。此作乃就蘇非派神祕主義體驗而言。蘇非派倡人主合一，主在我心，最終心靈寂滅於真主，崇拜者與被崇拜者統一於一身。

XXXIV

Then of the THEE IN ME who works behind
The Veil, I lifted up my hands to find
　　A lamp amid the Darkness; and I heard,
As from Without — "THE ME WITHIN THEE BLIND!"

其三十五

誰主此生心欲參，脣前瓦缶語呢喃。生時荷鍤長歡醉，埋罷黃泉絶此甘。

譯箋：《晉書‧劉伶傳》："常乘鹿車，攜一壺酒，使人荷鍤而隨之，謂曰死便埋我。"○參看溫譯其二百七十四與其四百三十一。

XXXV

Then to the Lip of this poor earthen Urn

I lean'd, the Secret of my Life to learn:

  And Lip to Lip it murmur'd — "While you live,

"Drink! — for, once dead, you never shall return."

其三十六

姑酌金罍晤語輕，憐卿前世醉平生。因歡絳口千回接，授受相親不解酲。

譯箋：《詩經·周南·卷耳》："我姑酌彼金罍。"《詩經·陳風·東門之池》："可以晤歌。"毛傳："晤，遇也。"鄭玄箋："晤，猶對也。"漢徐幹《車渠椀賦》："因歡接口，媚于君顏。"○《説文解字》："酲，病酒也。"《詩經·小雅·節南山》："憂心如酲。"毛傳："病酒曰酲。"《世説新語·任誕》："天生劉伶，以酒爲名。一飲一斛，五斗解酲。"參看溫譯其三十二。

XXXVI

I think the Vessel, that with fugitive

Articulation answer'd, once did live,

  And drink; and Ah! the passive Lip I kiss'd,

How many Kisses might it take — and give!

其三十七

憶昔游方半道棲，佇觀陶匠正搏坯。泥中鳩舌悄聲語，楚毒輕加但緩稽。

譯箋：《説文解字》："搏，圜也。"《韻會》引《説文》："搏，以手圜之也。"《説文解字》："批，手擊也。"○鴃舌，《孟子·滕文公上》："今也南蠻鴃舌之人，非先王之道，子倍子之師而學之，亦異於曾子矣。"原作謂已湮滅之語言也。○《墨子·明鬼下》："播棄黎老，賊誅孩子，楚毒無罪，刳剔孕婦，庶舊鰥寡，號咷無告也。"○菲注謂詩人阿塔爾曾有故事云，一旅者泉邊以手掬飲。時復有一人至，以陶缶盛之飲，飲罷遺缶。前旅者拾缶復飲，然驚覺泉甚苦澀，全不似以手掬飲之甘美也。時有聲自天而告之，此缶前世爲人，故無論化成何形，終難失凡人苦之況味。○參看溫譯其二百五十二。

XXXVII

For I remember stopping by the way
To watch a Potter thumping his wet Clay;
    And with its all-obliterated Tongue
It murmur'd — "Gently, Brother, gently, pray!"

其三十八

一抔濕土女媧搏，造作人形獨有天。亙古綿延今不絕，渺茫此説代相傳。

譯箋：文理本《舊約·創世紀》第二章："耶和華上帝搏土爲人，噓生氣於其鼻，乃成生靈。"《太平御覽》卷七八引《風俗通》："俗説天地開闢，未有人民，女媧搏黄土作人。劇務，力不暇供，乃引繩於泥中，舉以爲人。故富貴者，黄土人；貧賤者，引繩人也。"林松譯《古蘭經韻譯》第六章第二節："他用泥土創造了你們。"張暉譯《魯達基詩集》："不論傻子還是智者，都是由泥土塑成，他們死後又都回到泥土之中。"又："由於你用泥土塑成，你的歸宿便是土地，你和用泥搏制的姑娘，都將塞進土裏。"張鴻年譯薩迪《果園》："聖潔的主把你用泥土塑成，主的奴僕啊，你應似泥土一樣謙恭。"○參看溫譯其四百六十六與四百九十三。

XXXVIII

And has not such a Story from of Old
Down Man's successive generations roll'd
　　Of such a clod of saturated Earth
Cast by the Maker into Human mould?

其三十九

香醪酹地入冥藏，滴滴潛行土未嚐。千歲游魂深隱在，熾心灼目得清涼。

譯箋：酹地，《漢書・外戚傳》："爲人有才略，善事人，下至宮人左右，飲酒酹地，皆祝延之。"顏師古：注"酹，以酒沃地。"宋蘇軾《念奴嬌・赤壁懷古》詞："人生如夢，一樽還酹江月。"菲注謂波斯有會飲時酹地習俗。○參看溫譯其二百零三。

XXXIX

And not a drop that from our Cups we throw
For Earth to Drink of，but may steal below
　　To quench the fire of Anguish in some Eye
There hidden — far beneath，and long ago.

其四十

仙露晨思降玉皇，紅塵儼儼鬱金香。空樽可擬君宜儆，地轉天翻作醉狂。

譯箋：《說文解字》："儼，昂頭也。"唐來鵠《聖政紀頌》："若儼見旒，若俯見冕。"○參看溫譯其四十四。

XL

As then the Tulip for her morning sup

Of Heav'nly Vintage from the soil looks up,

　　Do you devoutly do the like, till Heav'n

To Earth invert you — like an empty Cup.

其四十一

性天不復惑人神，明日亂蔴風解紛。擁醉當壚誰氏子，指間青髮掌中身。

譯箋：當壚，《史記·司馬相如列傳》："買一酒舍酤酒，而令文君當鑪。"裴駰集解："韋昭曰：'鑪，酒肆也。以土爲墮，邊高似鑪。'"《漢書·司馬相如列傳》："乃令文君當盧。"顏師古注："賣酒之處累土爲盧以居酒甕，四邊隆起，其一面高，形如鍛盧，故名盧耳。而俗之學者，皆謂當盧爲對溫酒火盧，失其義矣。"王先謙補注："字當作壚。"漢辛延年《羽林郎》詩："胡姬年十五，春日獨當壚。"○唐羅隱《贈雲英》詩："鍾陵醉別十餘春，重見雲英掌上身。"○參看溫譯其一百九十一、其三百三十二與其四百二十六。

XLI

Perplext no more with Human or Divine,

To-morrow's tangle to the winds resign,

　　And lose your fingers in the tresses of

The Cypress-slender Minister of Wine.

其四十二

倘付芳屑與綠醪，色空生滅莫宜逃。今之汝即昨之汝，明日安傷汝髮毫。

譯箋：綠醪，唐徐夤《驕侈詩》："古今人事惟堪醉，好脱霜裘換綠醪。"○佛家言，色，變壞之義，變礙之義，質礙之義。空，因緣所生之法，究竟而無實體曰空。又謂理體之空寂。蘇非派寂滅説則謂與真主合一。○參看溫譯其二百八十二。

XLII

And if the Wine you drink, the Lip you press,
End in what All begins and ends in — Yes;
　　Think then you are TO-DAY what YESTERDAY
You were — TO-MORROW you shall not be less.

其四十三

神差尋汝至西崦，澤畔終逢濁酒拈。捉汝元神來對酌，羽觴飛舉勿相謙。

譯箋：崦，崦嵫也，山名。《山海經·西山經》："鳥鼠同穴山西南三百六十里曰崦嵫之山。"郭璞注："日没所入山也。"戰國楚屈原《離騷》："吾令羲和弭節兮，望崦嵫而勿迫。"○澤畔，戰國楚屈原《漁父》："游於江潭，行吟澤畔。"○參看溫譯其二百五十四。

XLIII

So when that Angel of the darker Drink
At last shall find you by the river-brink,

And, offering his Cup, invite your Soul
Forth to your Lips to quaff — you shall not shrink.

其四十四
玉宇憑虛浩浩翔，天爲棟宇屋爲裳。泥骸跼蹐何其辱，未若元神棄濁囊。

譯箋：憑虛，宋蘇軾《赤壁賦》："浩浩乎如憑虛禦風，而不知其所止；飄飄乎如遺世獨立，羽化而登仙。"○《世說新語·任誕》："劉伶恒縱酒放達，或脫衣裸形在屋中。人見譏之，伶曰：'我以天地爲棟宇，屋室爲褌衣，諸君何爲入我褌中！'"○《詩經·小雅·正月》："謂天蓋高，不敢不局。謂地蓋厚，不敢不蹐。"毛傳："局，曲也。"陸德明《經典釋文》："局，本或作跼。"毛傳："蹐，累足也。"《說文解字》："蹐，小步也。"○參看溫譯其四百三十六。

XLIV
Why, if the Soul can fling the Dust aside,
And naked on the Air of Heaven ride,
　　Were't not a Shame — were't not a Shame for him
In this clay carcase crippled to abide?

其四十五
一日之閑憩帳廬，六龍御駕赴酆都。法曹淵默收供具，留待新賓復此趨。

譯箋：酆都，傳爲冥司所在。○法曹，英譯原爲波斯語 Ferrásh 侍從，當暗喻司命者。《後漢書·百官志》："法曹主郵驛科程事。"《淮南子·泰族訓》："齊明盛服，淵默而不言。"據其它譯本，帳廬乃借喻身體，君王則喻靈魂。○參看溫譯其八十二。

XLV

'Tis but a Tent where takes his one day's rest
A Sultán to the realm of Death addrest;
　　The Sultán rises, and the dark Ferrásh
Strikes, and prepares it for another Guest.

其四十六
簿錄全憑帝力終，何憂往事不能重。億千酒沫皆如我，仙女不停傾玉鍾。

譯箋：仙女，原譯作 The Eternal Sáki 長生薩吉。薩吉，波斯語，指斟酒伴飲之人，多爲女性。長生薩吉，喻造化或支配命運之力。○參看溫譯其一百六十一。

XLVI

And fear not lest Existence closing your
Account, and mine, should know the like no more;
　　The Eternal Sáki from that Bowl has pour'd
Millions of Bubbles like us, and will pour.

其四十七
緇帷穿越逝聯翩，浮世悠悠過億年。卿我往來誰又見，石投於海浪依然。

譯箋：參看溫譯其八十七、其一百七十六與其一百五十。

XLVII

When You and I behind the Veil are past,

Oh, but the long, long while the World shall last,

　　Which of our Coming and Departure heeds

As the Sea's self should heed a pebble-cast.

其四十八

駐軒片暇大荒中，遽飲神泉行色匆。征轡丁令如蜃影，自空處出復歸空。

譯箋：文理本《舊約·傳道書》："虛空之虛空，虛空之虛空，萬事虛空，人於日下所勞力之操作，何益之有。"此作亦謂人生於無而歸於無，無亦蘇非寂滅之言歟？○參看溫譯其一百三十六與其三百三十八。

XLVIII

A Moment's Halt — a momentary taste

Of BEING from the Well amid the Waste —

　　And Lo! —the phantom Caravan has reach'd

The NOTHING it set out from — Oh, make haste!

其四十九

毋俟日終而見幾，錦衣玉飾盡拋飛。僞真其間但容髮，悵惘此生何處依。

譯箋：《周易·繫辭下》："君子見幾而作，不俟終日。"○漢枚乘《上書諫吳王》："繫絕於天，不可復結，墜入深淵，難以復出，其出不出，間不容髮。"間爲間隙。

XLIX

Would you that spangle of Existence spend
About THE SECRET — quick about it, Friend!
　　A Hair perhaps divides the False and True —
And upon what, prithee, may life depend?

其五十
偽真其間但容髮，一字能尋拯迷沒。直上昆侖崒崔宮，或逢真宰傲然兀。

譯箋：一字，英譯指 Alif，爲阿拉伯文第一個字母，亦爲真主一詞之首字母。〇《昆侖記》曰："昆侖之山三級，下曰樊桐，一名板桐；二曰玄圃，一名閬風；上曰層城，一名天庭，是謂太帝之居。"〇真宰，英譯 THE MASTER，當指真主。《莊子·齊物論》："若有真宰，而特不得其眹。"〇赫榮-愛倫云上二首宜合參。參看溫譯其四百五十八、其二十四與其一百零九。

L

A Hair perhaps divides the False and True;
Yes; and a single Alif were the clue —
　　Could you but find it — to the Treasure-house,
And peradventure to THE MASTER too.

其五十一
萬類幽攤問太玄，遹行如汞慰憂煎。雜然魚月流形賦，運化惟其獨不遷。

譯箋：太玄，原文 secret presence 也。漢揚雄《太玄·攤》："玄者，幽攤萬類而不見形者也。"《老子·第一章》:"道可道,非常道;名可名,非常名。無,名天地之始;有,名萬物之母。故常無,欲以觀其妙;常有,欲以觀其徼。此兩者同出而異名,同謂之玄,玄之又玄,衆妙之門。"○南朝宋僧肇《物不遷論》:"人命逝速,速如川流。"莪默則謂世界速如流汞之轉,其譬喻義頗類。○宋文天祥《正氣歌》:"天地有正氣,雜然賦流形。下則爲河嶽,上則爲日星。於人曰浩然,沛乎塞蒼冥。"菲注謂 from Máh to Máhi 即 from Fish to Moon 從魚至月,指波斯神話中造物之序。○南朝宋僧肇《物不遷論》:"功業不可朽,故雖在昔而不化,不化故不遷。不遷故,則湛然明矣。"僧肇之不遷乃謂萬物言,莪默之不遷乃謂造物主言。○參看溫譯其七十五與五十七。

LI

Whose secret Presence, through Creation's veins
Running Quicksilver-like eludes your pains;
　　Taking all shapes from Máh to Máhi; and
They change and perish all — but He remains.

其五十二

猜疑片刻返雲屏,軸戲連連隱闇冥。無數流光怎消得,自爲優孟自觀聽。

譯箋:《史記·滑稽列傳》:"楚有優孟。"司馬貞索隱:"優者,倡優也。"○吳經熊譯《新經全集·聖保祿致格林多人書一》第四章:"蓋天主已使我輩爲其宗徒者,似成爲最卑賤之人,一若擬死之囚,又似優伶演劇於世,以博人神之一笑者。"○參看溫譯其四百七十五。

LII

A moment guess'd — then back behind the Fold
Immerst of Darkness round the Drama roll'd
    Which, for the Pastime of Eternity,
He doth Himself contrive, enact, behold.

其五十三

仰察天文閉網羅，俯觀地理恨蹉跎。汝身有汝惟今日，明日成非汝奈何。

譯箋：《周易·繫辭上》："仰以觀於天文，俯以察於地理，是故知幽明之故。"○參看温譯其五十二。

LIII

But if in vain, down on the stubborn floor
Of Earth, and up to Heav'n's unopening Door,
    You gaze TO-DAY, while You are You — how then
TO-MORROW, when You shall be You no more?

其五十四

爭求支詘有何功，盡付韶華逝水中。當與蒲桃恣歡謔，莫吞苦果墮虛空。

譯箋：《史記·周本紀》："非吾能教子支左詘右也。"○唐李白《將進酒》詩："斗酒十千恣歡謔。"○參看温譯其二百一十六與三百零四。

LIV

Waste not your Hour, nor in the vain pursuit

Of This and That endeavour and dispute;

　　Better be jocund with the fruitful Grape

Than sadden after none, or Bitter, Fruit.

其五十五

慧根乏嗣耄倥侗，卷帳遣教棲冷宮，喜瑞盈門宴賓友，蒲桃新婦笑嫣紅。

譯箋：漢揚雄《法言序》："天降生民，倥侗顓蒙。"莪默或謂真主之奧秘非理性所能探究，而惟憑迷醉之體悟方可得之。參看溫譯其一百九十六。

LV

You know, my Friends, with what a brave Carouse

I made a Second Marriage in my house;

　　Divorced old barren Reason from my Bed,

And took the Daughter of the Vine to Spouse.

其五十六

因明可據識崇卑，物則有無能探微。知也無涯競蠡測，誰從我向酒池歸。

譯箋：因明，佛學術語，五明之一。相當於西學之邏輯。〇《詩經・大雅・烝民》："天生烝民，有物有則。"有無，英譯作"IS"and"IS-NOT"是與不是，指存在與不存在。〇參看溫譯其三百三十六。

LVI

For "IS" and "IS-NOT" though with Rule and Line

And "UP-AND-DOWN" by Logic I define,

Of all that one should care to fathom, I

Was never deep in anything but — Wine.

其五十七
身厠疇人研曆算，新頒正朔歲宜短。昨天已死但刪除，明日未生當不選。

譯箋：莪默於波斯塞爾柱朝曾修訂曆法，建天文臺。阿魯孜依《文苑精英》亦列其爲天文學家。〇參看温譯其三百五十與其二十六。

LVII

Ah, but my Computations, People say,

Reduced the Year to better reckoning? — Nay,

　'Twas only striking from the Calendar

Unborn To-morrow and dead Yesterday.

其五十八
熹微茅店入門堂，忽睹金身顯異光。原是仙人扛甕至，蒲桃佳釀命余嘗。

譯箋：參看温譯其二百八十四。

LVIII

And lately, by the Tavern Door agape,

Came shining through the Dusk an Angel Shape

    Bearing a Vessel on his Shoulder; and

He bid me taste of it; and 'twas — the Grape!

其五十九

酒德堪依至道行,坐談橫議盡消冥。土鈃忽化瑚璉器,無上真仙獨顯靈。

譯箋:《孟子·滕文公下》:"聖王不作,諸侯放恣,處士橫議,楊朱、墨翟之言盈天下。"坐談橫議,英譯原作 The Two-and-Seventy jarring Sects(相互爭執的七十二派)。阿布杜拉·本·阿穆勒《傳述》:"穆聖説:'以色列的後代將分爲七十二夥,我的教生將分爲七十三夥,除過一派外,其餘的全部進火獄。'衆人問:'貴聖啊!哪一夥人進天堂?'穆聖説:'依照我和我的弟子們所遵循的那一派。'"菲注謂指世界有七十二教之説,或含伊斯蘭,或否。○《漢書·司馬遷傳》:"堯舜飯土簋,歠土鈃。"《論語·公冶長》:"子貢問曰:'賜也何如?'子曰:'女,器也。'曰:'何器也?'曰:'瑚璉也。'"原譯以化鉛爲金喻酒所予生命之變化。○參看温譯其一百九十四。

LIX

The Grape that can with Logic absolute

The Two-and-Seventy jarring Sects confute;

    The sovereign Alchemist that in a trice

Life's leaden metal into Gold transmute.

其六十

千憂萬懼黯銷魂，黑帳壓城如黑雲。天祐聖王拔劍起，一麾江海散愁軍。

譯箋：南朝梁江淹《別賦》："黯然銷魂者，唯別而已矣。"○唐李賀《雁門太守行》："黑雲壓城城欲摧。"黑帳，原譯 black Horde。Horde，指遊牧民族之帳篷。中國蒙藏民族亦有以帳篷顏色區分部落之習俗，藏族史詩《格薩爾王》中即有黑帳汗。菲注謂暗喻瑪赫穆德征伐印度及其黑人部隊。Misbelieving，乃指異族之非伊斯蘭信仰，此未譯。○神王，原文 The mighty Mahmúd，瑪赫穆德乃古波斯伽茲尼王朝國王。《三國志·魏書·徐邈傳》："酒清者爲聖人，濁者爲賢人。"原注以爲此處莪默以瑪赫穆德王喻酒，蓋酒可消愁。○唐杜牧《將赴吳興登樂游原》詩："欲把一麾江海去，樂遊原上望昭陵。"此借其語。○參看溫譯其二百零三。

LX

The mighty Mahmúd, Allah-breathing Lord,
That all the misbelieving and black Horde
    Of Fears and Sorrows that infest the Soul
Scatters before him with his whirlwind Sword.

其六十一

天教碩果成佳釀，何謗蠻藤爲穽網。福至堪承直可承，詛災莫問由誰降。

譯箋：參看溫譯其一百九十七。

LXI

Why, be this Juice the growth of God, who dare
Blaspheme the twisted tendril as a Snare?
　　A Blessing, we should use it, should we not?
And if a Curse — why, then, Who set it there?

其六十二

生當歸靜未曾忘，券契還憂貫滿償。碾作香塵尚何冀，但求仙液滿離觴。

譯箋：《老子·第十六章》："夫物云云，各歸其根。歸根曰靜，靜曰復命，復命曰常，知常曰明。"〇宋陸游《卜算子·詠梅》詞："零落成泥碾作塵，只有香如故。"〇參看溫譯其四百二十七。

LXII

I must abjure the Balm of Life, I must,
Scared by some After-reckoning ta'en on trust,
　　Or lured with Hope of some Diviner Drink,
To fill the Cup — when crumbled into Dust!

其六十三

地獄天堂愛憎分，歲華荏苒怎重溫。萬紅飛盡葬青塚，色界惟斯可實聞。

譯箋：參看溫譯其一百零七。

LXIII

Oh threats of Hell and Hopes of Paradise!
One thing at least is certain —*This* Life flies;
　　One thing is certain and the rest is Lies;
The Flower that once has blown for ever dies.

其六十四

怪哉千萬往匆匆，俱入冥關十二峯。欲問前津皆不返，漫漫求索恨追從。

譯箋：戰國楚屈原《離騷》："路曼曼其修遠兮，吾將上下而求索。"○參看溫譯其一百二十九與二百五十八。

LXIV

Strange, is it not? that of the myriads who
Before us pass'd the door of Darkness through,
　　Not one returns to tell us of the Road,
Which to discover we must travel too.

其六十五

漫道先知遭火焚，聖賢示道代相聞。夢醒說此傳奇事，談罷復歸槐蟻羣。

譯箋：火焚，疑指蘇非前賢哈拉智被處死焚屍一事。○槐蟻，見唐李公佐《南柯太守傳》。○參看溫譯其二百零九。

LXV

The Revelations of Devout and Learn'd
Who rose before us, and as Prophets burn'd,
　　Are all but Stories, which, awoke from Sleep
They told their comrades, and to Sleep return'd.

其六十六

指麾吾魄入希夷，遽報來生消息知。飄渺須臾來返告，天堂地獄一身持。

譯箋：《老子·第十四章》："視之不見，名曰夷；聽之不聞，名曰希；搏之不得，名曰微。"○參看溫譯其一百一十四。

LXVI

I sent my Soul through the Invisible,
Some letter of that After-life to spell:
　　And by and by my Soul return'd to me,
And answer'd, "I Myself am Heav'n and Hell".

其六十七

九如幻相即天堂，煉魄光成地獄場。吾輩俱投幽闇去，且明且隱兩茫茫。

譯箋：九如，語出《詩經·小雅·天保》："如山如阜，如岡如陵，如川之方至，以莫不增。"又："如月之恒，如日之升。如南山之壽，不騫不崩。如松柏之茂，無不爾或承。"○參看溫譯其九十二。

LXVII

Heav'n but the Vision of fulfill'd Desire,

And Hell the Shadow from a Soul on fire,

　　Cast on the Darkness into which Ourselves,

So late emerged from, shall so soon expire.

其六十八
日燭庭燎誰取明，司烜中夜獨能擎。憧憧來往惟吾輩，幻影光前隊隊行。

譯箋：《周禮・秋官・司寇》："司烜氏，掌以夫遂取明火於日，以鑒取明水於月，以共祭祀之明齍、明燭，共明水。凡邦之大事，共墳燭、庭燎。"○《周易・咸卦》："憧憧往來。"○參看溫譯其三百一十。

LXVIII

We are no other than a moving row

Of Magic Shadow-shapes that come and go

　　Round with the Sun-illumined Lantern held

In Midnight by the Master of the Show.

其六十九
困窮碁石任移挪，枰局陰陽立網羅。馳突沙場攻殺罷，終歸一匣沒行窩。

譯箋：宋邵伯溫《聞見前錄》卷二十："十餘家如康節先公所居安樂窩，起屋以待其來，謂之行窩。故康節先公沒，鄉人挽詩有云：春風秋月嬉遊處，冷落行窩十二家。"○艾哈邁德・愛敏《阿拉伯-伊斯蘭文化史》稱，"穆斯林就是從印度人那裡學會下象棋的，盡管人們對學習的途徑，即直接從印度，還是通過波斯學到的——有不同的看法。"並云："阿拉伯人也寫了很多有關象棋的詩，如伊本·魯米。"〇參看溫譯其二百七十。

LXIX

But helpless Pieces of the Game He plays
Upon this Chequer-board of Nights and Days;
　　Hither and thither moves, and checks, and slays,
And one by one back in the Closet lays.

其七十

縱橫宛轉逐人飛，蹴鞠焉能辨是非。唯有蹙卿場圃者，因緣獨識理無違。

譯箋：英譯 The Ball，指馬球。〇《說文解字》："鞠，蹋鞠也。"漢劉向《別錄》："蹵鞠者，傳言黃帝所作。"〇參看溫譯其四百零一。

LXX

The Ball no question makes of Ayes and Noes,
But Here or There as strikes the Player goes;
　　And He that toss'd you down into the Field,
He knows about it all — HE knows — HE knows!

其七十一

柔荑巧運瀰洋洋,書罷焉能削半行。黠智齋莊皆枉用,滂沱難洗一詞章。

譯箋:《詩經‧衛風‧碩人》:"手如柔荑,膚如凝脂。"○《文選‧宋玉〈登徒子好色賦〉》李善注:"齋,莊也,言自潔貌。"譯文取絜祀意。爲人由己,縱有所悔,亦是徒然,譬如書跡,不得刪改,禱祝、文過,實皆無補。○《詩經‧陳風‧澤陂》:"寤寐無爲,涕泗滂沱。"○參看溫譯其三十五。

LXXI

The Moving Finger writes; and, having writ,
Moves on: nor all your Piety nor Wit
　　Shall lure it back to cancel half a Line,
Nor all your Tears wash out a Word of it.

其七十二

昊蒼如簋覆羣生,六道輪迴伏楅衡。舉手何須籲天祐,其如兀者亦難行。

譯箋:此首之天指自然天穹。《詩經‧魯頌‧閟宮》:"秋而載嘗,夏而楅衡。"《說文解字》:"楅,以木有所畐束也。衡,牛觸橫大木。"○六道,又稱六趣。地獄、餓鬼、畜生、阿修羅、人間、天上是也。此六者,乃衆生輪迴之道途,故曰六道。衆生各乘因業而趣之,故謂之六趣。就佛理言,天亦六道之一,未出輪回,人禱之,彼宜無應。此雖非莪默信奉之義理,聊作譬況似亦無不可。○《莊子‧德充符》:"魯有兀者叔山無趾,踵見仲尼。仲尼曰:無趾,兀者也。"○參看溫譯其四百零八與其九十六。

LXXII

And that inverted Bowl they call the Sky,

Whereunder crawling coop'd we live and die,

　　Lift not your hands to *It* for help — for It

As impotently moves as you or I.

其七十三

造人摶土功才足，末日豐田已播穀。太始噉熹何所書，劫終拂曙當吟讀。

譯箋：參看溫譯其二百五十七。

LXXIII

With Earth's first Clay They did the Last Man knead,

And there of the Last Harvest sow'd the Seed:

　　And the first Morning of Creation wrote

What the Last Dawn of Reckoning shall read.

其七十四

今日狂狷昨日生，喜憂明日默然迎。何來何去又何故，酣飲忘機不願醒。

譯箋：唐陳子昂《酬暉上人秋夜山亭有贈》詩："多謝忘機人，塵憂未能整。"
〇參看溫譯其四百八十九與其八十七。

LXXIV

YESTERDAY *This* Day's Madness did prepare;

TO-MORROW'S Silence, Triumph, or Despair:

　　Drink! for you know not whence you came, nor why:

Drink! for you know not why you go, nor where.

其七十五
旄頭木曜下長鞭，更越炎炎天馬肩。一出紫垣靈土寄，蒲桃根畔共纏綿。

譯箋：英譯 Parwin, Mushtari, 皆波斯語，指昴宿七星與木星。唐李賀《塞下曲》："秋静見旄頭，沙遠席羈愁。"《史記·天官書》："昴曰旄頭。"○天馬，原文作 the Foal Of Heav'n，譬日也。《史記·大宛列傳》："初，天子發書《易》，云'神馬當從西北來'。得烏孫馬好，名曰天馬。及得大宛汗血馬，益壯，更名烏孫馬曰西極，名大宛馬曰天馬云。"○紫垣，英譯原作 Goal。《史記·孝武本紀》司馬貞索隱："天神貴者太一。案：《樂汁微圖》云：'紫微宮，北極。天一，太一。'"《宋史·天文志一》："極星之在紫垣，爲七曜、三垣、二十八宿衆星所拱，是謂北極，爲天之正中。"○菲譯此章當與下章連讀。參看温譯其一百四十。

LXXV

I tell you this — When, started from the Goal,

Over the flaming shoulders of the Foal

　　Of Heav'n, Parwin and Mushtari they flung,

In my predestined Plot of Dust and Soul.

其七十六

蒲桃根畔共纏綿，那管游僧笑我頹。門外呼號亦何益，賤囊磨鑰別開天。

譯箋：游僧，原作 Dervish，亦源自波斯語達爾維什，指苦行、禁欲、安貧之蘇非。張鴻年《波斯文學史》引安薩里《心聲》："達爾維什是何許人也？達爾維什外表莊重平靜，內心不急躁浮動；不慕虛名，受辱不驚，無所謂與人和解，因與人不爭；達爾維什的飲水在井，大餅在於冥冥；達爾維什心無思慮，袋無黃金。"莪默似不與之。

LXXVI

The Vine had struck a fibre: which about
If clings my Being — let the Dervish flout;
    Of my Base metal may be filed a Key,
That shall unlock the Door he howls without.

其七十七

真光一任化慈皦，或作荼毗焚坐身。但得歌筵捉其影，勝於祠廟永沉淪。

譯箋：吳經熊譯《新經全集・福音若望傳》一章："天主遣使，名曰如望。如望之來，惟以證光。俾我元元，藉以起信。渠非真光，真光之證。惟彼真光，普照生靈。"真光者，真道也。○荼毗，梵語，譯言焚燒。唐賈島《哭柏巖和尚》詩："寫留行道影，焚卻坐禪身。"蘇非之法，不重廟儀，故此作意謂得其道而棄其儀可也。○參看溫譯其二百六十二。

LXXVII

And this I know; whether the one True Light

Kindle to Love, or Wrath-consume me quite,

　　One Flash of It within the Tavern caught

Better than in the Temple lost outright.

其七十八

有情物出絕情空，卻恨偷歡轇輵中。但恐他年脫斯縛，又遭永劫泣瘝恫。

譯箋：有情，對譯原文之 conscious。梵語薩埵 Sattva，舊譯曰衆生，新譯曰有情。有情識者，有愛情者。總名動物。○參看溫譯其一百與二百六十五。

LXXVIII

What! out of senseless Nothing to provoke

A conscious Something to resent the yoke

　　Of unpermitted Pleasure, under pain

Of Everlasting Penalties, if broke!

其七十九

些微熔滓許人得，卻索真金償彼值。逋債何來本不知，此般貿物甭何則。

譯箋：南朝梁沈約《宋書・武帝紀下》："逋租宿債勿復收。"○參看溫譯其二百二十一。

LXXIX

What! from his helpless Creature be repaid

Pure Gold for what he lent him dross-allay'd —

    Sue for a Debt he never did contract,

And cannot answer — Oh the sorry trade!

其八十

汝命通塗機網充，教余躑躅勒青驄。復教罪罟由天降，強墮人於惡彀中。

譯箋：文理本《舊約·約伯記》第十八章："健壯之步履，將見狹隘，自設之計謀，轉致傾覆。其足陷之於網羅，自行於羈絆。樊籠鉗其踵，機檻拘其身。繩索爲之藏於土，罟攫爲之設於塗。"○《古詩爲焦仲卿妻作》："金車玉作輪，躑躅青驄馬。"○《詩經·大雅·召旻》："天降罪罟，蟊賊內訌。"○參看溫譯其四百三十二。

LXXX

Oh Thou, who didst with pitfall and with gin

Beset the Road I was to wander in,

    Thou wilt not with Predestined Evil round

Enmesh, and then impute my Fall to Sin!

其八十一

既搏賤質造元元，復設毒蟲藏樂園。按罪黥刑汝皆宥，人兮宥汝亦無言。

譯箋：《周禮·考工記》："搏埴之工二。"鄭玄注："搏之言拍也，埴粘土也。"

漢賈誼《過秦論上》："元元之民冀得安其性命，莫不虛心而仰上。"唐陳子昂《感遇》詩其十九："聖人不利已，憂濟在元元。"○樂園，原文作 Paradise，即天堂伊甸。英彌爾頓有詩曰《失樂園》。○赫榮-愛倫引考維爾教授言，云原作無言及蛇虺之詩句，且疑末行係菲氏誤讀尼柯拉斯版其二百三十六章，其文云："O thou who knowest the secrets of every one's mind, / Who graspest evey one's hand in the hour of weakness, / O God, give me repentance, and accept my excuses, /O thou who givest repentance and acceptest the excuses of every one.（嗚呼！惟爾知羣生之幽祕，惟爾扶衆肱之將傾。嗚呼！真主！伏願賜吾懺心而納吾辭辯。嗚呼！惟爾徧賜羣生懺心而納辭辯。）"菲氏誤解文中賜納之義，故有末行自撰之句。○參看溫譯其九十三、其二百七十六與其四百七十一。

LXXXI

Oh Thou, who Man of baser Earth didst make,
And ev'n with Paradise devise the Snake:
　　For all the Sin wherewith the Face of Man
Is blacken'd — Man's forgiveness give — and take!

其八十二
西山薄暮消殘照，齋月飢腸方欲了。重謁陶坊獨佇覬，行行瓦缶身前繞。

譯箋：菲譯首版自此章至其九十爲《陶缶篇》（KUZA-NAMA, Pot-book）。○萊麥丹，Ramazán 或 Ramadan，指伊斯蘭曆第九月，即齋月。其後爲閃瓦魯 Shawwal，開齋節開始。○其八十二、其八十三與其八十七宜與溫譯其二百八十三與其一百八十八。

LXXXII

As under cover of departing Day

Slunk hunger-stricken Ramazán away,

　　Once more within the Potter's house alone

I stood, surrounded by the Shapes of Clay.

其八十三

長短肥癯形不齊，行行立地壁前棲。懸河或有滔滔說，或默無言若耳提。

譯箋：《詩經・大雅・抑》："匪面命之，言提其耳。"

LXXXIII

Shapes of all Sorts and Sizes, great and small,

That stood along the floor and by the wall;

　　And some loquacious Vessels were; and some

Listen'd perhaps, but never talk'd at all.

其八十四

有物自言凡埏挺，挺成又毀豈徒然。幾經蹂躪還歸土，形復無形本在天。

譯箋：《老子・第十一章》："埏埴以爲器，當其無有，器之用。"埴，亦作挺，河上公注："挺，和也；埴，土也。和土以爲飲食之器"。○參看溫譯其二百九十。

LXXXIV

Said one among them — "Surely not in vain

My substance of the common Earth was ta'en

　　And to this Figure moulded, to be broke,

Or trampled back to shapeless Earth again."

其八十五

縱有狡童常醉癡，歡餘焉忍碎金卮。一如瓦缶彼親作，矧以衝冠毀棄之。

譯箋：吳經熊譯《新經全集・聖保祿致羅馬人書》第九章："嗟爾蒼生，爾何人斯？乃敢質問天主！被製之物，豈能反詰製之者，曰：'汝何爲而造我如此耶？'抑陶人於泥無自由處置之權，而不能於同一撮土中，製成貴賤不同之器耶？若天主欲宣其威而彰其德，對於可惡可毀之器，已予百般容忍，而對於吾人預定爲榮貴之器，沛加恩澤，以揚其無窮之榮，且從猶太及天下萬國之中，甄而別之，召而集之；果有何不可乎？"○參看溫譯其四十二。

LXXXV

Then said a Second — "Ne'er a peevish Boy

Would break the Bowl from which he drank in joy;

　　And He that with his hand the Vessel made

Will surely not in after Wrath destroy."

其八十六

稍定訥訥忽語詹，咨嗟物怪似無鹽。人皆笑我籧篨貌，豈是陶人顫手拈。

譯箋：《莊子・齊物論》："大言炎炎，小言詹詹。"成玄英疏："詹詹，詞費也。"○《詩經・邶風・新臺》："燕婉之求，籧篨不鮮。"毛傳："籧篨，不能俯者。"

謂醜疾之人也。○此首無較吻合之原作。

LXXXVI

After a momentary silence spake

Some Vessel of a more ungainly make;

　　"They sneer at me for leaning all awry:

What! did the Hand then of the Potter shake?"

其八十七

蘇非小甕發霆雷，鼓舌滔滔驚四維。陶器陶人莫煩絮，二端敢問本爲誰。

譯箋：蘇非，本阿拉伯語，意爲"穿粗毛衫者"。伊斯蘭蘇非教派謂主在萬物之中，萬物之中亦皆有主。

LXXXVII

Whereat some one of the loquacious Lot —

I think a Súfi pipkin — waxing hot —

　　"All this of Pot and Potter — Tell me, then,

Who is the Potter, pray, and who the Pot?"

其八十八

不成器者有何辜，譴降陰曹任鬼誅。謬執斯論二三子，未明洵美降恩殊。

譯箋：《詩經·鄭風·有女同車》："彼美孟姜，洵美且都。"洵美，原譯作善者，指真主。據艾敏《阿拉伯-伊斯蘭文化史》，哈拉智《塔辛之書》謂無始以來，除了真主別無他物,他見其自我本體,便生愛意,此愛即萬物起因,即萬物存在之緣由。○參看溫譯其一百二十六與其一百九十三。

LXXXVIII
"Why," said another, "Some there are who tell
Of one who threatens he will toss to Hell
  The luckless Pots he marr'd in making — Pish!
He's a Good Fellow, and 'twill all be well."

其八十九
器成待賈且由它,余乃乾泥葬冷花。一得千年玉膏饗,迴光返照病漸瘥。

譯箋:《論語・子罕》:"沽之哉,沽之哉,我待賈者也。"○《山海經・西山經》:"丹水出焉,西流注於稷澤,其中多白玉。是有玉膏,其原沸沸湯湯,黃帝是食是饗。"○參看溫譯其三百三十。

LXXXIX
"Well," murmur'd one, "Let whoso make or buy,
My Clay with long Oblivion is gone dry:
  But fill me with the old familiar Juice,
Methinks I might recover by and by."

其九十
一干瓦缶雜諓諓,新月待窺清牖前。鳩聚相呼四美至,酒罌已壓酒人肩。

譯箋:《說文解字》:"諓,善言也。"《春秋公羊傳・文公十二年》:"惟諓諓善竫言。"○唐王勃《秋日登洪府滕王閣餞別序》:"四美具,二難並。"○按穆斯林教法,萊麥丹月(第九月)封齋二十九或三十日,以見新月止,次日爲開齋節。菲注另錄莪默絶句一章云:"樂復樂兮愁月終,嬋娟必不負情衷。艱時戒食摧人老,僂影癯顔正泯空。"○參看溫譯其二百一十八。

XC

So while the Vessels one by one were speaking,
The little Moon look'd in that all were seeking:
    And then they jogg'd each other, "Brother! Brother!
Now for the Porter's shoulder-knot a-creaking!"

其九十一

供我殘生以碧醪,百年骸骨可淋澆。葬余蓊郁芳園側,絡繹凴臨不寂寥。

譯箋:阿魯兹依《四類英才》云,莪默在巴里黑曾言己將葬於春風吹拂之鮮花叢中。廿餘年後,阿魯兹依重訪納霞堡,莪默已離世,其墓果如其所説,上覆樹葉鮮花。○參看溫譯其六與其一百三十九。

XCI

Ah, with the Grape my fading life provide,
And wash the Body whence the Life has died,
    And lay me, shrouded in the living Leaf,
By some not unfrequented Garden-side.

其九十二
骸灰既葬化藤叢，更共蒲桃架碧空。往聖熙熙皆未覺，不知我已踵其風。

譯箋：參看温譯其十七。

XCII
That ev'n my buried Ashes such a snare
Of Vintage shall fling up into the Air
　　As not a True-believer passing by
But shall be overtaken unaware.

其九十三
誤將清譽今生葬，祇爲久崇諸偶像。榮寵消沉於淺斟，浮名終把換低唱。

譯箋：宋柳永《鶴沖天》詞："忍把浮名，換了淺斟低唱。"○參看温譯其一百八十。

XCIII
Indeed the Idols I have loved so long
Have done my credit in this World much wrong:
　　Have drown'd my Glory in a shallow Cup,
And sold my Reputation for a Song.

其九十四

幾番立誓恨前衷,疑在當時醉夢中。舊悔逢春花在握,又隨落瓣破東風。

譯箋:參看溫譯其四百二十五。

XCIV

Indeed, indeed, Repentance oft before
I swore — but was I sober when I swore?
    And then and then came Spring, and Rose-in-hand
My thread-bare Penitence apieces tore.

其九十五

奪我紫緋羞我顏,誤人儀狄果妖端。當壚既已得珍物,賤售如斯爲那般。

譯箋:唐韓愈《送區弘南歸》詩:"佩服上色紫與緋。"○《呂氏春秋·勿躬》:"儀狄作酒。"《戰國策·魏策二》:"昔者帝女令儀狄作酒而美,進之禹,禹飲而甘之,遂疏儀狄,絕旨酒,曰:'後世必有以酒亡其國者。'"○當壚,英譯原作 Vintner, 酒店老闆。參其四十一譯箋。○參看溫譯其二百零八。

XCV

And much as Wine has play'd the Infidel,
And robb'd me of my Robe of Honour — Well,
    I wonder often what the Vintners buy
One half so precious as the stuff they sell.

其九十六

薔薇終挽好春回，壯歲芳箋化錦灰。枝上黃鸝獨啼囀，誰知何去復何來。

譯箋：宋黃庭堅《清平樂》詞："春歸何處，寂寞無行路。若有人知春去處，喚取歸來同住。春無蹤跡誰知，除非問取黃鸝。百囀無人能解，因風飛過薔薇。"○參看溫譯其一百五十五。

XCVI

Yet Ah, that Spring should vanish with the Rose!
That Youth's sweet-scented manuscript should close!
　　The Nightingale that in the branches sang,
Ah whence, and whither flown again, who knows!

其九十七

甘泉荒漠盼深眸，縱是矇騰亦解愁。一眺行人病中起，恰如偃草復昂頭。

譯箋：甘泉當是真理之譬喻。行人喻塵世之寄居者。○參看溫譯其四百四十二。

XCVII

Would but the Desert of the Fountain yield
One glimpse — if dimly, yet indeed, reveal'd,
　　To which the fainting Traveller might spring,
As springs the trampled herbage of the field!

其九十八

神差振翼徙如鵬，冥簿應猶封束縢。亟命判官更舊録，或勾一筆滅前徵。

譯箋：《莊子·逍遥游》："北冥有魚，其名爲鯤。鯤之大，不知其幾千里也。化而爲鳥，其名爲鵬。鵬之背，不知其幾千里也。怒而飛，其翼若垂天之雲。是鳥也，海運則將徙于南冥。"○《説文解字》："縢，緘也。"《詩經·秦風·小戎》："竹閉緄縢。"毛傳："縢，約。"○參看温譯其四百八十六。

XCVIII

Would but some wingéd Angel ere too late
Arrest the yet unfolded Roll of Fate，
　　And make the stern Recorder otherwise
Enregister，or quite obliterate!

其九十九

當攜鴛侶禱天工，造化樞機執掌中。願得毀之重鑄範，從心所欲樂融融。

譯箋：菲譯此章流行甚廣，羅素《西方哲學史》卷三曾引此詩後三句。○參看温譯其三百七十九。

XCIX

Ah，Love! could you and I with Him conspire
To grasp this sorry Scheme of Things entire，
　　Would not we shatter it to bits — and then

Re-mould it nearer to the Heart's Desire!

其一百

玉壺光轉又升空，清苑盈虛未有窮。升復升兮焰復焰，佼人一逝覓無蹤。

譯箋：宋辛棄疾《青玉案‧元夕》詞："鳳簫聲動，玉壺光轉，一夜魚龍舞。"○《詩經‧陳風‧月出》："月出皎兮，佼人僚兮。"陸德明《經典釋文》："佼字又作姣。《方言》云：'自關而東河濟之間，凡好謂之姣。'"○參看溫譯其七。

C

Yon rising Moon that looks for us again —
How oft hereafter will she wax and wane;
    How oft hereafter rising look for us
Through this same Garden — and for *one* in vain!

其一百零一

侑酒玉人難得覯，嘉賓星散沒荒楱。殷勤倘造我幽栖，但請覆杯空對月。

譯箋：侑酒玉人，原作薩吉，見其菲譯四十六譯箋。參看溫譯其二百三十四與二百零五。

CI

And when like her, oh Sáki, you shall pass
Among the Guests Star-scatter'd on the Grass,
    And in your joyous errand reach the spot

Where I made One — turn down an empty Glass!

（篇終）

（TAMAM）

外編

一、見於菲氏譯介諸篇

致知織帳枉辛勞，卻墮愁爐烈火熬。鬻盡一身無所得，命絲竟付斷魂刀。

譯箋：參看溫譯其八十三。

Khayyam, who stitched the Tents of Science,
Has fallen in Grief's furnace and been suddenly burned;
　　The shears of Fate have cut the tent-ropes of his life,
And the Broker of Hope has sold him for nothing!

人投獄火汝心焦，亦入熊熊將己燒。長喚天恩自天降，誰教誰效恨中宵。

譯箋：參看溫譯其四百八十八。

Oh, Thou who burn'st in Heart for those who burn
In Hell, whose fires thyself shall feed in turn;
　　How long been crying, "Mercy on them, God!"
Why, who art Thou to teach, and He to learn?

律例洋洋隨意觀，善行寶鏈偶能攢。儜斯亦可祈天恕，獨一真神未錯看。

譯箋：參看溫譯其二百六十八。

If I myself upon a looser Creed

Have loosely strung the Jewel of Good deed,

    Let this one thing for my Atonement plead

That one for Two I never did misread.

二、見於注釋諸篇

其十八

宮闕雕梁挂絳霄，列王匍匐拜前朝。而今我向此間望，幾處鶌鴣悲寂寥。

譯箋：參看溫譯其三百九十二。

XVIII

The Palace that to Heav'n his pillars threw,

And Kings the forehead on his threshold drew —

    I saw the solitary Ringdove there,

And "Coo, coo, coo," she cried; and "Coo, coo, coo."

其九十

樂復樂兮愁月終，嬋娟必不負情衷。艱時戒食摧人老，傻影癯顏正泯空。

XC

Be of Good Cheer — the sullen Month will die,

And a Young Moon requite us by and by：

　　Look how the old one, meager, bent and wan

With Age and Fast, is fainting from the Sky!

三、僅見首版諸篇

其三十三

周天行健我高呼，稚子趑趄在閽廬。歧路何燈堪指引，但憑智瞽又何如。

譯箋：與第四、五版其三十二異文。

XXXIII

Then to the rolling Heav'n itself I cried,

Asking, "What Lamp had Destiny to guide

　　Her little Children stumbling in the Dark?"

And— "A blind Understanding!" Heav'n replied.

其四十五

且任羣賢辯不窮，但聽愚叟說鴻蒙。喧筵亦有嘲卿者，吾亦嘲之側座中。

XLV

But leave the Wise to wrangle, and with me

The Quarrel of the Universe let be：

　　And, in some corner of the Hubbub coucht,

Make Game of that which makes as much of Thee.

其三十七

金樽常滿莫嗟愁，無限韶光足底流。明日未生昨日死，眼前好景但優游。

譯箋：參看溫譯其一百一十二。

XXXVII

Ah, fill the Cup:—what boots it to repeat
How Time is slipping underneath our Feet:
　　Unborn TO-MORROW, and dead YESTERDAY,
Why fret about them if TO-DAY be sweet!

四、僅見第二版諸篇

其十四

莫傚蜘蛛織網中，浮生到了總成空。人間一點浩然氣，吐納難知異與同。

譯箋：蘇非主義認爲，真主以吐納所賜予之靈氣乃購成宇宙萬有動力之根源，如同《古蘭經》所言之亞當被創造的過程。〇參看溫譯其四百一十一。

XIV

Were it not Folly, Spider-like to spin
The Thread of present Life away to win—
　　What? for ourselves, who know not if we shall

Breathe out the very Breath we now breathe in!

其四十四
蒙恩世上日無多，披戴縗蔴嘆奈何。黃土招魂終一去，渺茫託體與山阿。

譯箋：參看温譯其一百八十一。

XLIV
Do you, within your little hour of Grace,
The waving Cypress in your Arms enlace,
　　Before the Mother back into her arms
Fold, and dissolve you in a last embrace.

其六十五
倘恃絕情逃飲功，能登仙界白雲宮。我疑仙界樂園裏，漠漠恐如斯掌空。

譯箋：參看温譯其三百八十一與其六十七。

LXV
If but the Vine and Love-abjuring Band
Are in the Prophet's Paradise to stand,
　　Alack, I doubt the Prophet's Paradise
Were empty as the hollow of one's Hand.

其七十七

且看賢哲笑談間，己意紛逞執一環。天道無窮有分節，不能蹣越不能刪。

譯箋：據西方研究者稱，是章無原作或近似之作。恐係菲氏自創。

LXXVII

For let Philosopher and Doctor preach

Of what they will, and what they will not — each

    Is but one Link in an eternal Chain

That none can slip, nor break, nor over-reach.

其八十六

聖顏不悅衆心驚，敢對弘恩懷不平。濟濟盈堂醉鄉客，亦留懦者與同行。

LXXXVI

Nay, but, for terror of his wrathful Face,

I swear I will not call Injustice Grace；

    Not one Good Fellow of the Tavern but

Would kick so poor a Coward from the place.

其九十

又聞詁讕聚相言，欹舌欺聰語絕源。如爐復燃吾耳熱，犀通不必待輶軒。

譯箋：《文選·張協〈七命〉》："語不傳於輶軒。"李善注引《風俗通》："秦周常以八月輶軒使採異代方言，藏之秘府。"

XC

And once again there gather'd a scarce heard

Whisper among them; as it were, the stirr'd

　　Ashes of some all but extinguisht Tongue,

Which mine ear kindled into living Word.

其九十九

契友茫茫宜問存，縱然蕭索別青春。飄搖牆外疏枝下，一樹繁花落滿身。

譯箋：參看第四版其九十一。

XCIX

Whither resorting from the vernal Heat

Shall Old Acquaintance Old Acquaintance greet,

　　Under the Branch that leans above the Wall

To shed his Blossom over head and feet.

其一百零七

涓涓春恨匯濤奔，騰越砰訇破海門。何若一翻生死卷，揮毫勾卻黯然魂。

譯箋：參看第四版其九十八。

CVII

Better, oh better, cancel from the Scroll

Of Universe one luckless Human Soul,

Than drop by drop enlarge the Flood that rolls

Hoarser with Anguish as the Ages roll.

五、異譯諸篇

首版

其一

覺起夜穹侵昧旦，一投弩石星飛散。扶桑后羿正馳歸，金索長揮落宮觀。

譯箋：與第四、五版其一異文。

I

Awake! for Morning in the Bowl of Night

Has flung the Stone that puts the Stars to Flight:

　　And Lo! the Hunter of the East has caught

The Sultán's Turret in a Noose of Light.

其二

夢榻熏微天際招，酒廛聲喝似寒鴉。人生當得金樽滿，莫待杯空剩寂寥。

譯箋：與第四、五版其二異文。

II

Dreaming when Dawn's Left Hand was in the Sky

I heard a Voice within the Tavern cry,

　　"Awake, my Little ones, and fill the Cup

Before Life's Liquor in its Cup be dry."

其八
朝花白日繽紛舞，夢散紛紛飛作土。孟夏常攜羣豔來，復攜列帝逍遥去。

譯箋：與第四、五版其九微異。

VIII
And look — a thousand Blossoms with the Day
Woke — and a thousand scatter'd into Clay：
　　And this first Summer Month that brings the Rose
Shall take Jamshýd and Kaikobád away.

其九
帝業千秋何足評，但隨老叟飲千觥。食魚彈鋏歌漸歇，猛士沙場不復行。

譯箋：與第四、五版其十微異。

IX
But come with old Khayyám, and leave the Lot
Of Kaikobád and Kaikhosrú forgot：
　　Let Rustum lay about him as he will，
Or Hátim Tai cry Supper — heed them not.

其十二

凡塵權勢或心甘，福滿樂園亦有談。但執貨泉餘盡棄，鼉音哪管震龍龕。

譯箋：與第四、五版其十二文異。

XII

"How sweet is mortal Sovranty!" — think some;
Others — "How blest the Paradise to come!"
　　Ah, take the Cash in hand and wave the Rest;
Oh, the brave Music of a *distant* Drum!

其二十六

但求我默莫求賢，生若逝川斯獨全。斯獨全兮它盡妄，落花難再舞新妍。

譯箋：與第四、五版其六十三異文。

XXVI

Oh, come with old Khayyám, and leave the Wise
To talk; one thing is certain, that Life flies;
　　One thing is certain, and the Rest is Lies;
The Flower that once has blown for ever dies.

其三十六

燕市閑遊日正西，佇觀陶匠正搏坯。泥中鳩舌悄聲語，楚毒輕加兄緩稽。

譯箋：與第四、五版其三十七微異。

XXXVI

For in the Market-place, one Dusk of Day,

I watch'd the Potter thumping his wet Clay:

 And with its all obliterated Tongue

It murmur'd — "Gently, Brother, gently, pray!"

其三十八

荒原虛寂暫停車,邊飲仙泉歎道遐。征響丁令沉旦昧,星移斗轉自橫斜。

譯箋:與第四、五版其四十八異文。

XXXVIII

One Moment in Annihilation's Waste,

One Moment, of the Well of Life to taste —

 The Stars are setting and the Caravan

Starts for the Dawn of Nothing — Oh, make haste!

其四十三

酒德依循至道行,坐談橫議盡消冥。土釧忽化瑚璉器,大智真仙獨顯靈。

譯箋:與第四、五版其五十九微異。

XLIII

The Grape that can with Logic absolute

The Two-and-Seventy jarring Sects confute:

The subtle Alchemist that in a Trice
Life's leaden Metal into Gold transmute.

其四十六

出入降升還往復，憧憧皮影鬧中籠。燭光如日映周遭，夢幻人生來去速。

譯箋：與第四、五版其六十八異文。

XLVI

For in and out, above, about, below,
'Tis nothing but a Magic Shadow-show,
　　Play'd in a Box whose Candle is the Sun,
Round which we Phantom Figures come and go.

其四十七

香唇佳釀兩茫茫，萬物歸空信有常。試想汝身將曷在，一朝寂滅又何傷。

譯箋：與第四、五版其四十二異文。

XLVII

And if the Wine you drink, the Lip you press,
End in the Nothing all Things end in —Yes—
　　Then fancy while Thou art, Thou art but what
Thou shalt be — Nothing — thou shalt not be less.

其四十八
薔薇灼灼發河湄，花下老夫傾赤醑。神使殷勤獻汝壽，莫因酒醨拒金卮。

譯箋：與第四、五版其四十三異文。

XLVIII
While the Rose blows along the River Brink,
With old Khayyám the Ruby Vintage drink:
　　And when the Angel with his darker Draught
Draws up to Thee — take that, and do not shrink.

其五十九
嬋娟耿耿未升空，知是行行齋月終。獨佇滄桑陶匠屋，悄聽泥偶坐談中。

譯箋：與第四、五版其八十二異文。

LIX
Listen again. One Evening at the Close
Of Ramazán, ere the better Moon arose,
　　In that old Potter's Shop I stood alone
With the clay Population round in Rows.

其六十
歷歷泥坯豈怪乎，或能謏謏或支吾。中聞率爾高聲問，陶缶陶工何別殊。

譯箋：與第四、五版其八十七異文。

LX

And, strange to tell, among that Earthen Lot

Some could articulate, while others not:

　　And suddenly one more impatient cried —

"Who *is* the Potter, pray, and who the Pot?"

其六十四

酒塵惡役孰知之，阿鼻煙灰滿面施。莫說千般試煉苦，天工獨善不須疑。

譯箋：與第四、五版其八十六異文。

LXIV

Said one — "Folks of a surly Tapster tell,

And daub his Visage with the Smoke of Hell；

　　They talk of some strict Testing of us — Pish!

He's a Good Fellow, and 'twill all be well."

其七十四

玉壺光轉又升空，樂復樂兮焉有終。升復升兮照復照，佼人何處去無蹤。

譯箋：與第四、五版其一百微異。

LXXIV

Ah, Moon of my Delight who know'st no wane,

The Moon of Heav'n is rising once again:

How oft hereafter rising shall she look
Through this same Garden after me — in vain!

第二版
其二十八
依稀枕夢妙聲連，但說花開拂曙天。覺起喁喁聞耳語，荼蘼放罷百花眠。

譯箋：宋王淇《春暮遊小園》詩："一叢梅粉褪殘妝，塗抹新紅上海棠。開到荼蘼花事了，絲絲夭棘出莓牆。"○參看第四、五版其六十三。

XXVIII
Another Voice, when I am sleeping, cries,
"The Flower should open with the Morning skies."
　　And a retreating Whisper, as I wake—
"The Flower that once has blown for ever dies."

其九十四
死生殊道所歸同，難悟因緣搔首中。忽有金剛怒目叱，誰爲陶缶與陶工。

譯箋：參看第四版其八十七。

XCIV
Thus with the Dead as with the Living, *What*?
And *Why*? so ready, but the *Wherefor* not,
　　One on a sudden peevishly exclaim'd,

"Which is the Potter, pray, and which the Pot?"

其一百零六

倘如創世可重來,冥錄金縢應可開。須鐫吾名汗青上,或教雨打滅泉臺。

譯箋:參看第四版其九十八。

CVI

Oh if the World were but to re-create,

That we might catch ere closed the Book of Fate,

    And make The Writer on a fairer leaf

Inscribe our names, or quite obliterate!

其一百零九

玉壺搖影轉清桐,佼客憭兮何處逢。升復升兮照復照,萬花葉底影無蹤。

譯箋:參看第四版其一百。

CIX

But see! The rising Moon of Heav'n again

Looks for us, Sweet-heart, through the quivering Plane:

    How oft hereafter rising will she look

Among those leaves — for one of us in vain!

菲茨傑拉德傳

M·科爾尼 撰　　石任之 譯　　眭謙 校

　　菲茨傑拉德氏，諱愛德華，薩福克郡不萊德菲爾德鎮人也，生欲隱其名，而終聞諸天下，乃同代詩人之罕有。菲茨傑拉德誕於一千八百零九年三月三十一日，行三，其父曰約翰·珀塞爾氏，愛爾蘭國基爾肯尼郡人，聘沃特福德郡威廉斯敦鎮約翰·菲茨傑拉德氏之女瑪麗·法蘭西斯·菲茨傑拉德氏爲妻，故菲氏乃承此卓異之姓，而彼未來之莪默遂具雙重愛爾蘭之血胤焉。蓋珀塞爾與菲茨傑拉德二族，皆自稱爲十一世紀諾曼武士之苗裔。現代人類學草創之際，多以伊蘭（Iran）與愛爾蘭（Erin）爲互易之辭，故或謂愛德華之研習波斯詩學，乃緣家族淵源之影響也。菲氏初問學於聖艾德蒙茲堡文法學校，一千八百二十六年入劍橋三一學院，同學少年各逞奇才，多早負盛名者，而菲氏尤眷眷於其日閑靜親睦之交遊也。時丁尼生氏、斯佩丁氏、但恩氏、肯布林氏、薩克雷氏皆有與焉，交誼綿綿，彼桂冠詩人發乎中情而獻辭於終響，用以追懷菲氏。菲氏早歲刊《幼發拉底人》之作，勾畫其爲學交遊行跡，足稱妙筆。其述士林流談，實事真體，皆託乎比興經典之名，顯於假託妙隱之中。出言莊以諧，致思誕而和，此固異人處，而終身亦如是。初版於一千八百五十一年，數年後二版三版，皆匿其名。後二版有所改易，然扉頁未註明焉。

　　《幼發拉底人》肆其藻繪，於研究本世紀三十年代劍橋士林，甚有神益。《榮譽磐石》作者可奈爾姆·蒂格，其去劍橋也，先於《幼發拉底人》之點染新語。而憶其爲人，栩然如生，謂其頎碩黧黑，若自乃父廊間之騎士畫像中出者，又神肖教堂翹足塑像下長眠者之重生。菲氏早年事略行誼，及眷眷於學園與終身知己之態，皆歷歷載諸《幼發拉底人》也。故其後日，屢造劍橋，追撫故習舊雨。菲氏實乃多情誤身之性，每自嘲"天予之黜"，以明自知己短，以爲愛爾蘭人之天性尤彰著於其身。其性藹藹，大得異趣殊品之士相親。蓋因聲氣相應，其所交遊學問之士博學過之而拙於言者，所得多矣。菲氏遊歷劍橋歲有常期，時與一少年名曰考埃爾者相綢繆。考氏於東方學造詣非凡，其熱忱親和，類於菲氏，而尤恭謹謙遜。自考埃爾，菲氏乃得聞上古詞源學中愛爾蘭（Erin）與伊蘭（Iran）二名之同源擬構。然渺遠絕學之誘終爲誦詩之樂所代，少年賞析文章，才力相侔，相與披瀝，遂爲常務。考埃爾先生才如淵海，其選誦伽亞謨遺作，取捨之間，即足以明之。莪默·伽亞謨身名未墜，其著於波斯文學，差可擬之吾國之奧里科夫與高爾。彼國吟士傳聞舊錄，往往恭談援引。然其作涉於異端，罪在無神，故蔑有問津。加之讀者並無好尚，是以傳誦之作，較之於菲爾多西以下諸家尤爲鮮見。其阿拉伯文代數學專論之外，歐羅巴學者知伽亞謨者甚罕。是以考埃爾先生發覆之功，而免其詩於堙沒。幸有先生精妙之趣及菲氏化金之才，今波斯詩人名揚泰西，無有逾於納霞堡天幕織工易卜拉欣之子莪默者，其風雲之氣宛似諾曼人之征英格蘭，而詩名（筆名）蓋得自其父所操之業。四行詩者，非賦數章之謂也。章非連綴，各借聲律以託深思。宴樂之外，亦無一旨。篡集體式頗隨意，率據尾字字母次第相連屬。若尾韻字母爲 a，則入首部，若爲 b，則爲次部，諸如此類。宿世業緣，不朽永生，人之所來所歸，今日基督世界化育之士以爲固有之宗教命題，伽亞謨俱有妙想獨見萌於奇篇之間，殊可欽仰。其爲穆斯林之虔誠，亦不稍遜於吾輩之奉天主。其哲思瑰想，豐贍於抒情雅麗，堪與賀拉斯並駕。其妙意生輝，羅馬詩歌無以過之。其鍛煉陶染菲氏之思，致其越乎譯家疆域，而菲氏重塑原作之神形，較之言辭比附有跡者，尤切元旨。人多以菲氏英譯再造，乃菲氏之《魯拜集》，非伽亞謨之《魯拜集》也，古波斯僅以詩材供盎格魯－愛爾蘭人炫能而已，實大謬不然。其如法蘭西譯者 J·B·尼古拉斯，英格蘭譯者溫菲爾德先生，分章譯意，信言可采。惟菲茨傑拉德先生或遣妙辭，允爲精當，或剪裁諸篇，衍爲新什，畢此詩歌傳輸之偉績。復常據義討源，溯爲異象，斯即温菲爾德先生以爲應代以尋常易解之詞者。域外芳菲，移來瓊苑，英華敷榮，宛若天然。問途此道，皆菲氏天才之力也。

菲茨傑拉德先生之伍德布里奇朋儕中，有伯納德·巴頓者，貴格會教徒詩人也。先生與其相厚經年，且以巴頓之女露西爲室。巴頓身後，詩集付梓，附菲氏所書友人傳略。菲氏本心親仁，然其秉性奇僻不羈，宜於鰥獨，未善齊眉。結縭日短，遂相約分袂。其時菲氏慷慨忘私，昭昭可察，奇思異想，亦未遜行止慎密。觀菲氏一生，其仁善温良之心，匪石不移，亦未嘗輕負一人。其樂也至簡無邪，所好不過自羅夫特斯特放舟，浮海一二日間，所攜不過二舟師及摯友考埃爾，所供不過餅一枚、酒數瓶耳。舟中自載書卷，可會古聖前賢之神思，啓當世友朋之月旦。菲氏激賞格言警句之睿智，運以精微妙切之言詞，窺其嫻習蒙田隨筆、賽維涅夫人書信及所纂箴言集《珀洛尼厄斯》廣徵博引諸家著作，可知矣。斯趣本諸其典則雅馴之愛，故菲氏特賞克雷布之雅正幽思，竟卒於乃孫之室宇。

其次槧刻之書，即前所謂《珀洛尼厄斯》，刊於一千八百五十二年。此集臚列所耽群書，擷篇撮要，或短章雋語，或長文思述，各存條目。偶用詹森博士語，固所欽服，然詹森氏拙重矯飾，失于天然，菲氏好之不若常引之培根、富勒、湯瑪斯·布朗尼爵士、柯勒律治爲甚。擷取卡萊爾妙語尤夥。卡萊爾自出機杼，識力雄健，菲氏友愛之，推重之，坐惑於此，無睹此"切爾西聖人"【按：十九世紀英國作家之謂】風格之粗豪不文（薩克雷引見二人相識於四十年前，而菲氏傾蓋如故，不渝忠信①）。《珀洛尼厄斯》亦見其寄心波斯學之初

---

① 菲氏與卡萊爾持久厚誼顯見於《史林》論斯夸爾文獻一文之中。此紀念檔案據稱乃克倫威爾時代之實錄。克萊爾以爲真跡，然亦有學者以其文内義斷言率皆時人僞作。然不管如何定論，茲涉吾輩之事者乃菲氏調停於斯夸爾與卡萊爾之間，而與後者就此論題鴻書往來，亦足見其二人親厚之狀也。

懷，其中援及蘇非詩歌巨匠哲拉魯丁・魯米，其作《瑪斯納維》未久由瑞德豪斯博士譯爲英文，而彼時菲氏所覽猶原典也。惟拼寫其名誤作 Jallaladin，而譯莪默・伽亞謨時不復見斯詞形之舛，亦可知是時也，其耽研伊朗文學猶未久。菲氏愛蒙田《隨筆》、帕斯卡爾《沉思錄》尤深，而《珀洛尼厄斯》於伏爾泰則頗有輕鄙之意。德人中，菲氏之所大爲忻慕者，讓・保爾、歌德、亞歷山大・馮・洪堡與奧古斯特・威廉・施萊格爾也，然似未通德語，所采者似亦皆譯文。所尚之銘曰："儉素其身，超逸其志。"雅慕丈夫氣，尚簡好真。至目吾國三尺之法先王之制爲至貴至尊。是以於愛爾蘭固有桑梓之情，而無地方自治之想，未稍改其尊仰聯邦之初衷。《珀洛尼厄斯》卷尾自作無韻詩數行，即其明證。詩繫《美學》下，此帕麥爾斯頓勳爵所作，稱頌格拉德斯通先生那不勒斯讞獄之行也。

菲氏又次之作，乃一千八百五十三年刊行之《卡爾德隆六幕劇》譯本。不見稱於當時，每不欲重刻。扉頁署名，是其罕爲，度之，友人強之以便梓行耳。是書爲無韻詩，固菲氏心手相應之體裁也。不事敷衍，不爲蕪漫之詞。神形絕似莎士比亞時代之作，措辭同源相諧，語言排奡直截。此扛鼎之作，終乏知音，菲氏特怏怏於署名，不爲爲之。歎抑之性，蓋其自恥之所由來。其後莪默・伽亞謨雖洛陽紙貴，菲氏尤言署名扉頁即爲幸名，而其移化波斯詩人，殊不足稱之。

菲氏之譯者特權觀，見諸卡爾德隆戲劇、埃斯庫羅斯《阿伽門儂》譯本前言。菲氏堅執，倘無至善之詩人以其本語再造原作之神體二端，則其至也，莫過於守義通神之重述，斯謂文字之輪回也。菲氏之譯卡爾德隆、埃斯庫羅斯、莪默・伽亞謨也，於形式無偏倚，而後者尤隨性適分，所造可觀，振英詩之文華，充異域之真趣。其譯波斯詩歌也，似羅馬而少憂鬱，似希臘而少靡麗詭秘，似西班牙而較轉譯抒情流麗，且神不稍失。無此卓絕之才，何以收此堂堂之績，菲茨傑拉德先生廁身本世紀詩人之俊乂者在此。卡爾德隆譯作重刻之時，學者D・F・麥克凱西譯本亦刊印。麥克凱西深諳西班牙文學，勝於菲氏，亦詩才不凡，然於譯者使命則持異議。麥氏譯本膾炙人口，形義皆達，足代原作，殊爲可貴。西班牙人之熟稔英文者推崇其作，然亦不稍減菲茨傑拉德先生於英國文學撰述之功。甚矣，唯此道可觀吾國譯作之得。菲氏之譯莪默，既爲英國詩歌，復調和異國風情以厚其味。與其曰譯詩，毋寧曰英詩，且美利堅人好之，倍於各色不列顚讀者也。

一千八百五十八年既半，菲茨傑拉德先生予夸里奇先生其所譯《魯拜集》，此書飽饜百千讀者之心，而菲氏聲望由是日熾。《魯拜集》爲小四開本，鐫刻者姓字而無譯者之名。初無人問津，書商遂慨然以之歸贈，菲茨傑拉德先生深慚盛意逾於自憐。此書由五先令降而爲一便士，以其價廉，流播甚速。一入書肆，二百印本即告售罄。購書者，有但丁・加布里爾・羅賽蒂，思威本先生、波頓上尉（今已爲理查爵士），及威廉姆斯・辛普森，《倫敦新聞插畫》之傑出藝術家也。時有青年集社（與者後皆聲名鵲起），前三人施諸影響，羅賽蒂尤最，乃使時人矚目此綺麗波斯詩歌之匿名譯者。其爲僞托乎，譯作乎，稱人不可得而知。縱波頓上尉亦乏親見《魯拜集》手稿之緣。東方意象典故寥落其間，人皆以爲英國作家自創也。讀者雖負賞鑒之能，仍多輕疑"譯者"實爲作者也，捉刀人也。衆皆好奇，而假匿名之庇，菲氏得享純眞之樂趣。初刻既盡，訪書者日多。一千八百六十八年，菲氏以第二版手稿歸夸里奇先生，《魯拜集》得再刊行，改訂增補，多於原作七十五節之數。修訂一如所期，潤色孔多，然亦有見作者品味與率性之處，首章尤甚。緣抱抉剔之心，此版力避巴羅克風、矯飾之態及剿襲之嫌。抑或鑒於賈米《薩拉曼》之移譯，乃摘剔首章瑰奇意象，代以尋常之筆。然菲氏雖深惡濫出己意，亦不必如履薄冰至此耳，蓋其措置《魯拜集》全文，自由更易、調轉、操持波斯四行詩，若有無上之權。菲氏昵呼己作曰"老莪默"，是名日漸風行，而美利堅讀者執卷尤切切。彼時，偶談及莪默・伽亞謨，即足使二萍水邂逅之人陡生天涯淪落之感，至以是訂交。更有奇觀：有美國莪默信徒，於重印詩集之前，購書甚巨，贈人而不取值。念會心此書妙趣者之有限，此版重刊之數不可謂少。一千八百七十二年之第三版，更加修訂，實爲作者之定本，蓋較一千八百七十九年第四版幾無出入。文集《莪默・伽亞姆〈魯拜集〉，賈米〈薩拉曼與阿布薩爾〉：英譯本》，即以第三版爲首篇。《薩拉曼》傳寫神秘主義愛情傳奇，原作一韻到底，譯爲無韻詩，間以諸韻點綴，一千八百五十六年曾單刻刊行。有別莪默・伽亞謨，賈米乃名副其實之蘇非，且才智穎異，以虔敬穆斯林士學者與詩家並名。居十五世紀文學盛衰之際，賈米之爲詩也，生機彌滿，汪洋恣肆，聲色繁蕪，窮極譬喻，竭盡摹畫，視伽亞謨辭采之簡而矯，不啻冰炭。先世詩人鮮用阿拉伯語，其好鄉音過於撒拉遜征服者後裔習用之混雜語，然賈米之文多以阿拉伯語爲緣飾。

　　菲茨傑拉德先生之交結克雷布家族也早。喬治・克雷布教士，詩人克雷布之孫，爲其密友，菲氏即逝於其訪莫頓教區之時。固知相交之厚，惑人亦深。菲氏尊尚克雷布詩歌恐非中立不倚，斯言未爲妄語。將死之歲，菲氏試刊刻小冊《克雷布讀本》，再推介克雷布詩歌於世，未果。而其《阿伽門儂：取自埃斯庫羅斯之悲劇》運命殊途，先由其私刻，後於一千八百七十六年修訂梓行。此書發揮希臘文頗自由，極富詩歌之美，然於埃斯庫羅斯之關聯乃非全豹。《阿伽門儂》所臻聲望與仰服難與莪默・伽亞謨相侔，所得不但方家之欽賞也。菲茨傑拉德先生演繹希臘文不止此，更作索福克勒斯之《俄狄浦斯》劇兩幕，然未卒章。幸得七八年前艾略特・諾頓先生瞥顧，遂相迫促，足有完章。既成，乃鏤版，惟樣稿少量刊印，英國不過一二件由作者流出。其所印卡爾德隆劇二幕未收入《六幕劇》者，亦如是。爲《人生如夢》、《神奇魔術師》，並爲西班牙文學之瑰寶也。皆不事發行，僅賫二三子而已。

　　菲氏之老舟師物化以後，垂十載，絕浮海之樂，小舟永棄。暮年所常至，劍橋也，卡雷布寓所也，別業之建於小格蘭治也。別業地近伍德布里奇，親舊時相過訪。

茲刊是版《莪默・伽亞謨》，惟以謙謙之想，追懷謙謙之士，先生非凡卓越之作，增華於英國文學之苑。其墓誌銘之最切當者，莫過一千八百八十三年刊諸丁尼生氏所著《忒瑞西阿斯及其他》者，時斯人升遐未久，享壽七十有五。

一八八七年一月

根據 E・H・温菲爾德（E. H. Whinfield）《莪默・伽亞謨四行詩》
（*The Quatrains of Omar Khayyám*，1883）轉譯

其一

拂曙華亭聞鶴鳴，狐朋狗友夢中驚。趁時斟得金樽滿，祇恐百齡將滿盈。

譯箋：《世説新語·尤悔》："陸平原河橋敗，爲盧志所讒，被誅。臨刑歎曰：'欲聞華亭鶴唳，可復得乎！'"○南朝梁劉勰《文心雕龍·徵聖》："百齡影徂，千載心在。"

At dawn a cry through all the tavern shrilled,
"Arise, my brethren of the revelers' guild,
  That I may fill our measure full of wine
Or e'er the measure of our days be filled."

其二

誰導卿身趁夜濃，一離粉陣入香叢。倘卿未在焚如火，吹皺春池盡熱風。

譯箋：南唐馮延巳《謁金門》詞："風乍起，吹皺一池春水。"

Who was it brought thee here at nightfall, who?
Forth from the harem in this manner, who?
  To him who in thy absence burns as fire,
And trembles like hot air, who was it, who?

其三

一日逡巡寄此間，累累所獲盡憂患。人生大義迷難覺，鶴翼歸遼負恨山。

譯箋：晉陶潛《搜神後記》卷一："丁令威，本遼東人，學道於靈虛山。後化鶴歸遼，集城門華表柱。時有少年，舉弓欲射之。鶴乃飛，徘徊空中而言曰：'有鳥有鳥丁令威，去家千年今始歸。城郭如故人民非，何不學仙塚壘壘。'遂高上衝天。"

'Tis but a day we sojourn here below,
And all the gain we get is grief and woe,
　　Then, leaving our life's riddles all unsolved,
And burdened with regrets, we have to go.

其四
茲惟一事待和加，早降祝詞收俐牙。爾去宜先醫拙目，莫將正道視如邪。

譯箋：和加，又作火者、和卓，波斯文 Khwaja，意爲顯貴或富有者，伊斯蘭教用於對聖裔和學者之尊稱。

Khaja! grant one request, and only one,
Wish me God-speed, and get your preaching done;
　　I walk aright, 'tis you who see awry;
Go! heal your purblind eyes, leave me alone.

其五
汝來肯否善相悅，解我倦心千萬結。抱缶今宵醉有時，他年作缶他人挈。

Arise! and come, and of thy courtesy
Resolve my weary heart's perplexity,

And fill my goblet, so that I may drink,

Or e'er they make their goblets out of me.

其六

瓊漿可沃寂然身，狂醉以歌當祭文。終劫若尋身所在，酒壚閫下弔清墳。

譯箋：參看菲譯其九十一。

When I am dead, with wine my body lave,

For obit chant a bacchanalian stave,

  And, if you need me at the day of doom,

Beneath the tavern threshold seek my grave.

其七

未央長樂棄今憂，誰執明朝爲爾留。夜宇嬋娟映澂酒，他年何處覓吾儔。

譯箋：參看菲譯其一百。

Since no one can assure thee of the morrow,

Rejoice thy heart to-day, and banish sorrow

  With moonbright wine, fair moon, for heaven's moon

Will look for us in vain on many a morrow.

其八

情癡當似我狂乖，酒海浮沉得所諧。萬事醒看盡舛謬，飲時惟任命安排。

Let lovers all distraught and frenzied be,
And flown with wine, and reprobates, like me;
　　When sober, I find everything amiss,
But in my cups cry, "Let what will be, be."

其九

仰問芸芸智者聰，靈心何故宅虛空。時來想息塵勞夢，執手閻君共赴酆。

譯箋：清俞樾《茶香室叢鈔》"酆都陰君"："酆都縣平都山爲道書七十二福地之一，宜爲神仙窟宅，而世乃傳爲鬼伯所居，殊不可解。"

In Allah's name, say, wherefore set the wise
Their hearts upon this house of vanities?
　　Whene'er they think to rest them from their toils,
Death takes them by the hand, and says, "Arise."

其十

天數雖言蘊古蘭，洋洋卷帙少人看。度量刻畫金壺上，惟此奇文可永觀。

譯箋：英譯原注謂缽盆上刻有綫條，用以測定水量。〇古蘭，《古蘭經》之畧。得魚忘筌，得意忘言，莪默其亦欲廢文字乎？

Men say the Koran holds all heavenly lore,

But on its pages seldom care to pore;

 The lucid lines engraven on the bowl, —

That is the text they dwell on evermore.

其十一

有緣吾亦戒醲醇，醒者休疵中聖身。爾輩鳶飛戾天者，罪深百倍飲中人。

譯箋：中聖，《春秋左氏傳·襄公二十二年》："二十二年春，臧武仲如晉，雨，過御叔。御叔在其邑，將飲酒，曰：'焉用聖人！我將飲酒而已，雨行，何以聖爲？'穆叔聞之曰：'不可使也，而傲使人，國之蠹也。'令倍其賦。"《三國志·魏書·徐邈傳》："魏國初建，爲尚書郎，時科禁酒，而邈私飲至於沈醉。校事趙達問以曹事，邈曰：'中聖人。'達白之太祖，太祖甚怒。度遼將軍鮮于輔進曰：'平日醉客謂酒清者爲聖人，濁者爲賢人，邈性修慎，偶醉言耳。'竟坐得免刑。"唐李白《贈孟浩然》詩："醉月頻中聖，迷花不事君。"○《詩經·大雅·旱麓》："鳶飛戾天，魚躍於淵。"南朝梁吳均《與朱元思書》："鳶飛戾天者，望峰息心。"

Blame not the drunkards, you who wine eschew,

Had I but grace, I would abstain like you,

 And mark me, vaunting zealot, you commit

A hundredfold worse sins than drunkards do.

其十二

懿範形人未足奇，天工旨意劇難知。何將塵世淒涼殿，盡飾花容與柏姿。

譯箋：《尚書·皋陶謨》："天工人其代之。"

What though 'tis fair to view, this form of man,
I know not why the heavenly Artizan
　　　Hath set these tulip cheeks and cypress forms
To deck the mournful halls of earth's divan.

其十三

一腔烈火淨煙寰，囤貨皆虧築債山。浪得高陽酒徒號，醉鄉難覓此塵間。

譯箋：愛敏《阿拉伯-伊斯蘭文化史》："沒有完全點燃的火只能生煙，但若燃燒起來就會產生火和光。人心是否去愛亦形同於此。"〇《史記·酈食其列傳》："酈生瞋目案劍叱使者曰：'走！復入言沛公，吾高陽酒徒也，非儒人也。'"

My fire gives forth no smoke-cloud here below,
My stock-in-trade no profit here below,
　　　And you, who call me tavern-haunter, know
There is indeed no tavern here below.

其十四

茫然偶像詢香客，何故良人求木石。祇為天覩自爾覩，與卿若剖靈符冊。

譯箋：漢揚雄《劇秦美新》："與天剖靈符，地合神契。"〇蘇非主義者將安拉與自然界與一切存在物視爲一體。英譯原注：一切皆由眞主而生，包括偶像。

Thus spake an idol to his worshiper,
"Why dost thou worship this dead stone, fair sir?
　'Tis because He who gazeth through thine eyes,
Doth some part of His charms on it confer."

其十五

莫向友于興忿塵，莫摧其寂莫傷神。欲嚐長樂未央福，但惱爾心休惱人。

譯箋：《尚書·君陳》："惟孝友于兄弟。"三國魏曹植《求通親親表》："今之否隔，友于同憂。"

Whate'er thou doest, never grieve thy brother,
Nor kindle fumes of wrath his peace to smother;
　Dost thou desire to taste eternal bliss,
Vex thine own heart, but never vex another!

其十六

天堂地獄主敷施，嗔愛均須自領持。君有行宫築天上，緣何拒我一居之。

譯箋：女蘇非拉比爾阿德維雅稱，其崇拜安拉，非因懼怕，亦非因貪享天園，惟因愛安拉，嚮往安拉。英譯原注稱，此作乃致先知穆罕默德。蘇非主義喜以眞主兼具美善與可畏二重神性對觀。

O Thou! to please whose love and wrath as well,

Allah created heaven and likewise hell;

 Thou hast thy court in heaven, and I have naught,

Why not admit me in thy courts to dwell?

其十七

生當一飲百千樽，會有馨香徹我墳。來往行人必停足，盤桓共挹此清芬。

譯箋：唐李白《贈孟浩然》詩："高山安可仰，徒此挹清芬。"○參看菲譯其九十二。

So many cups of wine will I consume,

Its bouquet shall exhale from out my tomb,

 And every one that passes by shall halt,

And reel and stagger with that mighty fume.

其十八

吉士春心妙術擒，天人歡得去駸駸。一心可抵天房百，勿覓天房覓一心。

譯箋：蘇非主義重視人内心之直覺經驗。天房 Ka'ba，又曰克爾白，阿拉伯語意爲方形房屋，今沙特阿拉伯麥加城聖寺中央之立方形高大石殿，乃伊斯蘭教徒朝覲聖地。○蘇非派不重教法。伊瑪目阿里云："認識了你自己，就認識了你的主。"哈拉智曾謂在家朝覲即可，無須赴聖地。

Young wooer, charm all hearts with lover's art,

Glad winner, lead thy paragon apart!
　　A hundred Ka'bas equal not one heart,
Seek not the Ka'ba, rather seek a heart!

其十九

當日持杯啜飲連，迷心醉夢忽成仙。欲看妙跡何能現，疢首湧歌如汨泉。

譯箋：是章以喻蘇非主義所追求之直覺經驗與神跡。《說文解字》："疢，熱病也。"《詩經·小雅·小弁》："疢如疾首。"

What time, my cup in hand, its draughts I drain,
And with rapt heart unconsciousness attain,
　　Behold what wondrous miracles are wrought,
Songs flow as water from my burning brain.

其二十

日看駒隙飲芳醇，生命安能再轉輪。已任光陰俘世界，更教殘酒虜斯身。

譯箋：駒隙，英譯原作 a breathing space，呼吸之間。《莊子·知北游》："人生天地之間，若白駒之過郤，忽然而已。"陸德明《經典釋文》本亦作隙。

To-day is but a breathing space, quaff wine!
Thou wilt not see again this life of thine;
　　So, as the world becomes the spoil of time,
Offer thyself to be the spoil of wine!

其二十一

俛首甘爲酒軛牛，捨生博得酒渦浮。小廝但執金罍頸，漫注蒲桃艷血流。

'Tis we who to wine's yoke our necks incline,
And risk our lives to gain the smiles of wine;
　　　The henchman grasps the flagon by its throat
And squeezes out the life blood of the vine.

其二十二

且來酒肆築棲巢，暫把身魂換碧醪。那管歡愁由禍福，氤氳天地樂遊遨。

譯箋：氤氳天地，英譯原作水、土、火、氣。《周易·繫辭下》："天地絪縕，萬物化醇。"

Here in this tavern haunt I make my lair,
Pawning for wine, heart, soul, and all I wear,
　　　Without a hope of bliss, or fear of bale,
Rapt above water, earth, and fire, and air.

其二十三

清谿汩汩正愁魚，但恐相濡在涸渠。凫雁未憂身後事，酒川漫賞想端居。

譯箋：《莊子·大宗師》："泉涸，魚相與處於陸，相呴以濕，相濡以沫，不如相忘於江湖。"

Quoth fish to duck, "'Twill be a sad affair,
If this brook leaves its channel dry and bare";
　　To whom the duck, "When I am dead and roasted
The brook may run with wine for aught I care."

其二十四

入信出疑斯息間，更看一氣化忠姦。生能享此何其貴，死罷游魂赴鬼關。

譯箋：參看菲譯其四十九與其五十。

From doubt to clear assurance is a breath,
A breath from infidelity to faith;
　　O precious breath! enjoy it while you may,
'Tis all that life can give, and then comes death.

其二十五

洪鈞酷虐肆其心，恨惡司空見慣臨。大塊如教裂其腑，中藏何寶可蒐尋。

譯箋：洪鈞，英譯原作 wheel of heaven（天之穹輪）。莪默多以此詞喻命運，而非指造物主。《文選·賈誼〈鵩鳥賦〉》："雲蒸雨降兮，糾錯相紛。大鈞播物兮，坱圠無垠。"李善注："如淳曰：'陶者作器於鈞上，此以造化為大鈞。'應劭曰：'陰陽造化，如鈞之造器也。'"晉張華《答何劭》詩："洪鈞陶萬類，大塊稟羣生。"

Ah! wheel of heaven to tyranny inclined,

'Twas e'er your wont to show yourself unkind;

 And, cruel earth, if they should cleave your breast,
What store of buried jewels they would find!

其二十六
生涯苦短能幾日，馳沙湍流逝何疾。獨有二日渾不知，來日未來去日失。

譯箋：參看菲譯其二十九與其五十七。末句義與溫譯其一百一十五類。〇是譯未入律。

My life lasts but a day or two, and fast
Sweeps by, like torrent stream or desert blast,
 Howbeit, of two days I take no heed, —
The day to come, and that already past.

其二十七
滄海何人識泣珠，瑕痕不易辨瓊琚。述恩當作殊方語，腹臆心猜盡幻虛。

譯箋：漢郭憲《洞冥記》卷二："乘象入海底取寶，宿於鮫人之舍，得淚珠，則鮫所泣之珠也，亦曰泣珠。"晉張華《博物志》卷九："南海外有鮫人，水居如魚，不廢織績，其眼能泣珠。從水出，寓人家，積日賣綃。將去，從主人索一器，泣而成珠滿盤，以與主人。"〇《詩經·衛風·木瓜》："投我以木瓜，報之以瓊琚。"〇唐王維《曉行巴峽》詩："人作殊方語，鶯爲舊國聲。"〇英譯原注云：意謂真主之真愛異於常人觀念。

That pearl is from a mine unknown to thee,
That ruby bears a stamp thou canst not see,
　　The tale of love some other tongue must tell,
All our conjectures are mere phantasy.

其二十八

韶華無限正歡逢，迷笛橫吹醉飲空。休怨杯中滋味苦，人生本與苦交融。

Now with its joyful prime my age is rife,
I quaff enchanting wine, and list to fife;
　　Chide not at wine for all its bitter taste,
Its bitterness sorts well with human life!

其二十九

世事無常忍久淹，漣如泣血痛承砭。幽魂既是終須去，何向斯軀暫隱潛。

譯箋：《周易·屯卦》："乘馬班如，泣血漣如。"

O soul! whose lot it is to bleed with pain,
And daily change of fortune to sustain,
　　Into this body wherefore didst thou come,
Seeing thou must at last go forth again?

其三十

惜茲命息假於天，一世應無再得緣。倘有今朝莫虛度，明朝冀望盡愁煎。

To-day is thine to spend, but not to-morrow,
Counting on morrows breedeth naught but sorrow;
　　Oh! squander not this breath that heaven hath lent thee,
Nor make too sure another breath to borrow!

其三十一

多門匍匐實徒然，禍福何如並仔肩。遊戲人間誰得免，呼盧喝雉但凴天。

譯箋：《詩經・周頌・敬之》："佛時仔肩。"○宋陸游《風順舟行甚疾戲書》詩："呼盧喝雉連暮夜，擊兔伐狐窮歲年。"

'Tis labor lost thus to all doors to crawl,
Take thy good fortune, and thy bad withal;
　　Know for a surety each must play his game,
As from heaven's dice-box fate's dice chance to fall.

其三十二

情愁曾共一壺澆，寶髻香釵紛繞繚。曲炳而今卿所見，昔時常並美人腰。

譯箋：參看菲譯其三十六。

This jug did once, like me, love's sorrows taste,

And bonds of beauty's tresses once embraced,
　　This handle, which you see upon its side,
Has many a time twined round a slender waist!

其三十三

未生卿我歲無窮，日月相推豈有終。足下微塵毋輕踢，恐爲異代美人瞳。

Days changed to nights, ere you were born, or I,
And on its business ever rolled the sky;
　　See you tread gently on this dust — perchance
'Twas once the apple of some beauty's eye.

其三十四

净祠佛刹滿嚁咶，神殿鼓鐘雲畔鏗。十架月星昭宇寺，同懸寰内祀天聲。

譯箋：《玉篇・口部》："嚁咶，市人聲。"《文選・司馬相如〈長門賦〉》："擠玉户以撼金鋪兮，聲嚁咶而似鐘音。"李善注："嚁咶，聲也。"〇英譯原注云：意謂信仰形式無關緊要。〇據愛敏《阿拉伯-伊斯蘭文化史》，蘇非派以爲，所有宗教皆爲通向主的道路。伊本・阿拉比云："我之心可包羅萬象：僧侶的修道院，羚羊的牧場，拜物教徒的廟宇，朝覲者的天方；聖經的文字，古蘭經的篇章。我信奉愛的宗教，不管它來自何方；愛，是我的宗教，我的信仰。"

Pagodas, just as mosques, are homes of prayer,
'Tis prayer that church-bells chime unto the air,
　　Yea, Church and Ka'ba, Rosary and Cross

Are all but divers tongues of world-wide prayer.

其三十五

一世因緣筆已落,何曾盺顧人憂樂。吮毫削牘既呵成,腹誹廷爭皆妄作。

譯箋:《漢書·游俠傳》:"削牘爲疏,具記衣被棺木,下至飯含之物,分付諸客。"《史記·呂太后本紀》:"於今面折廷爭,臣不如君。"筆牘之義可參看温譯其一百一十四譯箋。○英譯原注云:意謂命運無情亦不可抗拒。○參看菲譯其七十一。

'Twas writ at first, whatever was to be,
By pen, unheeding bliss or misery,
　　Yea, writ upon the tablet once for all,
To murmur or resist is vanity.

其三十六

俛仰太玄知本原,災祥於世未能論。文辭拙澀苦無奈,曲徑通幽不可言。

譯箋:三國魏嵇康《贈兄秀才入軍》:"俛仰自得,游心太玄。"

There is a mystery I know full well,
Which to all, good and bad, I can not tell;
　　My words are dark, but I can not unfold
The secrets of the "station" where I dwell.

其三十七

莫教阿堵繞吾牀，擁彗須當掃室光。酒舍喜聽賢達語，愁年消得醉眠長。

譯箋：《世説新語•規箴》："王夷甫雅尚玄遠，常疾其婦貪濁，口未嘗言錢。婦欲試之，令婢以錢繞牀，不得行。夷甫晨起，見錢閡行，令婢：'舉阿堵物！'"○晉郭璞《爾雅序》："輒復擁彗清道，企望塵躅者，以將來君子爲亦有涉乎此也。"○英譯原注云：意謂毛拉無稽之談難被信從。

No base or light-weight coins pass current here,
Of such a broom has swept our dwelling clear;
　　Forth from the tavern comes a sage and cries,
"Drink! for ye all must sleep through ages drear."

其三十八

旨意惟須聽帝君，儀形徒可惑愚羣。縱憑黠智深謀慮，定命安能拒半分。

譯箋：英譯原注云：意謂人之掌控力與天命之力相比甚爲屠弱。

With outward seeming we can cheat mankind,
But to God's will we can but be resigned;
　　The deepest wiles my cunning e'er devised,
To balk resistless fate no way could find.

其三十九

詭忠私友棄如讎，諍黨明誠敬可酬。苦藥原爲療毒劑，蜜漿或隱斷魂鈎。

譯箋：英譯 eisel，含義不明。據尼科拉斯由法語轉譯之散體本，此章後兩句譯作 If poison cures you, consider it an antidote, and if the antidote does not agree with you, regard it as a poison。嘗轉託求教旅美友人。覆云，後兩句意謂 If a sweet drink does not agree with you, it acts like a sting (the word that has been translated to eisel is "sting" …… like bee sting。意遂豁然，故如是譯。

Is a friend faithless? spurn him as a foe;
Upon trustworthy foes respect bestow;
　　Hold healing poison for an antidote,
And baneful sweets for deadly eisel know.

其四十

慕卿容色視何純，別後傷心瀝血痕。縱使如斯卿未覩，爲卿愁絕自銷魂。

譯箋：卿，指真主。傳拉比爾·阿德維雅曾祈求真主不要禁止她看到主的尊容和永恒的俊美。

No heart is there but bleeds when torn from Thee,
No sight so clear but craves Thy face to see;
　　And though perchance Thou carest not for them,
No soul is there but pines with care for Thee.

其四十一

醉罷神魂溺淵壑，醒來盡失當時樂。吾生允得執其中，半醉半醒浮復落。

譯箋：《論語・堯曰》："天之曆數在爾躬，允執其中。"〇英譯原注云：伊壁鳩魯主義（享樂主義）之黃金分割。參看文理本《舊約傳道書》第七章："有義人行義而隕没，有惡人行惡而長久，我於虛空之日，皆見之矣。勿過於義，勿過於智，何爲自取敗亡耶。勿作極惡，勿爲愚昧，何爲未及期而死耶。"

Sobriety doth dry up all delight,
And drunkenness doth drown my sense outright;
　　There is a middle state, it is my life,
Not altogether drunk, nor sober quite.

其四十二

太上屈尊搏衆杯，豈能盡破恣狂詭。芸芸手足美頭顱，何愛造之何怒毁。

譯箋：太上，英譯原作 He，祂，指造物主。Cups，杯，喻所造之物。〇參看菲譯其八十五。

Behold these cups! Can He who deigned to make them,
In wanton freak let ruin overtake them,
　　So many shapely feet and hands and heads,—
What love drives Him to make, what wrath to break them?

其四十三

億年靈樹死中萌，傷逝悼亡由幻成。永劫金盆已洗手，耶穌一氣化新生。

譯箋：參看《舊約創世紀》第二章："耶和華上帝搏土爲人，噓生氣於其鼻，乃成生靈。耶和華上帝植囿於東方之伊甸，置所造之人於其間。耶和華上帝使地生諸樹，觀可娛目，食可適口。當囿之中，有生命之樹，及別善惡之樹。"○耶穌，英譯原作 Isa，爾薩，伊斯蘭教以阿拉伯語稱耶穌，參看菲譯其四譯箋。

Death's terrors spring from baseless phantasy,
Death yields the tree of immortality;
　　Since 'Isa breathed new life into my soul,
Eternal death has washed its hands of me!

其四十四

春甌仰若鬱金香，更遣花容侑羽觴。莫待青穹驟風起，徒教杯覆濺瑤漿。

譯箋：《楚辭・招魂》："瑤漿蜜勺，實羽觴些。"王逸注："羽，翠羽也。觴，觚也。"○參看菲譯其四十。

Like tulips in the Spring your cups lift up,
And, with a tulip-cheeked companion, sup
　　With joy your wine, or e'er this azure wheel
With some unlooked-for blast upset your cup.

其四十五

休誇人力須知足，萬事難遷遂人慾。寄世煩憂重泰山，生何晚也死何速。

譯箋：英譯原注云，意謂與定命抗爭乃是徒勞。

Facts will not change to humour man's caprice,
So vaunt not human powers, but hold your peace;
　　Here must we stay, weighed down with grief for this,
That we were born so late, so soon decease.

其四十六

人生莫泣百般哀，骨立神傷何益哉。義者安須覓恩典，慈恩但爲罪人來。

譯箋：《世説新語・德行》："王戎雖不備禮，而哀毀骨立。"○吳經熊譯《福音馬竇傳》第九章："耶穌聞之曰：'康健者不需醫，惟病者需之。予愛仁慈，不愛祭祀。爾其歸而玩索斯語之義。蓋予之來，非召義者，惟召罪人耳。'"

Khayyam! why weep you that your life is bad?
What boots it thus to mourn? Rather be glad.
　　He that sins not can make no claim to mercy,
Mercy was made for sinners — be not sad.

其四十七
凡塵識見隔緇帷，縱是離婁眼亦衰。幽土蒼茫人所寄，傳奇千古道深悲。

譯箋：緇帷，英譯原作 veil，帷幕，藉以喻人神之隔。參看菲譯其三十二譯箋。〇《孟子・離婁上》："離婁之明，公輸子之巧，不以規矩，不能成方圓。"

All mortal ken is bounded by the veil,
To see beyond man's sight is all too frail;
　　Yea! earth's dark bosom is his only home;—
Alas! 'twere long to tell the doleful tale.

其四十八
霜姿嚴若柏亭亭，更想容暉璧月清。悖世羈身深切問，此間誰可比卿卿。

This faithless world, my home, I have surveyed,
Yea, and with all my wit deep question made,
　　But found no moon with face so bright as thine,
No cypress in such stateliness arrayed.

其四十九
諸教廟壇人若林，鬼憂仙樂滿胸襟。但看妙悟天機者，不撒粃糠欺己心。

譯箋：英譯原注云，意謂靈魂源自神性之本質，與物質性之天堂地獄無關。

In synagogue and cloister, mosque and school,

Hell's terrors and heaven's lures men's bosoms rule,
　　But they who master Allah's mysteries,
Sow not this empty chaff their hearts to fool.

其五十

須彌所見渺然空，所說所聞安有蹤。四大部洲皆若幻，何來祕寶貯房中。

譯筆：《春秋公羊傳·桓公二年》："所見異辭，所聞異辭，所傳聞異辭。"○佛經謂四大部洲在須彌山四方鹹海之中，一南贍部洲，二東勝神洲，三西牛貨洲，四北瞿盧洲。○英譯原注云：一切皆爲虛幻。竊謂此即物質世界而言，房或喻肉體。

You see the world, but all you see is naught,
And all you say, and all you hear is naught,
　　Naught the four quarters of the mighty earth,
The secrets treasured in your chamber naught.

其五十一

芳歲無由夢裡遷，枕中安有杏花天。鄚都本與南柯近，終任墓風吹永眠。

I dreamt a sage said, "Wherefore life consume
In sleep? Can sleep make pleasure's roses bloom?
　　For gather not with death's twin-brother sleep,
Thou wilt have sleep enough within thy tomb!"

其五十二

玄命如能覺在茲，欲探神蹟但終時。有身之日不能悟，他日喪身何可知。

譯箋：參看菲譯其五十三。

If the heart knew life's secrets here below,
At death 'twould know God's secrets too, I trow;
　But, if you know naught here, while still yourself,
To-morrow, stripped of self, what can you know?

其五十三

迢迢河漢暗沉淪，惶恐觀天恨劫辰。號泣牽裾問太一，無辜定死乃何因。

譯箋：英譯原注謂可參《古蘭經》第八十二章與第五十章有關創世與死時報應之教誨。太一，英譯原作 the Loved One，所愛獨一之神。《史記‧封禪書》："天神貴者太一，太一佐曰五帝，古者天子以春秋祭太一東南郊。"

On that dread day, when wrath shall rend the sky,
And darkness dim the bright stars' galaxy,
　I'll seize the Loved One by His skirt, and cry,
"Why hast Thou doomed these guiltless ones to die?"

其五十四

頑劣安能曉道玄，愚癡不必識其淵。羣生定數何迍邅，奢望重重盡隱先。

To knaves Thy secret we must not confide,
To comprehend it is to fools denied,
    See then to what hard case Thou doomest men,
Our hopes from one and all perforce we hide.

其五十五

難寄此身安樂鄉，運交華蓋又何妨。手擎真道引吾向，但請長斟此夜光。

譯箋：《三命通會·論將星華蓋》："華蓋者，喻如寶蓋，天有此星，其形如蓋，常覆乎大常之座，故以三合底處得庫，謂之華蓋。……凡人命得華蓋，多主孤寡，縱貴亦不免孤獨作僧道。"○夜光，英譯原作 the bright wine cup，晶瑩之酒杯。《海內十洲記·鳳麟洲》："周穆王時，西胡獻昆吾割玉刀及夜光常滿杯。刀長一尺，杯受三升。刀切玉如切泥，杯是白玉之精，光明夜照。冥夕出杯於中庭以向天，比明而水汁已滿於杯中也。汁甘而香美，斯實靈人之器。"

Cupbearer! what though fate's blows here betide us,
And a safe resting-place be here denied us,
    So long as the bright wine-cup stands between us,
We have the very Truth at hand to guide us.

其五十六
紫薇玉液樂長耽，猶是生涯苦塞淹。佳釀終難遂人願，一朝棄絶不濡沾。

Long time in wine and rose I took delight,
But then my business never went aright;
　　Since wine could not accomplish my desire,
I have abandoned and forsworn it quite.

其五十七
醉靈偃蹇舞裾飄，命數昏昏夢未消。白日光陰飛若箭，青春火焰退如潮。

譯箋：《楚辭·九歌·東皇太一》："靈偃蹇兮姣服，芳菲菲兮滿堂。"○參看菲譯其五十一。

Bring wine! my heart with dancing spirit teems,
Wake! fortune's waking is as feeting dreams;
　　Quicksilver-like our days are swift of foot,
And youthful fire subsides as torrent streams.

其五十八
不是天民與聖軍，黃泉螻蟻聚愛墳。衰顔襤褸何能樂，亦匱綾綢與裠分。

譯箋：聖軍，英譯原作 Solomons，所羅門之人。《聖經舊約》中的所羅門即《古蘭經》中先知蘇萊曼（或譯蘇萊曼尼），以色列國家創建者大衛（伊斯蘭教中先知達烏德）之子，在位期間國家達至鼎盛。《古蘭經》第二十七章："蘇萊曼尼繼承了達烏德,他說:'人們啊!我們對禽言鳥語能夠領悟,我們被賜予各種事物,這確實是明顯的幸福。'蘇萊曼尼的隊伍,——由神類、人類、禽類編組,已被徵集,他們被整編部署,直至他們抵達螞蟻之谷,一個母蟻說:'螞蟻們啊!快藏進你們的住處,以防蘇萊曼尼和他的隊伍,會無意識地踩得你們粉身碎骨。'"○《戰國策·楚策一》:"楚王游於雲夢,仰天而笑曰:'今日之游也!寡人萬歲千秋之後,誰與樂此矣?'安陵君泣數行而進曰:'臣入則編席,出則陪乘。大王萬歲千秋之後,願得以身試黃泉、蓐螻蟻,又何得如此樂而樂之。'"

Love's devotees, not Moslems here you see,
Not Solomons, but ants of low degree;
　Here are but faces wan and tattered rags,
No store of Cairene cloth or silk have we.

其五十九

花徑堪迷理必遊,冥談玄義辯應休。新人倖拒妝奩事,但樂嘉賓無所求。

My law it is in pleasure's paths to stray,
My creed to shun the theologic fray;
　I wedded Luck, and offered her a dower,
She said, "I want none, so thy heart be gay."

其六十

神何搏我這般惡,一教深懺一教謫。復若淫僧與醜妓,仰無冀望俛無樂。

譯箋:英譯 mosque,清真寺,代指伊斯蘭教。Church,教堂,代指基督教。

From mosque an outcast, and to church a foe,
Allah! of what clay didst thou form me so?
　　Like sceptic monk, or ugly courtesan,
No hopes have I above, no joys below.

其六十一

慾如家犬吠淫狂，徒以狺狺擾陋房。疑似綏狐狡似兔，苛如猛虎詭如狼。

譯箋：《詩經·衛風·有狐》："有狐綏綏，在彼淇梁。心之憂矣，之子無裳。"毛傳："綏綏，匹行貌。"《戰國策·齊策四》："狡兔有三窟，僅得免其死耳。"《禮記·檀弓下》："苛政猛於虎也。"狼之詭詐見明馬中錫《中山狼傳》。人之物慾，犬、狐、兔、虎、狼斯五物可象之。

Men's lusts, like house dogs, still the house distress
With clamour, barking for mere wantonness;
　　Foxes are they, and sleep the sleep of hares;
Crafty as wolves, as tigers pitiless.

其六十二

溪水之涯碧草春，盈盈如繞妙仙脣。應從花塚香塵發，慎勿輕之踐玉身。

譯箋：妙仙，英譯原作 cherub，基路伯，原指猶太傳統中一類天使。○參看菲譯其二十。

Yon turf, fringing the margent of the stream,

As down upon a cherub's lip might seem,

　　Or growth from dust of buried tulip cheeks;

Tread not that turf with scorn, or light esteem!

其六十三

清祠神廟衆心停，愛火生光放大明。俛畏仰嘆安足惱，惟於慈典著嘉名。

譯箋：清祠神廟，英譯原作 mosque or synagogue，前者指伊斯蘭清真寺，後者則爲猶太教會堂。○英譯原注謂可參哈菲兹詩云："何處有愛，何處即有尊神顏面之榮光。"

Hearts with the light of love illumined well,

Whether in mosque or synagogue they dwell,

　　Have *their* names written in the book of love,

Unvexed by hopes of heaven or fears of hell.

其六十四

瓊漿一呷得長歡，不與諸王易冕冠。攘攘徒吟世間怨，何如愛侶夢醒歎。

譯箋：英譯 Kobad, Kai Kawus，父子皆古波斯傳說中凱揚王朝國王，參看菲譯其十譯箋。

One draught of wine outweighs the realm of Tus,

Throne of Kobad and crown of Kai Kawus;

　　Sweeter are sighs that lovers heave at morn,

Than all the groanings zealot breasts produce.

其六十五

暗通偶像入旁門,清教今添一罪人。酣死須尋酒壚去,管它何劫降斯身。

譯箋:偶像,喻酒也。

Though Moslems for my sins condemn and chide me,
Like heathens to my idol I confide me;
  Yea, when I perish of a drunken bout,
I'll call on wine, whatever doom betide me.

其六十六

天條未敢悖毫纖,豈願無端臥酒簾。自性潛機思一悟,方醺瓊液醉掀髯。

In drinking thus it is not my design
To riot, or transgress the law divine,
  No! to attain unconsciousness of self
Is the sole cause I drink me drunk with wine.

其六十七

醉客俱投火獄中,欺人駭世信難通。倘無飲者知門徑,天界當如吾掌空。

譯箋:菲譯第二版其六十五即此。

Drunkards are doomed to hell, so men declare,
Believe it not, 'tis but a foolish scare;
 Heaven will be empty as this hand of mine,
If none who love good drink find entrance there.

其六十八

中吕蓁賓當戒飲，先知真主享其寢。古經何復設林鐘，專爲渴人忍所禁。

譯箋：中吕，孟夏之月，英譯作 Rajab，賴哲卜，伊斯蘭曆七月。蓁賓，仲夏之月，英譯作 Sha'ban 舍爾邦，伊斯蘭曆八月。林鐘，季夏之月，英譯作 Ramadan 萊麥丹，伊斯蘭曆九月。九月乃齋月，自破曉至日落，成人禁食禁飲。○先知，謂穆罕默德也。古經，古蘭經也。

'Tis wrong, according to the strict Koran,
To drink in Rajab, likewise in Sha'ban,
 God and the Prophet claim those months as theirs;
Was Ramazan then made for thirsty man?

其六十九

素蟻浮醪熱月泯，歡愉奄忽若飆塵。窖藏佳釀須停飲，輩美絳脣難一親。

譯箋：熱月，即齋月，阿拉伯語萊麥丹。○《古詩十九首》其四："人生寄一世，奄忽若飆塵。"

Now Ramazan is come, no wine must flow,

Our simple pastimes we must now forego,
　　The wine we have in store we must not drink,
Nor on our mistresses one kiss bestow.

其七十
塵世悠悠羈旅鄉，戲臺命夬轉陰陽。才開列帝鐘鳴宴，又架羣王墓寢牀。

譯箋：參看菲譯其十七。

What is the world? A *caravanserai*,
A pied pavilion of night and day;
　　A feast whereat a thousand Jamshids sat,
A couch whereon a thousand Bahrams lay.

其七十一
薔薇灼灼樂天工，對席持觥手勿鬆。刻漏憎人當盡飲，如斯良讌再難逢。

Now that your roses bloom with flowers of bliss,
To grasp your goblets be not so remiss;
　　Drink while you may! Time is a treacherous foe,
You may not see another day like this.

其七十二
野鹿離雛虎失林，獵王此殿昔曾臨。嗚呼雄主今安在，司命追魂隻手擒。

譯箋：獵王，英譯原作 Bahram，巴赫拉姆。參看菲譯其十八譯箋。

Here in this palace, where Bahram held sway,
The wild roes drop their young, and tigers stray;
　　And that great hunter king — ah! well-a-day!
Now to the hunter death is fallen a prey.

其七十三

陰曀層天涕淚垂，羣芳啜飲更葳蕤。欣欣蓓蕾令余樂，花發骸塵我爲誰。

譯箋：參看菲譯其二十三。

Down fall the tears from skies enwrapt in gloom,
Without this drink, the flowers could never bloom!
　　As now these flowerets yield delight to me,
So shall my dust yield flowers, — God knows for whom.

其七十四

時逢週五穆民忙，暢飲連觥又幾場。常日一盅今必倍，此天乃是日中王。

譯箋：星期五爲穆斯林主麻日。主麻，阿拉伯語聚集之義。

To-day is Friday, as the Moslem says,
Drink then from bowls served up in quick relays;
　　Suppose on common days you drink one bowl,
To-day drink two, for 'tis the prince of days.

其七十五

葡萄美酒百千身,暫寄鱗蟲草木魂。莫道菁華皆已死,其形雖滅有神存。

譯箋:參看菲譯其五十一。

The *very* wine a myriad forms sustains,
And to take shapes of plants and creatures deigns
    But deem not that its essence ever dies,
Its forms may perish, but its self remains.

其七十六

羣生香火但餘煙,安樂誰能顧我憐。從命但教雙手捉,卻無衣縐可稍牽。

'Tis naught but smoke this people's fire doth bear,
For my well-being not a soul doth care;
    With hands fate makes me lift up in despair,
I grasp men's skirts, but find no succour there.

其七十七

密友如斯可深賴,卻爲庸智敵同愾。勿從側陋擇良朋,速避其言若疫穢。

譯箋:《尚書·堯典》:"明明揚側陋。"

This bosom friend, on whom you so rely,
Seems to clear wisdom's eyes an enemy;

Choose not your friends from this rude multitude,
Their converse is a plague 'tis best to fly.

其七十八

愚者須知輿地空,天穹光駁亦空空。死生一息人間寄,除卻是空仍是空。

O foolish one! this moulded earth is naught,
This particolored vault of heaven is naught;
  Our sojourn in this seat of life and death
Is but one breath, and what is that but naught?

其七十九

青青溪畔自深吟,天女婀娜持酒臨。既有人間樂園在,何勞汲汲上天尋。

Some wine, a Houri (Houris if there be),
A green bank by a stream, with minstrelsy; —
  Toil not to find a better Paradise
If other Paradise indeed there be!

其八十

曾視哲人遊醉宮,拜氈酒盞抱懷中。欲詢長老此深意,飲罷方知塵世空。

To the wine-house I saw the sage repair,
Bearing a wine-cup, and a mat for prayer;
  I said, "O Shaikh, what does this conduct mean?"

Said he, "Go drink! the world is naught but air."

其八十一
夜鶯翔囿唱雲和，百合薔薇語笑多。樂說眼前須惜取，良辰難再逝如波。

譯箋：宋晏殊《浣溪沙》詞："不如憐取眼前人。"

The Bulbul to the garden winged his way,
Viewed lily cups, and roses smiling gay,
    Cried in ecstatic notes, "O live your life,
You never will re-live this fleeting day."

其八十二
穹廬作體奉王靈，片暇逍遙即起行。司命須臾拆帷幕，又移別處演新聲。

譯箋：參看菲譯其四十五。

Thy body is a tent, where harbourage
The Sultan spirit takes for one brief age;
    When he departs, comes the tent-pitcher death,
Strikes it, and onward moves, another stage.

其八十三
求知織帳枉辛勞，卻墮熔爐烈火熬。身賤全教運所賣，命絲竟付斷魂刀。

Khayyam, who long time stitched the tents of learning,

Has fallen into a furnace, and lies burning,

    Death's shears have cut his thread of life asunder,

Fate's brokers sell him off with scorn and spurning.

其八十四

草岸芳春覓昔時，婉孌天女奉仙卮。任人謂我鄙如犬，縱有天堂亦不思。

In the sweet spring a grassy bank I sought,

And thither wine, and a fair Houri brought;

    And, though the people called me graceless dog,

Gave not to Paradise another thought!

其八十五

金樽美酒笑紅嫣，琴瑟歡諧舞自旋。對盞狂徒伴不顧，尚離廿步已陶然。

譯箋：英譯 roundelay，疑即指蘇非宗教儀式中圍圈頌經，或類於莫拉維教團之回旋舞。

Sweet is rose-ruddy wine in goblets gay,

And sweet are lute and harp and roundelay;

    But for the zealot who ignores the cup,

'Tis sweet when he is twenty leagues away!

其八十六

笛吟琴酒倘皆無，寂寞人間何足趣。獨立蒼茫看世界，百年苦果幾歡愉。

譯箋：英譯原注：參看其九十六覆此。

Life, void of wine, and minstrels with their lutes,
And the soft murmurs of Irakian flutes,
　　Were nothing worth: I scan the world and see:
Save pleasure, life yields only bitter fruits.

其八十七

塵世匆匆若逝暉，穿帷越幕悟玄機。得行樂處且行樂，來去不知何所依。

譯箋：參看菲譯其四十七。

Make haste! soon must you quit this life below,
And pass the veil, and Allah's secrets know;
　　Make haste to take your pleasure while you may,
You wot not whence you come, nor whither go.

其八十八

何益徒然慾滿衷，既知終逝步仍匆。昊天未賜棲身位，誰向蘭臺定轉蓬。

譯箋：唐李商隱《無題二首》其一："走馬蘭臺類轉蓬。"

Depart we must! what boots it then to be,
To walk in vain desires continually?
　　Nay, but if heaven vouchsafe no place of rest,
What power to cease our wanderings have we?

其八十九

酒頌日吟閑閉園，杯壺歷歷作籩樊。狂夫仗智爲承擯，吾擯反求吾指門。

譯箋：《禮記‧聘義》："卿爲上擯，大夫爲承擯，士爲紹擯。"孔穎達疏："承者，承副上擯也。紹者，繼續承擯也。"

To chant wine's praises is my daily task,
I live encompassed by cup, bowl, and flask;
　　Zealot! if reason be thy guide, then know
That guide of me doth ofttimes guidance ask.

其九十

胡教市虎謗吾身，但問芸芸大德人。酒色誠爲寡人疾，除斯何罪任君陳。

譯箋：《韓非子‧內儲說上》："夫市之無虎也明矣，然而三人言而成虎。"○《孟子‧梁惠王下》："王曰：'寡人有疾，寡人好色。'"

O men of morals! why do ye defame,
And thus misjudge me? I am not to blame.
　　Save weakness for the grape, and female charms,

What sins of mine can any of ye name?

其九十一

紅塵將棄怨窮鰥，貧寠難行步履艱。爾乃何人自何出，復因何事入何山。

Who treads in passion's footsteps here below,
A helpless pauper will depart, I trow;
　　Remember who you are, and whence you come.
Consider what you do, and whither go.

其九十二

幕宇如環困倦魂，滂沱涕泗若河奔。偷安天國暫如瞬，禍起悲愁陰火吞。

譯箋：英譯 Jihun，源自阿拉伯語，即 Oxus 烏滸水，今名阿姆河。《詩經‧陳風‧澤陂》："寤寐無爲，涕泗滂沱。"○參看菲譯其六十七。

Skies like a zone our weary lives enclose,
And from our tear-stained eyes a Jihun flows;
　　Hell is a fire enkindled of our griefs;
Heaven but a moment's peace, stolen from our woes.

其九十三

大光仰待賜幽魂，溺海還期救苦尊。天國如憑勞力得，此爲償值不爲恩。

譯箋：吳經熊譯《聖保羅致羅馬人書》第三章："故人之稱義，惟憑耶穌基督之救贖；此實天主之慈恩，不勞而獲者也。"○參看菲譯其八十一。

I drown in sin — show me Thy clemency!
My soul is dark — make me Thy light to see!
　　A heaven that must be earned by painful works,
I call a wage, not a gift fair and free.

其九十四

霄壤殊途不可云，佳人琴酒怎攜分。休將今世真金錠，換得天堂債券文。

譯箋：參看菲譯其十三。

Did He who made me fashion me for hell,
Or destine me for heaven? I can not tell.
　　Yet will I not renounce cup, lute and love,
Nor earthly cash for heavenly credit sell.

其九十五

傷良毀善酒須絶，聖旨監官傳兩列。既是敬虔之寇讎，天何不許吮其血。

From right and left the censors came and stood,
Saying, "Renounce this wine, this foe of good";
　　But if wine be the foe of holy faith,
By Allah, right it is to drink its blood!

其九十六

人心善惡雜相承，禍福由天命九層。有恨何關乾象轉，乾穹比爾更無能。

譯箋：英譯原注云，命運即真主之命。〇參看菲譯其七十二。

The good and evil with man's nature blent,
The weal and woe that heaven's decrees have sent, —
　　Impute them not to motions of the skies, —
Skies than thyself ten times more impotent.

其九十七

比干怎拒死神戈，富貴榮華又抵何。塵世漫尋總無益，除非善德盡蹉跎。

譯箋：《尚書・牧誓》："稱爾戈，比爾干。"孔傳："干，楯也。"孔穎達疏："楯則並以捍敵，故言比。"〇英譯原注云，或係某虔誠讀者書於頁緣以覆其八十六。則此章非我默之作矣。

Against death's arrows what are buckles worth?
What all the pomps and riches of the earth?
　　When I survey the world, I see no good
But goodness, all beside is nothing worth.

其九十八

弱魄安能與世爭，憂煎拘縛共今生。心無塵慮福祉積，異想沉淪禍種萌。

Weak souls, who from the world can not refrain,

Hold life-long fellowship with rule and pain;
    Hearts free from worldly cares have store of bliss,
All others seeds of bitter woe contain.

其九十九

已栽慧種入成胸，一日未曾虛作功。既得殷勤順神旨，亦從己意舉金盅。

He, in whose bosom wisdom's seed is sown,
To waste a single day was never known;
    Either he strives to work great Allah's will,
Or else exalts the cup, and works his own.

其一百

真宰搏泥造體靈，未來行止定冥冥。百行既乃承其預，火獄加身豈義刑。

譯箋：此章乃質疑神定論。

When Allah mixed my clay, He knew full well
My future acts, and could each one foretell;
    Without His will no act of mine was wrought;
Is it then just to punish me in hell?

其一百零一

閑時杯爵未曾捐，週五何庸独改遷。暮去晨來日无別，敬神豈是敬諸天。

譯箋：伊斯蘭教稱週五爲主麻日，義爲聚禮。

Ye, who cease not to drink on common days,
Do not on Friday quit your drinking ways;
　　Adopt my creed, and count all days the same,
Be worshipers of God, and not of days

其一百零二

斥逐阿丹出樂園，怎言真宰廣懷恩。苦行邀寵寵何有，遘罪蒙憐寵滿門。

譯箋：阿丹，即亞當。〇參看溫譯其四十六與九十三。我默此意與正統蘇非派之苦行觀有異。

If grace be grace, and Allah gracious be,
Adam from Paradise why banished He?
　　Grace to poor sinners shown is grace indeed;
In grace hard earned by works no grace I see。

其一百零三

司命娘娘笑隱刀，一揮利刃斷秋毫。偶教蜜餞落卿口，鴆毒宴安輕勿饗。

譯箋：《春秋左氏傳·閔公元年》："宴安鴆毒，不可懷也。"杜預注："以宴安比之鴆毒。"

Dame Fortune's smiles are full of guile, beware!
Her scimitar is sharp to smite, take care!
　　If e'er she drop a sweetmeat in thy mouth,

'Tis poisonous, — to swallow it forbear!

其一百零四

喋血賢君沃土芳，薔薇常伴鬱金香，紫英此處揚翎羽，蟫首曾親黑痣孃。

譯箋：波斯人以痣爲美。參看菲譯其十九。

Where'er you see a rose or tulip bed,
Know that a mighty monarch's blood was shed
    And where the violet rears her purple tuft,
Be sure a black-moled girl hath laid her head.

其一百零五

樽泛瓊波蘊寶珍，靈爲佳釀盞爲身。夜光杯裡紅漪笑，卻似傷心血淚新。

Wine is a melting ruby, cup its mine;
Cup is the body, and the soul is wine;
    These crystal goblets smile with ruddy wine
Like tears, that blood of wounded hearts enshrine.

其一百零六

飲存永命慰勞形，秋實春花歲廩盈。朋飲花間一壺酒，及時行樂度今生。

Drink wine! 'tis life etern, and travail's meed,
Fruitage of youth, and balm of age's need;

'Tis the glad time of roses, wine, and friends;
Rejoice thy spirit — that is life indeed.

其一百零七

奄歹長眠不可問，煢煢誰共遣愁頰。眼前惟得一拚醉，萎落黃花不再開。

譯箋：參看菲譯其二十四。

Drink wine! long must you sleep within the tomb,
Without a friend, or wife to cheer your gloom;
　　Hear what I say, and tell it not again,
"Never again can withered tulips bloom."

其一百零八

人慕天仙作嫁孃，怎如醱色與醇香。真金不可換期券，空鼓由它響一旁。

譯箋：參看菲譯其十三。

They preach how sweet those Houri brides will be,
But I say wine is sweeter — taste and see!
　　Hold fast this cash, and let that credit go,
And shun the din of empty drums like me.

其一百零九

靈明屢屢問於斯，天道精微安可知。余告其心惟宅一，鴻蒙除此不須思。

譯箋：《尚書·大禹謨》："人心惟危，道心惟微。惟精惟一，允執厥中。"○英譯原注：哈菲茲《頌詩》有類似表述："知獨一即知一切。"案即謂認識真主即認識世界。英譯 Alif，阿拉伯文首字母，代指 Allah，真主。○參看菲譯其四十九與其五十。

Once and again my soul did me implore,
To teach her, if I might, the heavenly lore;
　　I bade her learn the *Alif* well by heart.
Who knows that letter well need learn no more.

其一百一十

來非所願去無由，玩偶生涯任戲游。但請佳人傾赤酒，一杯滌淨世間羞。

譯箋：參看菲譯其三十。

I came not hither of my own free will,
And go against my wish, a puppet still;
　　Cupbearer! gird thy loins, and fetch some wine;
To purge the world's despite, my goblet fill.

第一百一十一

海上何時了砌塼，枉崇偶像度虛年。本非地府飄零客，時作游魂時作仙。

How long must I make bricks upon the sea?
Beshrew this vain task of idolatry;
  Call not Khayyam a denizen of hell;
One while in heaven, and one in hell is he.

其一百一十二

薔薇花面拂春潮，佳境更添人面嬌。昨日悲淒今日美，芳辰恨別怎愁消。

Sweet is the breath of Spring to rose's face,
And thy sweet face adds charm to this fair place;
  To-day is sweet, but yesterday is sad,
And sad all mention of its parted grace.

其一百一十三

酬酢笙歌此夜歡，絳脣常點美人間。殷殷酒色映紅頰，擾擾春心亂綠鬟。

譯箋：唐杜牧《阿房宮賦》："綠雲擾擾，梳曉鬟也。"

To-night pour wine, and sing a dulcet air,
And I upon thy lips will hang, O fair;
  Yea, pour some wine as rosy as thy cheeks,
My mind is troubled like thy ruffled hair.

其一百一十四

筆牘鬼仙吾獨尋，九天亙古徧親臨。幸逢智者終相告，筆牘鬼仙懸爾心。

譯箋：英譯原注謂安拉以筆牘書寫律令。林松譯《古蘭經韻譯》第六十八章第一至第二節："努尼，以筆和他們所書寫的盟誓：你獲得養主的恩惠，你決不是瘋子。"〇鬼仙，原譯作 heaven and hell，天堂和地獄。此謂真主之律令教法皆在人心，故可內求。〇參看菲譯其六十六。

Pen, tablet, heaven and hell I looked to see
Above the skies, from all eternity;
　　At last the master sage instructed me,
"Pen, tablet, heaven and hell are all in thee".

其一百一十五

必信果殊難得撲，必由塗尚未曾復。本枝安敢手搖之，今失但睎明日福。

譯箋：英譯原注謂以明朝爲重來之日。

The fruit of certitude *he* can not pluck,
The path that leads thereto who never struck,
　　Nor ever shook the bough with strenuous hand;
To-day is lost; hope for to-morrow's luck.

其一百一十六

春潮帶雨盪煙垓，但奏薰琴活潑來。淑氣吹醒塵世夢，梨花万樹應聲開。

譯箋：此章與下其二百零一意類。〇淑氣，英譯原作 Isa's breath，爾薩之噓氣，爾薩即耶穌。文理本《舊約‧創世紀》第二章："耶和華上帝搏土爲人，噓生氣於其鼻，乃成生靈。"《約翰福音》第二十章："耶穌又曰：'願爾曹安，我遣爾，如父遣我。'遂噓於衆曰：'受聖神。'"梨花，英譯原作 Musa's hand，穆薩之手，穆薩即摩西。詳參看菲譯其四譯箋。

Now spring-tide showers its foison on the land,
And lively hearts wend forth, a joyous band,
　　For 'Isa's breath wakes the dead earth to life,
And trees gleam white with flowers, like Musa's hand.

其一百一十七

心冷如灰不再燃，歡情不解醉狂癲。一簾春夢總難挽，多少韶華若逝煙。

Alas for that cold heart, which never glows
With love, nor e'er that charming madness knows;
　　The days misspent with no redeeming love; —
No days are wasted half as much as those!

其一百一十八

金風又送爾芳芬，誘我春心棄主人。直入香懷不我顧，與卿並蒂化同身。

譯箋：據英譯原注，是篇或非莪默所作。

The zephyrs waft thy fragrance, and it takes
My heart, and me, his master, he forsakes;
　Careless of me he pants and leaps to thee,
And thee his pattern and ensample makes!

其一百一十九

酒酣頓似穆王驕，天樂聞傳奏九韶。來日昔時何足顧，華年不負但今朝。

譯箋：穆王，英譯原作 Mahmud，瑪赫穆德，波斯伽茲尼王朝之國王。詳參菲譯其十一譯箋。○九韶，英譯原作 David's strain，大衛之樂章。大衛，詳參菲譯其六譯箋。《莊子·至樂》："奏《九韶》以爲樂。"成玄英疏："《九韶》，舜樂名也。"

Drink wine! and then as Mahmud thou wilt reign,
And hear a music passing David's strain:
　Think not of past or future, seize to-day,
Then all thy life will not be lived in vain.

其一百二十

十力九州八重天，七星六合五覺圓。四元三靈二世在，獨一如君惟人賢。

譯箋：英譯原注謂此係對伊斯蘭教"流溢説"之總括。流溢説本肇自古羅馬普羅提諾，謂萬物皆由某先驗本原而出。按英譯原注，三靈，指植物、動物與人之靈魂，若亞里士多德《論靈魂》所述。○五覺，指五種感覺色、聲、香、味、觸。四元，指構成世界之四種元素土、風、水、火。○是譯未入律。

Ten Powers, and nine spheres, eight heavens made He,
And planets seven, of six sides, as we see,

　　Five senses, and four elements, three souls,
Two worlds, but only one, O man, like thee.

其一百二十一

已閱羅浮無數仙，更嘆赤縣逝羣賢。金銀鑾殿幾家坐，宮闕煙塵誰永眠。

譯箋：Kasra's dome 疑即波斯語 Taq-i Kisra, Taq Kasra 或 Eyvān-e Kasra，意即 Iwan of Khosrau，霍斯魯之埃旺。Kasra、Kisra 皆 Khosrau 異名，《隋書》作庫薩和。Iwan 即波斯語拱頂。今伊拉克忒息封昔爲波斯安息王朝西部首都，其遺址今尤存一座巨大拱頂土坯磚建築，據稱乃薩珊國王沙普爾一世時代（Shapur Ⅰ，公元二四零至二七一年在位）所建。或謂建于薩珊王朝之前而重建于國王霍斯魯一世（Khosrau Ⅰ Anoushirvan，公元五三一至五七九年在位），疑即莪默是處所言。參看其二百三十三譯箋。

霍斯魯埃旺（Ctesiphon）遺址，位於今伊拉克忒息封（1932 年攝）

Jewry hath seen a thousand prophets die,
Sinai a thousand Musas mount the sky;
    How many Cæsars Rome's proud forum crossed!
'Neath Kasra's dome how many monarchs lie!

其一百二十二

錦茵困坐似樊籠，莫信黃金生慧聰。浪蕊浮翻紫薇笑，幽蘭垂首愧囊空。

譯箋：英譯原注謂暗指薔薇金色花蕊。可參看菲譯其十四。

Gold breeds not wit, but to wit lacking bread
Earth's flowery carpet seems a dungeon bed;
    'Tis his full purse that makes the rose to smile,
While empty-handed violets hang the head.

其一百二十三

新薇又作墜樓人，憔悴芳心怨大鈞。茁壯春華安足炫，幾多鈴蕾散風塵。

譯箋：唐杜牧《金谷園》詩："日暮東風怨啼鳥，落花猶似墜樓人。"大鈞，見菲譯其二十五譯箋。晉陶潛《神釋》詩："大鈞無私力，萬物自森著。"

Heaven's wheel has made full many a heart to moan,
And many a budding rose to earth has thrown;
    Plume thee not on thy youth and lusty strength,
Full many a bud is blasted ere 'tis blown.

其一百二十四

除非真道誰能制,其制誰能違厥旨。大命集身綏萬方,日光之下皆如是。

譯箋:《尚書‧太甲上》:"天監厥德,用集大命,撫綏萬方。"孔傳:"天視湯德,集王命於其身。"○英譯原注謂真道乃蘇非派稱神性之名。

What lord is fit to rule but "Truth"? Not one.
What beings disobey His rule? Not one.
    All things that are, are such as He decrees;
And naught is there beside beneath the sun.

其一百二十五

青穹湛湛挂金槃,歲月悠悠日換班。吾亦如隨命輪轉,匆匆來此去閑閑。

譯箋:英譯原注謂金槃指日。

That azure colored vault and golden tray
Have turned, and will turn yet for many a day;
    And just so we, impelled by turns of fate, —
Come here but for a while, then pass away.

其一百二十六

卿教諸器得完形,何使蒙羞與賤輕。玉我於成還復毀,心知此毀不干卿。

譯箋:參看菲譯其八十八。

The Master did himself these vessels frame,
Why should he cast them out to scorn and shame?
　　If he has made them well, why should he break them?
Yea, though he marred them, *they* are not to blame.

其一百二十七
施仁何別敵朋門，善即慈心自可論。暴虐徒教知己遠，溫良堪慰釋儷冤。

Kindness to friends and foes 'tis well to show,
No kindly heart can prove unkind, I trow:
　　Harshness will alienate a bosom friend,
And kindness reconcile a deadly foe.

其一百二十八
鴛侶何關媸與妍，情真安顧錦衣鮮。入凡遝舉不須慮，縱墮泉臺亦永牽。

To lovers true, what matters dark or fair?
Or if the loved one silk or sackcloth wear,
　　Or lie on down or dust, or rise to heaven?
Yea, though she sink to hell, he'll seek her there.

其一百二十九
萬壑千山踏翠微，海洲四部洗征衣。難逢朝聖回鄉客，一旦登程便不歸。

譯箋：海洲四部，參看溫譯其五十譯箋。○參看菲譯其六十四。

Full many a hill and vale I journeyed o'er;
Yea, journeyed through the world's wide quarters four,
    But never heard of pilgrim who returned;
When once they go, they go to come no more.

其一百三十

解飢救渴酒街喧，負悔如磐背上囤。無罪何須仰恩典，乃因我罪立慈恩。

譯箋：參看溫譯其四十六。

Wine-houses flourish through this thirst of mine,
Loads of remorse weigh down this back of mine;
    Yet, if I sinned not, what would mercy do?
Mercy depends upon these sins of mine.

其一百三十一

爾情乃出彼之情，爾在乃由他所在。覆面而思爾必知，遮前手爪亦他戴。

譯箋：英譯原注，意謂神乃唯一真實之中保。

Thy being is the being of Another,
Thy passion is the passion of Another.
    Cover thy head, and think, and thou wilt see
Thy hand is but the cover of Another.

其一百三十二

一去芸牕向缶樽,醴泉奧義獨陶熏。直將巾幘賃杯酒,額縈一條餘盡焚。

譯箋:醴泉,英譯原作 Kausar。原注云考賽爾爲樂園之酒泉。《古蘭經》第一零八章名"豐盛(考賽爾)"。考賽爾含義,其説不一,其中一説指樂園中一條清谿或風景宜人的水池。波斯傳説,考賽爾爲天堂河源,一切河流均由此流出。穆罕默德云:"考賽爾就是我的養主在樂園中賜予我的河流。"

From learning to the cup your bridle turn;
All lore of world to come, save Kausar, spurn;
    Your turban pawn for wine, or keep a shred
To bind your brow, and all the remnant burn.

其一百三十三

何益紅塵爲我留,生涯何果手中收。靈杯既碎如何卜,光滅安能秉燭遊。

譯箋:靈杯,英譯原作 Jamshid's goblet,賈姆什德之杯,即照世杯,參看菲譯其五譯箋。兹章靈杯或譬肉體,則靈魂如光而滅,則皮囊亦無用矣。○《古詩十九首》其十五:"晝短苦夜長,何不秉燭遊。"

See! from the world what profit have I gained?
What fruitage of my life in hand retained?
    What use is Jamshid's goblet, once 'tis crushed?
What pleasure's torch, when once its light has waned?

其一百三十四

歿身雙邑尚如何，樽盡苦甘存幾多。此地他年難再飲，陰晴圓缺任蹉跎。

譯箋：雙城，原譯指巴里黑與納霞堡。巴里黑，在今阿富汗北部，《馬可波羅遊記》稱之為"名貴大城"，曾為祆教中心，終為成吉思汗所毀。○參看菲譯其八。

When life is spent, what's Balkh or Nishapore?
What sweet or bitter, when the cup runs o'er?
　　Come drink! full many a moon will wax and wane
In times to come, when we are here no more.

其一百三十五

頰紅大勝紫薇羣，更與羅敷秋色分。一瞥君王驚百媚，任教席捲奪千軍。

譯箋：原譯 Chin，指中國北部。漢樂府《陌上桑》："日出東南隅，照我秦氏樓。秦氏有好女，自名為羅敷。"○君王，英譯原作巴比倫王。○是章詠酒，以美人弈棋為喻。

O fair! whose cheeks checkmate red eglantine,
And draw the game with those fair maids of Chin;
　　You played one glance against the king of Babil
And took his pawns, and knights, and rooks, and queen.

其一百三十六

人生如旅隙駒過，莫慮煩憂明日多。酣飲良宵莫教逝，一場歡會任消磨。

譯箋：《古詩十九首》："今日良宴會，歡樂難具陳。"又："人生寄一世，奄忽若飆塵。"莪默所詠類此。○參看菲譯其四十八。

Life's caravan is hastening on its way;
Brood not on troubles of the coming day,
　　But fill the wine-cup, ere sweet night be gone,
And snatch a pleasant moment, while you may.

其一百三十七

元神久定世間基，日日傷摧胸臆凄。多少紅唇麝香髮，一棺入土混泉泥。

譯箋：英譯原注引《聖經·約伯記》第十章："爾手所造，則虐待之、輕視之。惡人之謀，則焜耀之，爾豈以是爲善乎。"

He, who the world's foundations erst did lay,
Doth bruise full many a bosom day by day,
　　And many a ruby lip and musky tress
Doth coffin in the earth, and shroud with clay.

其一百三十八

塵間暗算盡機關，愚者須諳此隱患。惜命休教風裡逝，遽尋醇酒對紅顏。

Be not beguiled by world's insidious wiles;

O foolish ones, ye know her tricks and guiles;
　　Your precious life-time cast not to the winds;
Haste to seek wine, and court a sweetheart's smile.

其一百三十九

須醫我疾以醒醴，病靨旋成瑪瑙紅。死後皮囊先滌酒，再盛藤蔓槨棺中。

譯箋：漢枚乘《七發》："況直眇小煩懣，醒醴病酒之徒哉。"○參看菲譯其九十一。

Comrades! I pray you, physic me with wine,
Make this wan amber face like rubies shine,
　　And, if I die, use wine to wash my corpse,
And frame my coffin out of planks of vine!

其一百四十

黃道周流帝執樞，更驅昴宿運星途，一生窮達定由命，陽錯陰差豈我辜。

譯箋：據英譯原注，此首作者當是 Afzul Kashi。參看菲譯其七十五。

When Allah yoked the courses of the sun,
And launched the Pleiades their race to run,
　　My lot was fixed in fate's high chancery;
Then why blame me for wrong that fate has done?

其一百四十一

偏將酥酒奉愚公，善器時常歸劣工。最是歡心突厥女，濫施巧笑與蒙童。

Ah! seasoned wine oft falls to rawest fools,
And clumsiest workmen own the finest tools;
　　And Turki maids, fit to delight men's hearts,
Lavish their smiles on beardless boys in school!

其一百四十二

當時未減少年狂，苦究人生謎萬行。齒慧同增今恨晚，空空腹笥誤韶光。

譯箋：《後漢書·文苑傳》："腹便便，五經笥。"

Whilom, ere youth's conceit had waned, methought
Answers to all life's problems I had wrought;
　　But now, grown old and wise, too late I see
My life is spent, and all my lore is naught.

其一百四十三

拜氈精織何其美，愚者織之誠大偽。莫怪莊嚴相所藏，盡皆悖信異端類。

譯箋：英譯原注：諺云魔鬼居於聖城。

They who of prayer-mats make such great display
Are fools to bear hypocrisy's hard sway;

Strange! under cover of this saintly show

They live like heathen, and their faith betray.

其一百四十四

自愆自作辯難盫，可聽虔詠再三。睿聖難窮智有限，孼由天作盡愚談。

譯箋：《逸周書·祭公》："王若曰：'祖祭公次予小子，虔虔在位。昊天疾威，予多時溥愆。'"○《尚書·太甲中》："天作孼，猶可違，自作孼，不可逭。"

To him who would his sins extenuate,

Let pious men this verse reiterate,

 "To call God's prescience the cause of sin

In wisdom's purview is but folly's prate."

其一百四十五

遣吾降此惑吾心，所獲爲何猜至今。碌碌生涯難率性，存亡來去秘何深。

譯箋：參看菲譯其二十九。

He brought me hither, and I felt surprise,

From life I gather but a dark surmise,

 I go against my will;—thus, why I come,

Why live, why go, are all dark mysteries.

其一百四十六

每憶生涯孽海深，焚胸火烈淚成霖。主前奴僕既哀悔，宜發慈憐恩恕心。

When I recall my grievous sins to mind,
Fire burns my breast, and tears my vision blind;
　　Yet, when a slave repents, is it not meet
His lord should pardon, and again be kind?

其一百四十七

天駒登送九霄煙，驚世賢才博識淵。皓首皆如大鈞轉，欲尋真宰卻茫然。

譯箋：天駒，原譯作 Borak，馬名。英譯原注云：卜拉格乃穆罕穆德夜行登霄所騎之天馬。林松譯《古蘭經韻譯》第十七章第一節："讚美安拉！他在一個夜晚，使他的僕人從禁寺夜行，到達我降福於四周的遠寺，以便把我的征跡對他顯現，他確實博聞而遠見。"登霄，傳說穆罕默德在傳教第十二年某夜，由天使吉卜利勒陪同，乘卜拉格仙馬由麥加禁寺飛至耶路撒冷阿克薩清真寺（即遠寺），並登霄遊七重天，見諸先知，領真主命，次日黎明重返麥加。詳情見《布哈里聖訓》與《穆斯林聖訓》。〇大鈞，見菲譯其二十五譯箋。〇參看菲譯其二十六。

They at whose lore the whole world stands amazed,
Whose high thoughts, like Borak, to heaven are raised,
　　Strive to know Thee in vain, and like heaven's wheel
Their heads are turning, and their brains are dazed.

其一百四十八

真神賜飲自天堂,何故人間入罪行。欲問其因應有一,蓋緣勇士醉沙場。

譯箋:勇士,英譯原作 Hamzah,哈姆宰,穆罕默德之叔父,喜獵善飲,死於戰。詳見《布哈里聖訓》。

Allah hath promised wine in Paradise,
Why then should wine on earth be deemed a vice?
　　An Arab in his cups cut Hamzah's girths, —
For that sole cause was drink declared a vice.

其一百四十九

舊歡惟剩假名存,舊友於今剩酒渾。傾蓋相逢當慍款,除非對盞樂何論。

譯箋:《楚辭‧卜居》:"吾寧悃悃款款樸以忠乎?將送往勞來斯無窮乎?"漢鄒陽《獄中上書自明》:"語曰:'白頭如新,傾蓋如故。'何則?知與不知也。"

Now of old joys naught but the name is left,
Of all old friends but wine we are bereft,
　　And that wine *new*, but still cleave to the cup,
For save the cup, what single joy is left?

其一百五十

縱然我默盛名收,不廢江河萬古流。曩歲悠悠我何在,今朝一逝復同疇。

譯箋:唐杜甫《戲爲六絕句》其二:"爾曹身與名俱滅,不廢江河萬古流。"

○參看菲譯其四十七。

The world will last long after Khayyam's fame
Has passed away, yea, and his very name;
　　Aforetime we were not, and none did heed.
When we are dead and gone, 'twill be the same.

其一百五十一
探秘尋幽有所思，海洲智者攬觀之。玄天妙構如何設，自度羣賢盡未知。

The sages who have compassed sea and land,
Their secret to search out, and understand, —
　　My mind misgives me if they ever solve
The scheme on which this universe is planned.

其一百五十二
空掌財錢插翅過，閻羅辣手倖災多。陰曹安有逃歸者，苦旅迢迢竟若何。

譯箋：後二句與菲譯其六十四、溫譯其一百二十九義類。

Ah! wealth takes wings, and leaves our hands all bare,
And death's rough hands delight our hearts to tear;
　　And from the nether world none e'er escapes,
To bring us news of the poor pilgrims there.

其一百五十三

雖是塵軀負重羈，冠緌貴冑固離奇。明知窮賤能忘役，亦罕屈尊人偶之。

譯箋：人偶，《儀禮・聘禮》"公揖，入每門，每曲揖。"漢鄭玄注："每門輒揖者，以相人偶爲敬也。"《禮記・中庸》："仁者，人也。"鄭玄注："人也，讀如相人偶之人，以人意相存問之言。"

'Tis passing strange, those titled noblemen
Find their own lives a burden sore, but when
　　They meet with poorer men, not slaves to sense,
They scarcely deign to reckon them as men.

其一百五十四

峻極洪鈞日日旋，不來苦界寄垂憐。偶逢一客心傷瘁，反欲更施一老拳。

譯箋：洪鈞，參見溫譯其二十五譯箋。

The wheel on high, still busied with despite,
Will ne'er unloose a wretch from his sad plight;
　　But when it lights upon a smitten heart,
Straightway essays another blow to smite.

其一百五十五

韶華歌闋奏將終，花發春潮摘欲空。觀爾新禽自來去，獨留孤客坐𮖐𮖐。

譯箋：參看菲譯其九十六。

Now is the volume of my youth outworn,

And all my spring-tide blossoms rent and torn.

　　Ah, bird of youth! I marked not when you came,

Nor when you fled, and left me thus forlorn.

其一百五十六

濟濟羣氓本下愚，超凡上智妄思居。巧言訾訾如邪道，天下安能覓此驢。

譯箋：英譯原注引《聖經·約伯記》第十二章："爾曹爲民，無疑也，智慧將與爾偕亡。"

These fools, by dint of ignorance most crass,

Think they in wisdom all mankind surpass;

　　And glibly do they damn as infidel,

Whoever is not, like themselves, an ass.

其一百五十七

嘈雜歡吟滿酒廛，律師竟未覺衫燃。襤褸青袍皆墜地，任教飲者踏歌連。

譯箋：律師，原作法利賽人，應代指猶太人。○英譯原注謂哈菲茲《頌詩》亦以袄僧青袍爲僞善象徵。○是章或刺猶太教與袄教。

Still be the wine-house thronged with its glad choir,

And Pharisaic skirts burnt up with fire;

　　Still be those tattered frocks and azure robes

Trod under feet of revellers in the mire.

其一百五十八
何苦癡迷幻景空，強尋善惡世塵中。眾生方若聖泉湧，又沒茫茫大地胸。

譯箋：聖泉，原譯作 Zamzam。滲滲泉，位於麥加禁寺內，傳由易卜拉欣之子易司瑪儀發現。

Why toil ye to ensure illusions vain,
And good or evil of the world attain?
　　Ye rise like Zamzam, or the fount of life,
And, like them, in earth's bosom sink again.

其一百五十九
友朋斟酌樂心間，天澤飛臨吻我顏。悔罪誠知須盡早，寵恩先賜化靈頑。

譯箋：英譯原注云，意即若無神恩人無力改其行。

Till the Friend pours his wine to glad my heart,
No kisses to my face will heaven impart:
　　They say, "Repent in time"; but how repent,
Ere Allah's grace hath softened my hard heart?

其一百六十

朽囊磨碾碎齏存，遺鑒應能警後昆。裹得黏泥摻酒和，可教吾體塞金樽。

When I am dead, take me and grind me small,
So that I be a caution unto all,
　　And knead me into clay with wine, and then
Use me to stop the wine-jar's mouth withal.

其一百六十一

人隔天帷青莽蒼，冥冥難視亦何妨。億千泡沫皆如我，永泛酒人之羽觴。

譯箋：參看菲譯其四十六。

What though the sky with its blue canopy
Doth close us in so that we can not see,
　　In the etern Cupbearer's wine methinks,
There float a myriad bubbles like to me.

其一百六十二

休倦墓中年月長，羣星依舊耀穹蒼。照君齏骨摶磚瓦，砌得宮樓峻一方。

Take heart! Long in the weary tomb you'll lie,
While stars keep countless watches in the sky,
　　And see your ashes moulded into bricks,
To build another's house and turrets high.

其一百六十三

安許歡心染玷微，拒披金紫炫榮輝。但如玄鳥入雲去，不作荒墟鴞黯飛。

譯箋：玄鳥，原譯 Simurgh，係波斯傳說中有翼動物，犬首獅足，偶作人面，波斯蘇非詩人常以隱喻玄祕之神。

Glad hearts, who seek not notoriety,
Nor flaunt in gold and silken bravery,
    Haunt not this ruined earth like gloomy owls,
But wing their way, Simurgh-like, to the sky.

其一百六十四

酒力能諳惟酒癡，寸光鼠目豈明斯。未曾驗效誠難怪，身未驗之安得知。

Wine's power is known to wine-bibbers alone,
To narrow heads and hearts 'tis never shown;
    I blame not them who never felt its force,
For, till they feel it, how can it be known.

其一百六十五

宜當買醉洗池醇，狼藉聲名怎耀身。且莫管它將進酒，纏巾已玷色難新。

Needs must the tavern-hunter bathe in wine,
For none can make a tarnished name to shine;
    Go! bring me wine, for none can now restore

Its pristine sheen to this soiled veil of mine.

其一百六十六

渺身空望恨悠悠，人世歡愉草草收。吾恐浮生須苦待，漫尋宿命復冤讎。

I wasted life in hope, yet gathered not
In all my life of happiness one jot;
　　Now my fear is that life may not endure,
Till I have taken vengeance on my lot!

其一百六十七

彷徨靈界必提心，塵事最宜持口噤。縱有聰明與簧舌，六根何若一時瘖。

譯箋：六根，眼、耳、鼻、舌、身、意。

Be very wary in the soul's domain,
And on the world's affairs your lips refrain;
　　Be, as it were, sans tongue, sans ear, sans eye,
While tongue, and ears, and eyes you still retain.

其一百六十八

簞食能持不改歡，鷦鷯仰見一枝安。役人人役皆非願，妙境斯臻誠可歎。

譯箋：《論語·雍也》："一簞食，一瓢飲，在陋巷，人不堪其憂，回也不改其樂。"〇《莊子·逍遙遊》："鷦鷯巢於深林，不過一枝。"

Let him rejoice who has a loaf of bread,
A little nest wherein to lay his head,
  Is slave to none, and no man slaves for him, —
In truth his lot is wondrous well bested.

其一百六十九

我愆瀆爾又何能，對越天威何可增。常發慈心而緩怒，爾爲赦宥不爲懲。

譯箋：《詩經·周頌·清廟》："對越在天，駿奔走在廟。"○是章言人之侍奉與罪愆于真主之威權皆無所影響。

What adds my service to Thy majesty?
Or how can sin of mine dishonor Thee?
  O pardon, then, and punish not, I know
Thou'rt slow to wrath, and prone to clemency.

其一百七十

雙手持甌啜醴醇，經書講席愧吾身。皆因飲性喜流濕，難與狂徒躁火親。

譯箋：《周易·乾卦》："水流濕，火就燥。"

Hands, such as mine, that handle bowls of wine,
'Twere shame to book and pulpit to confine;
  Zealot! thou'rt dry, and I am moist with drink,
Yea, far too moist to catch that fire of thine!

其一百七十一

蔷薇红颊衆心欢，荆棘生涯学苦攀。篦齿君知须痛割，方能理我美人鬟。

Whoso aspires to gain a rose-cheeked fair,

Sharp pricks from fortune's thorns must learn to bear.

　　See! till this comb was cleft by cruel cuts,

It never dared to touch my lady's hair.

其一百七十二

心慕天仙共婉变，但求把酒永言欢。悔愆须得天恩助，我得天恩悔亦难。

For ever may my hands on wine be stayed,

And my heart pant for some fair Houri maid!

　　They say, "May Allah aid thee to repent!"

Repent I could not, e'en with Allah's aid!

其一百七十三

时命哀哉偕与亡，珍珠无一串成行。千千真道随吾去，愚者未宜闻半章。

Soon shall I go, by time and fate deplored,

Of all my precious pearls not one is bored;

　　Alas! there die with me a thousand truths

To which these fools fit audience ne'er accord.

其一百七十四

新霖濯濯解園枯，淑氣沁人何美乎。杜宇欣從病薇唱，爾能共飲一杯無。

譯箋：參看菲譯其六。

To-day how sweetly breathes the temperate air,
The rains have newly laved the parched parterre;
　　And Bulbuls cry in notes of ecstasy,
"Thou too, O pallid rose, our wine must share!"

其一百七十五

悲恐終臨命墜亡，空樽傾盡赤瓊漿。君非殉葬黃金物，誰願辛勞掘北邙。

譯箋：北邙，山名，漢以來爲公卿墓地。晉陶潛《擬古》其四："一旦百歲後，相與還北邙。"○參看菲譯其十五。

Ere you succumb to shocks of mortal pain,
The rosy grape-juice from your wine-cup drain.
　　You are not gold, that, hidden in the earth,
Your friends should care to dig you up again!

其一百七十六

去不能加天壯猶，來無百祿進其羞。人間來去還如驛，充耳未聞何所由。

譯箋：《詩經・小雅・采芑》："方叔元老，克壯其猶。"毛傳："壯，大；猶，道也。"《詩經·小雅·天保》:"罄無不宜,受天百祿。"思高本《聖經·次經·德訓篇》:"上主的奇妙化工,人不能增損,也無法窮究。"〇參看菲譯其四十七。

My coming brought no profit to the sky,
Nor does my going swell its majesty;
　　Coming and going put me to a stand,
Ear never heard their wherefore nor their why.

其一百七十七

天聖安能相輕軒,筋髮莖莖數可言。其視衆心皆袒露,豈如凡俗可欺諼。

譯箋:吳經熊譯《新經全集·福音馬竇傳》第十章:"即爾頭上之髮,亦莖莖見數。"

The heavenly Sage, whose wit exceeds compare,
Counteth each vein, and numbereth every hair;
　　Men you may cheat by hypocritic arts,
But how cheat Him to whom all hearts are bare?

其一百七十八

酒齋雙翼倦人同,霞暈頻飛粉頰堆。齋月未曾沾一滴,良宵須飲百千杯。

譯箋:良宵,原譯爲有福之拜蘭夜。拜蘭,指開齋節。英譯原注謂拜蘭乃萊麥丹月之後沙瓦魯月初一之節慶。參看菲譯其八十二譯箋。

Ah! wine lends wings to many a weary wight,
And beauty spots to ladies' faces bright;
　　All Ramazan I have not drunk a drop,
Thrice welcome, then, O Bairam's blessed night!

其一百七十九

惶惑終宵飽醉愁，行行珠淚墜心頭。此顛翻覆成椑榼，來歲猶能大白浮。

譯箋：《漢書·張騫傳》"以其頭爲飲器。"顏師古注："韋昭曰：'飲器，椑榼也。'"

All night in deep bewilderment I fret,
With tear-drops big as pearls my breast is wet;
　　I can not fill my cranium with wine,
How can it hold wine, when 'tis thus upset?

其一百八十

祈頌持齋心欲從，萬般志意探私衷。玉身空被酒污玷，禱念虛拋一息風。

譯箋：參看菲譯其九十三。

To prayer and fasting when my heart inclined,
All my desire I surely hoped to find;
　　Alas! my purity is stained with wine,
My prayers are wasted like a breath of wind.

其一百八十一

薔薇紅頰拜神魂,隻手安能棄此樽。賤體微軀惟所用,何憂容彼整身吞。

譯箋:英譯原注謂暗指與真主之本質復合。案即蘇非派主張之在寂滅(或曰渾化)中與真主合一。

I worship rose-red cheeks with heart and soul,
I suffer not my hand to quit the bowl,
　I make each part of me his function do,
Or e'er my parts be swallowed in the Whole.

其一百八十二

塵歡俗愛假名淵,光熱全無焰怎延。真愛何曾需飲食,不眠不息續年年。

譯箋:真愛,謂對真主之愛,其永恒不熄,不可休止。對言之,對塵世之愛則虛空不實,轉瞬逝遷。

This worldly love of yours is counterfeit,
And, like a half-spent blaze, lacks light and heat;
　True love is his, who for days, months, and years,
Rests not, nor sleeps, nor craves for drink or meat.

其一百八十三

虛榮一世枉圖功,檢點人間有與空。司命漸來按君踵,何如醉逝夢鄉中。

譯箋:有與空,原譯作 Being and Not-being,存在與非存在,或是與非是。英譯原注謂存在即神性，惟一真實之存在。非存在，指反映其屬性之虛無。

Why spend life in vainglorious essay
All Being and Not-being to survey?
  Since Death is ever pressing at your heels,
'Tis best to drink or dream your life away.

其一百八十四

狂逐天仙妙影過，太虛幻境逝婀娜。捲簾顒望尋卿處，隔岸迢迢嘆奈何。

譯箋：參看菲譯其十三。

Some hanker after that vain phantasy
Of Houris, feigned in Paradise to be;
  But, when the veil is lifted, they will find
How far they are from Thee, how far from Thee.

其一百八十五

樂園聞說女仙棲，蜜酒泉流可潤滋。彼境漱芳當合禮，信哉亦可饗於斯。

譯箋：我默數寫飲酒之辯，蓋飲酒宴樂乃波斯傳統生活方式，與伊斯蘭教禁酒之禮不無扞格。

In Paradise, they tell us, Houris dwell,
And fountains run with wine and oxymel;

If these be lawful in the world to come,
Surely 'tis right to love them here as well.

其一百八十六

頑徒斜睨酒盈甌，一啜羣山舞未休。有酒爲靈身乃振，空談戒飲約宜收。

A draught of wine would make a mountain dance,
Base is the churl who looks at wine askance;
　　Wine is a soul our bodies to inspire,
A truce to this vain talk of temperance!

其一百八十七

精魂長恨哭幽囚，樂棄皮囊舊侶儔。不是天條絆其足，寧爲玉碎出塵憂。

譯箋：英譯原注謂若非全能者禁自戕之律條吾必自去。○是章莪默哭酒也。幽囚謂酒，侶儔乃杯。

Oft doth my soul her prisoned state bemoan,
Her earth-born co-mate she would fain disown,
　　And quit, did not the stirrup of the law
Upbear her foot from dashing on the stone.

其一百八十八

如鉤新月望樓臺，從此金樽不得開。八月終宵須飲足，直教醉至拜蘭來。

譯箋：英譯者以爲此首非莪默作。拜蘭，見前。按伊斯蘭曆，九月萊麥丹月爲齋月。八月舍爾邦月爲齋月前一月。○參看菲譯七八十二、其八十三與其八十七。

The moon of Ramazan is risen, see!
Alas, our wine must henceforth banished be;
　　Well! on Sha'ban's last day I'll drink enough
To keep me drunk till Bairam's jubilee.

其一百八十九
時飲仙漿時飲糟，今憨襦褸昨榮袍。斯人已在黃泉岸，俛仰隨波神不勞。

譯箋：黃泉，《春秋左氏傳・隱公元年》："不及黃泉，無相見也。"杜預注："地中之泉，故曰黃泉。"

From life we draw now wine, now dregs to drink,
Now flaunt in silk, and now in tatters shrink;
　　Such changes wisdom holds of slight account
To those who stand on death's appalling brink!

其一百九十
太玄解悟孰稱賢，自性誰離半步遷。師弟毚君轉睛辨，同胞一母貌相駢。

譯箋：蘇非追求忘我之境以求真實，此章或係譏刺教法學派。○參看菲譯其二十七與其二十八。

What sage the eternal tangle e'er unravelled,
Or one short step beyond his nature travelled?
　　From pupils to the masters turn your eyes,
And see, each mother's son alike is gravelled.

其一百九十一

休逐塵歡餍己心，輪困禍福豈宜尋。悠哉當傲九天上，止止行行旋默瘖。

譯箋：英譯原注謂諸天如人皆有定則，然未自憂。參看菲譯其四十一。

Crave not of worldly sweets to take your fill,
Nor wait on turn of fortune, good or ill;
　　Be of light heart, as are the skies above,
They roll a round or two, and then lie still.

其一百九十二

誰目能穿天命帷，且將后土謎窮推。春秋七十空思索，玄賾猶今恨未窺。

譯箋：英譯原注引《聖經·約伯記》第二十六章："至有力之雷霆，又孰能測之。"○參看菲譯其三十二。

What eye can pierce the veil of God's decrees,
Or read the riddle of earth's destinies?
　　Pondered have I for years threescore and ten,
But still am baffled by these mysteries.

其一百九十三

喪鐘終顯帝威能，判罰陰曹第幾層。善德終將存善報，何須戰戰履如冰。

譯箋：《詩經・小雅・小旻》："戰戰兢兢，如臨深淵，如履薄冰。"○參看菲譯其八十八。

They say, when the last trump shall sound its knell,
Our Friend will sternly judge, and doom to hell.
　　Can aught but good from perfect goodness come?
Compose your trembling hearts, 'twill all be well.

其一百九十四

科條七二亂如麻，一醉根除玄學芽。留得神奇煉金術，萬般願足此中誇。

譯箋：參看菲譯其五十九。

Drink wine to root up metáphysic weeds,
And tangle of the two-and-seventy creeds;
　　Do not forswear that wondrous alchemy,
'Twill turn to gold, and cure a thousand needs.

其一百九十五

飲雖非善須詳度，誰飲誰斟何可酌。能察斯三無飲憂，若非英士誰能作。

譯箋："舉杯邀明月，對影成三人"，此李白之飲也。"誰飲誰斟何可酌"，察斯三者而後飲，此㦲默之飲也。飲者，㦲默自謂也。斟者，長生之薩吉也，永恒之真主也。所飲者，生命之妙諦也。

Though drink is wrong, take care with whom you drink,
And who you are that drink, and what you drink;
　　And drink at will, for, these three points observed,
Who but the very wise can ever drink?

其一百九十六

臨筵暫擬飲連升，豐酒盈盈心欲騰。舊愛三休冷宮去，蒲桃之女獨歡承。

譯箋：英譯原注謂三休不可再復。林松譯《古蘭經韻譯》第二章第二百三十節："如果他已經將她休棄，那麼，她此後就不能做他的妻，直至她被另外一個丈夫聘娶。如果他將她休棄，那麼他倆也不妨恢復（夫妻）關係，如果雙方認為可以遵行安拉的律例。"舊愛，原譯作舊之信仰和理性。○參看菲譯其五十五。

To drain a gallon beaker I design,
Yea, two great beakers, brimmed with richest wine;
　　Old faith and reason thrice will I divorce,
Then take to wife the daughter of the vine.

其一百九十七

真神料不厭流斟，庸智凡常盡湎沉。太古已知吾必飲，安能抗命拒天音。

譯箋：參看菲譯起六十一。

True I drink wine, like every man of sense,
For I know Allah will not take offense;
 Before time was, He know that I should drink,
And who am I to thwart His prescience?

其一百九十八

長飲朱門棄俗緣，終如乞丐憾歸天。赤瓊管插碧瑤草，愁悒鰥魚亦可眠。

譯箋：碧瑤草，英譯原作 emerald hemp，綠寶色般的大麻。根據英譯原注，祖母綠（綠寶石）能使蛇目盲。○《釋名·釋親屬》："鰥，昆也。昆，明也。愁悒不寐，目恒鰥鰥然也。故其字從魚，魚目恒不閉者也。"宋陸游《晚登望雲》詩："衰如蠹葉秋先覺，愁似鰥魚夜不眠。"

Rich men, who take to drink, the world defy
With shameless riot, and as beggars die;
 Place in my ruby pipe some emerald hemp,
'Twill do as well to blind care's serpent eye.

其一百九十九

愚氓巡夜不燃燈，寸步移身本未曾。衣錦而行誰得見，奪人美譽闇中能。

These fools have never burnt the midnight oil
In deep research, nor do they ever toil
 To step beyond themselves, but dress them fine,
And plot of credit others to despoil.

其二百

蒲桃純血一杯持,影掠寒曦幻陸離。真道初嚐皆苦口,壺樽象道亦如斯。

When false dawn streaks the east with cold, gray line,
Pour in your cups the pure blood of the vine;
　　The truth, they say, tastes bitter in the mouth,
This is a token that the "Truth" is wine.

其二百零一

蒼茫大地碧成陰,一樹梨花展素心。淑氣橫吹醒萬木,密雲淚滿化甘霖。

譯箋:此章與其一百一十六意類。直譯作:一時大地碧成陰,穆薩花開素手心。草木醒因爾撒息,密雲淚滿化甘霖。○淑氣,英譯原作'Isa's breath,爾撒的氣息。《爾雅·釋詁》:"淑,善也。"爾撒或爾薩(Isa),即耶穌(Jesus)。在伊斯蘭教中,尔撒被視爲真主使者,並作爲猶太人先知帶去一部新經文《引支勒》,即《福音書》或《新約全書》。爾撒在伊斯蘭教中被尊稱爲麥爾彥(瑪麗亞)之子、麥西哈(彌賽亞)。然伊斯蘭教否認爾撒爲神之子。林松譯《古蘭經韻譯》第三章第四十九節列舉安拉所傳示於爾薩奇跡云:"我確已把你們的主所降示的一種跡象,帶來給你們了。我必定爲你們用泥做一個像鳥樣的東西,我吹口氣在裡面,它就奉真主的命令而飛動。我奉真主的命令,能醫治天然盲、大麻瘋。又能使死者復活。又能把你們所吃的和你們儲藏在家裡的食物告訴你們。"○《周易·小畜卦》:"密雲不雨。自我西郊。"○參看菲譯其四譯箋。

Now is the time earth decks her greenest bowers,

And trees, like Musa's hand, grow white with flowers!
　　As 'twere at 'Isa's breath the plants revive,
While clouds brim o'er, like tearful eyes, with showers.

其二百零二
毋服鹽車阪上瘅，千金散盡復來歡。高朋會讌氣曾熱，終饗豐肌螻蟻寒。

譯箋：《戰國策·楚策四》："夫驥之齒至矣，服鹽車而上太行。蹄申膝折，尾湛胕潰，漉汁灑地，白汗交流，中阪遷延，負轅不能上。伯樂遭之，下車攀而哭之，解紵衣以冪之。"○借李白《將進酒》："天生我材必有用，千金散盡還復來。"○陸機《挽歌詩三首》其二："豐肌饗螻蟻。"

Oh burden not thyself with drudgery,
Lord of white silver and red gold to be;
　　But feast with friends, ere this warm breath of thine
Be chilled in death, and earthworms feast on thee.

其二百零三
彩袖玉鍾紅雨傾，千憂百慮焰漸平。謝天賜降安魂藥，祓淨瘝愁救眾生。

譯箋：宋晏幾道《鷓鴣天》詞："彩袖殷勤捧玉鍾，當年拚卻醉顏紅。"○《國語·周語上》："是故祓除其心，以和惠民。"韋昭注："祓，猶拂也。"宋王質《臨江仙·宴向守簇》詞："曲水流觴修禊事，祓除洗淨春愁。"○參看菲譯其三十九與其六十。

The showers of grape juice, which cupbearers pour,
Quench fires of grief in many a sad heart's core.
　　Praise be to Allah, who hath sent this balm
To heal sore hearts, and spirits' health restore!

其二百零四

親承沾溉近豐神，僞者安知汝大仁。若說罪靈須火煉，此言但向路人陳。

Can alien Pharisees Thy kindness tell,
Like us, Thy intimates, who nigh Thee dwell?
　　Thou say'st, "All sinners will I burn with fire."
Say that to strangers, we know Thee too well.

其二百零五

有朋倘自遠方來，與共珍饈良宴開。仙飲斟時但相警，勿忘暫禱一停杯。

譯笺：仙飲，英譯原作 old Magh wine，麻葛陳酒。麻葛，祆教祭司稱謂，中國史籍作穆護。此或謂祆教祭司以聖草豪麻所搾製之飲料，祭禮中供人飲用，或譯胡姆，見祆教經典《阿維斯塔》。○參看菲譯其一百零一。

O comrades dear, when hither ye repair
In times to come, communion sweet to share,
　　While the cupbearer pours your old Magh wine,
Call poor Khayyam to mind, and breathe a prayer.

其二百零六

兜率未聞絲竹存，更無鈞樂壓驚魂。才離恨海滔天浪，又入深深愁院門。

譯箋：兜率，佛家謂慾界第四重天，未來佛彌勒所居。○《史記‧趙世家》："我之帝所甚樂，與百神游於鈞天，廣樂九奏萬舞，不類三代之樂，其聲動人心。"

For me heaven's sphere no music ever made,
Nor yet with soothing voice my fears allayed;
　　If e'er I found brief respite from my woes,
Back to woe's thrall I was at once betrayed.

其二百零七

志滿躊躇簞食調，啜漿瓢破自逍遙。何庸跛扈呈威福，亦不摧眉復折腰。

譯箋：志滿躊躇，英譯原作 contented，滿足。《莊子‧養生主》："提刀而立，爲之四顧，爲之躊躇滿志。"簞食，英譯原作 half a loaf，半個麵包。瓢，英譯原作 crock，甕、罌。《論語‧雍也》："子曰：'一簞食，一瓢飲，在陋巷，人不堪其憂，回也不改其樂。賢哉回也。'"○呈威福，英譯原作 lord over，作威作福。《尚書‧洪範》："惟辟作福，惟辟作威。"孔穎達疏："惟君作福得專賞人也，惟君作威得專罰人也。"○摧眉與折腰，英譯原作 to another bow the vassal knee，向他人彎曲奴僕之膝。唐李白《夢遊天姥吟留別》詩："安能摧眉折腰事權貴，使我不得開心顏。"

Sooner with half a loaf contented be,

And water from a broken crock, like me,
    Than lord it over one poor fellow-man,
Or to another bow the vassal knee.

其二百零八

美哉膏汁數蒲桃，更值良辰星月高。頗怪當壚甚愚暗，如斯賤價售珍醪。

譯箋：星月，英譯原作 Moon and Venus，月亮和金星。星月標誌，今象徵伊斯蘭教信仰，喻真主及其智慧充滿宇宙萬物。○參看菲譯其九十五譯箋。

While Moon and Venus in the sky shall dwell,
None shall see aught red grape-juice to excel:
    O foolish publicans, what can you buy
One half so precious as the goods you sell?

其二百零九

聰明天降擅羣科，師表人前盛譽多。形影方纔浮暗夜，一番夢語返南柯。

譯箋：參看菲譯其六十五。

They who by genius, and by power of brain,
The rank of man's enlighteners attain,
    Not even they emerge from this dark night,
But tell their dreams, and fall asleep again.

其二百一十

初霑朝露鬱金香，頷首紫英嬌弄妝。最愛薔薇閉華萼，風摧猶自守椒房。

譯箋：椒房，對譯原文 petal，花瓣。《漢書·車千秋傳》："未央椒房。"顏師古注："椒房，殿名，皇后所居也。以椒和泥塗壁，取其溫而芳也。"班固《西都賦》："後宮則有掖庭椒房，后妃之室。"李善注："《三輔黃圖》曰：'長樂宮有椒房殿。'"

At dawn, when dews bedeck the tulip's face,
And violets their heavy heads abase,
　　I love to see the roses' folded buds,
With petals closed against the wind's disgrace.

其二百一十一

一洗甘霖茉莉開，青原漠漠濕玫瑰。紫蘭花缶手中執，絳雪春傾百合杯。

譯箋：絳雪春，英譯原作 rosy wine。清李百川《綠野仙蹤》第三回："嚴嵩道：'日前吏部尚書邦謨夏大人，惠酒三壇，名爲絳雪春，真琬液瓊蘇也。'"

Like as the skies rain down sweet jessamine,
And sprinkle all the meads with eglantine,
　　Right so, from out this jug of violet hue,
I pour in lily cups this rosy wine.

其二百一十二

皓首堪憐自戴枷，數番信誓絕杯叉。發心築廈終成棄，衣紉懺祈今又睑。

譯箋：懺祈，英譯原作 penitence，懺悔。前蜀杜光庭《中元衆修金籙齋詞》："每因齋薦，皆爲懺祈，必離冥漠之鄉，更遂逍遥之適。"

Ah! thou hast snared this head, though white as snow,
Which oft has vowed the wine-cup to forego;
  And wrecked the mansion long resolve did build,
And rent the vesture penitence did sew!

其二百一十三

吾但憂存不懼亡，豈因形蛻日惶惶。人生寄世如駒隙，時日至兮終必償。

譯箋：形蛻，英譯原作 Death，死。唐鄭璧《和襲美傷顧道士》詩："形蛻遠山孤壙月，影寒深院曉松風。"

I am not one whom Death doth much dismay,
Life's terrors all Death's terrors far outweigh;
  This life, that Heaven hath lent me for a while,
I will pay back, when it is time to pay.

其二百一十四

衆辰列宿象垂天，搔首卜人嘆杜然。堪笑星官疑示兆，未諳常道怎知玄。

譯箋：《周易·繫辭上》："天垂象，見吉凶，聖人象之。"○英譯原注謂斥占星術。

The stars, who dwell on heaven's exalted stage,
Baffle the wise diviners of our age;
  Take heed, hold fast the rope of mother wit.
These augurs all distrust their own presage.

其二百一十五

朝聞夕往一何誠，爲飾天堂上下征。但與真神共長在，斯人永世享重生。

The people who the heavenly world adorn,
Who come each night, and go away each morn,
  Now on Heaven's skirt, and now in earth's deep pouch,
While Allah lives, shall aye anew be born!

其二百一十六

求知問道枉爲奴，竭智窮神索有無。賢達但須長飲醉，莫教腦汁若藤枯。

譯箋：有無，英譯原作 Being and Nonentity，存在與不存在。《老子·第一章》："故常無，欲以觀其妙；常有，欲一觀其徼。"又《老子·第二章》："有無相生，難易相成。"又《老子·第四十章》："天下萬物生於有，有生於無。"○參看菲譯其五十四。

Slaves of vain wisdom and philosophy,
Who toil at Being and Nonentity,

Parching your brains till they are like dry grapes,
Be wise in time, and drink grape-juice like me!

其二百一十七

忘憂耽樂苟營營，徼福六根渾不清。豈若離離原上草，今朝刈罷復還生。

譯箋：《論語·述而》："發憤忘食，樂以忘憂。"《莊子·庚桑楚》："全汝形，抱汝生，勿使汝思慮營營。"宋蘇軾《臨江仙》詞："長恨此身非我有，何時忘卻營營？"○六根，英譯原作 sense，感覺、知覺。六根本佛家語。丁福保《佛學大辭典》："眼耳鼻舌身意之六官也，根爲能生之義，眼根對於色境而生眼識，乃至意根對於法境而生意識，故名爲根。"○原上草，英譯原作 the meadow grass 牧場之草。唐白居易《賦得古原草送別》詩："離離原上草，一歲一枯榮。野火燒不盡，春風吹又生。"

Sense, seeking happiness, bids us pursue
All present joys, and present griefs eschew;
　　She says, we are not as the meadow grass,
Which, when they mow it down, springs up anew.

其二百一十八

暑消十月慶開齋，鼓瑟嘉賓樂允諧。販卒競肩珍釀至，橐囊車水沸喧街。

譯箋：十月，英譯原作 Shawwal，指伊斯蘭曆十月。○鼓瑟嘉賓，《詩經·小雅·鹿鳴》："我有嘉賓，鼓瑟吹笙。"《尚書·益稷》："庶尹允諧。"孔穎達疏："信皆和諧，言職事修理也。"○橐囊，英譯原作 wine-skin，盛酒皮囊。《詩經‧大雅‧公劉》:"乃裹餱糧,于橐于囊。"毛傳:"小曰橐,大曰囊。"《戰國策‧秦策一》:"負書擔橐。"高誘注:"無底曰囊,有底曰橐。"○參看菲譯其九十。

Now Ramazan is past, Shawwal comes back,
And feast and song and joy no more we lack;
　　The wine-skin carriers throng the streets and cry,
"Here comes the porter with his precious pack."

其二百一十九

羣友皆從遼鶴遊,恨悲相續碾塵溝。醒時饗宴交歡樂,醉後沉酣伏案頭。

譯箋:遼鶴,見溫譯其三。○宋王安石《桂枝香‧金陵懷古》詞:"念往昔、繁華競逐,歎門外樓頭,悲恨相續。"○三、四句,意類李白《月下獨酌》:"醒時同交歡,醉後各分散。"○參看菲譯其二十二。

My comrades are all gone; Death, deadly foe,
Has caught them one by one, and trampled low;
　　They shared life's feast, and drank its wine with me,
But lost their heads, and dropped a while ago.

其二百二十

浪得虛名遊士閑,棲街謀食乞人憐。稷下迂閣誇孔墨,空空腹笥衍談天。

譯箋:游士,英譯原作 hypocrites。漢劉向《戰國策敘錄》:"戰國時,遊士輔所用之國，爲之策謀，宜爲《戰國策》。"又稱戰國"棄仁義而用詐譎"、"詐僞並起"。宋曾鞏《戰國策目錄序》："戰國之遊士則不然，不知道之可信而樂於説之易合，其設心注意，偷爲一切之計而已。"○稷下，漢應劭《風俗通‧窮通》："孫況，齊威、宣王之時，聚天下賢士於稷下，尊寵之。"英譯原作 Karkh，卡爾赫，今伊拉克巴格達西半部，底格里斯河西岸。該詞源自敍利亞語"堡壘"。九世紀卡爾赫爲蘇非派流行之重要地區。○孔墨，英譯原作 Shibli and Junaid。巴格達祝奈德（Junayd al-Baghdadi）爲波斯蘇非派早期著名導師，長期在巴格達傳教。希伯里（Shibli）亦爲蘇非派重要人物，祝奈德之徒。○腹笥，《後漢書‧邊韶傳》："邊爲姓，孝爲字。腹便便，五經笥。"談天，《史記‧孟子荀卿列傳》："騶衍之術迂大而閎辯；奭也文具難施；淳于髡久與處，時有得善言。故齊人頌曰：'談天衍，雕龍奭，炙轂過髡。'"

Those hypocrites, all know so well, who lurk
In streets to beg their bread, and will not work,
 Claim to be saints, like Shibli and Junaid,
No Shiblis are they, though well known in Karkh!

其二百二十一

鏐金凡鐵混同熬，造物洪爐一例拋。洵美且都終不得，難歸初出大鈞陶。

譯箋：鏐金，英譯原作 gold。《説文解字》："鏐，黃金之美者。"《爾雅‧釋器》："黃金謂之璗，其美者謂之鏐。"注云："鏐即紫磨金。"凡鐵，英譯原作 baser metal，賤金屬。宋陸游《劍客行》："世無知劍人，太阿混凡鐵。"○洪爐，英譯原作 the great Founder，偉大創立者。晉葛洪《抱朴子‧勖學》："鼓九陽之洪爐，運大鈞乎皇極。"○洵美且都，英譯原作 Better or fairer，較善或較美。

《詩經・鄭風・有女同車》:"彼美孟姜,洵美且都。"毛傳:"都,閑也。"鄭玄箋:"洵,信也。言孟姜信美好,且閑習婦禮。"○大鈞,參見溫譯其二十五譯箋。是章可與其四百二十一章合參。

When the great Founder moulded me of old,
He mixed much baser metal with my gold;
　　Better or fairer I can never be
Than I first issued from his heavenly mould.

其二百二十二
聖徒龕廟禱伶丁,蕩子魂銷酒罄瓶。苦海同沉不見岸,衆人皆醉獨神醒。

譯箋:龕廟,英譯原作 mosques,清真寺。南朝梁劉孝綽《棲隱寺碑》:"誠敬所先,是歸龕廟。"伶丁,英譯原作 sad,憂傷。《文選・李密〈陳情表〉》:"零丁孤苦。"李善注引舊題漢李陵《贈蘇武》詩:"遠處天一隅,苦困獨伶丁。"○蕩子,《文選・古詩〈青青河畔草〉》:"蕩子行不歸,空牀難獨守。"李善注:"《列子》曰:'有人去鄉土游於四方而不歸者,世謂之爲狂蕩之人也。'"罄瓶,《詩經・小雅・蓼莪》:"瓶之罄矣,維罍之恥。"三國魏曹丕《又與吳質書》:"從我遊處,獨不及門,瓶罄罍恥,能無懷魏?"唐韓愈《答張徹》詩:"蘋甘謝鳴鹿,罍滿慚罄瓶。"○《朱子語類》卷五九:"知得心放,此心便在這裡,更何用求?適見道人題壁云:'苦海無邊,回頭是岸。'説得極好。"○《史記・屈原賈生列傳》:"舉世混濁而我獨清,衆人皆醉而我獨醒,是以見放。"英譯原注謂一即神。

The joyous souls who quaff potations deep,

And saints who in the mosques sad vigils keep,

　　Are lost at sea alike, and find no shore,

ONE only wakes, all others are asleep.

其二百二十三

無何有水和陶泥，直撲吾心苦火淒。終被世風漂雨襲，消殘土偶復西堤。

譯箋：無何有，英譯原作 Not-being，不存在。《莊子·逍遙遊》："今子有大樹，患其無用，何不樹之於無何有之鄉，廣莫之野。"成玄英疏："無何有，猶無有也。莫，無也。謂寬曠無人之處，不問何物，悉皆無有，故曰無何有之鄉也。"○世風，英譯原作 wind about the world，世上的風。宋蘇舜欽《高山別鄰幾》詩："世風隨日儉，俗態逐勢熱。"○《戰國策·齊策三》："今者臣來，過於淄上，有土偶人與桃梗相與語。桃梗謂土偶人曰：'子，西岸之土也，挺子以為人，至歲八月，降雨下，淄水至，則汝殘矣。'土偶曰：'不然，吾西岸之土也，土則復西岸耳。今子東國之桃梗也，刻削子以為人，降雨下，淄水至，流子而去，則子漂漂者將何如耳。'"○英譯原注謂此納四大元素土、風（氣）、水、火於一章。

Not-being's water served to mix my clay,

And on my heart grief's fire doth ever prey,

　　And blown am I like wind about the world,

And last my crumbling earth is swept away.

其二百二十四
青春老去怨蹉跎，塵俗求知獲幾多。何若愚癡不須學，偏蒙福運贈梨渦。

譯箋：宋羅大經《鶴林玉露》卷十二："胡澹庵十年貶海外，北歸之日，飲于湘潭胡氏園，題詩云：'君恩許歸此一醉，傍有梨頰生微渦。'謂侍妓黎倩也。"

Small gains to learning on this earth accrue,
They pluck life's fruitage, learning who eschew;
　　Take pattern by the fools who learning shun,
And then perchance shall fortune smile on you.

其二百二十五
幽魂已自桂宮遷，萬物歸根復本天。玉體金枝任飄碎，聚如春夢散如煙。

譯箋：桂宮，英譯原作 mansion，第宅。《文選・班固〈西都賦〉》："自未央而連桂宮。"李善注："《三輔舊事》曰：'桂宮內有明光殿。'"○《老子・第十六章》："致虛極，守靜篤。萬物並作，吾以觀其復。夫物芸芸，各復歸其根。歸根曰靜，是謂復命。復命曰常，知常曰明。不知常妄作凶。知常融，容乃公，公乃王，王乃天，天乃道，道乃久，沒身不殆。"○玉體金枝，英譯原作 silken furniture 光鮮的傢俱，指人之肉體。○借清富察明義《題〈紅樓夢〉絕句二十首》："莫問金姻與玉緣，聚如春夢散如煙。石歸山下無靈氣，總使能言亦枉然。"

When the fair soul this mansion doth vacate,
Each element assumes its primal state,

And all the silken furniture of life
Is then dismantled by the blows of fate.

其二百二十六

枉穿腐議念珠中，亂墜天花論不窮。至賾璿璣未能察，已微頷首夢周公。

譯箋：至賾璿璣，英譯原作 the riddle of the skies，天上之謎。《尚書·堯典》："在璿璣玉衡，以齊七政。"《大傳》曰："道正而萬事順成，故天道，政之大業。旋機者，何也？傳曰：旋者，還也。機者，幾也，微也。其變幾微，而所動者大，謂之旋機，是故旋機謂之北極。"《周易·繫辭上》："言天下之至賾而不可惡也。"〇英譯原注疑此章乃斥經院神學家。

These people string their beads of learned lumber,
And tell of Allah stories without number;
　　Yet never solve the riddle of the skies,
But wag the chin, and get them back to slumber.

其二百二十七

負炫技如驢出黔，鳴空鼓腹勢炎炎。卑身但受浮名役，邀譽甘親塵足尖。

譯箋：唐柳宗元《黔之驢》："噫！形之龐也類有德，聲之宏也類有能。向不出其技，虎雖猛，疑畏卒不敢取。今若是焉，悲夫！"〇炎炎，英譯原作 glittering 閃光貌。《莊子齊物論》："大言炎炎，小言詹詹。"陸德明《經典釋文》引梁簡文帝曰："美盛貌。"漢班固《東都賦》："羽旄掃霓，旌旗拂天，焱焱炎炎，揚光飛文。"〇文理本《舊約·以賽亞書》第四十九章："王爲養父，后爲乳母，面伏於地，拜於爾前，舐爾足塵。"

These folk are asses, laden with conceit,
And glittering drums, that empty sounds repeat,
　　And humble slaves are they of name and fame,
Acquire a name, and, lo! they kiss thy feet.

其二百二十八

閻羅十殿柏臺高，録鬼簿中分爾曹。在世須當修美質，届時循品得酬勞。

譯箋：閻羅，梵語 Yamarāja 音譯。《玄應音義》二十一："焰摩或作琰摩，聲之轉也。舊云閻羅，又云閻摩羅，此言縛，或言雙世也。謂苦樂並受，故云雙世，即鬼官總司也。"柏臺，即御史台。《漢書·朱博傳》："御史府吏舍百餘區井水皆竭；又其府中列柏樹，常有野烏數千棲宿其上，晨去暮來，號曰朝夕烏，烏去不來者數月，長老異之。"唐宋之問《和姚給事寓直之作》詩："柏臺遷烏茂，蘭署得人芳。"○晉陶潛《擬挽歌辭》其一："有生必有死，早終非命促。昨暮同爲人，今旦在鬼録。"鍾嗣成《録鬼簿序》："雖然，人之生斯世也，但知以已死者爲鬼，而未知未死者亦鬼也。"○品第，英譯原作 rate。南朝梁鍾嶸《詩品·總論》："諸英志録，並義在文，曾無品第。"唐封演《封氏聞見記·討論》："著作郎孔至，二十傳儒學，撰百家類例，品第海內族姓。"

On the dread day of final scrutiny
Thou wilt be rated by thy quality;
　　Get wisdom and fair qualities to-day,
For, as thou art, requited wilt thou be.

其二百二十九

天工妙手造顱元，俱按己形如缺盆。覆幬羣生一盆下，教人乾惕日驚魂。

譯箋：天工，英譯原作 the Brazier 銅匠。《尚書·皋陶謨》："無曠庶官，天工人其代之。"《集傳》："庶官所治，無非天事。"元，英譯原作 head。《春秋左氏傳·僖公三十三年》："狄人歸其元，面如生。"○覆幬，《中庸》："辟如天地之無不持載，無不覆幬。"○乾惕，英譯原作 afraid 害怕。《周易·乾卦》："君子終日乾乾，夕惕若厲，無咎。"○參看菲譯其八十四。

Many fine heads, like bowls, the Brazier made,
And thus his own similitude portrayed;
 He sets one upside down above our heads,
Which keeps us all continually afraid.

其二百三十

真我茫茫誰與存，短歌聯句一身論。憐卿獨愴離魂去，爲有卿憐又返魂。

譯箋：《樂府詩集·相和歌平調曲》有《短歌行》。短歌聯句，英譯原作 two short verses。波斯詩歌多由對句聯綴構成，對句亦即雙行詩別格。如頌體詩格綏德由十五個以上對句組成。與魯拜類似的兩聯詩都貝堤前兩行一韻、後兩行一韻。抒情詩體嘎扎勒（又譯加宰裡，維吾爾族讀作格則勒）多由五至十五個對句。敘事詩體瑪斯那維兩行一韻，之後可變韻。短詩卡埃特兩至十八個對句，全篇協同韻。○唐陳玄祐有傳奇《離魂記》，元鄭光祖據作《倩女離魂》雜劇。宋姜夔《踏莎行》詞："別後書辭，別時針綫，離魂暗逐郎行遠。"唐宣宗李忱《弔白居易》詩："一度思卿一愴然。"

My true condition I may thus explain

In two short verses which the whole contain:

　　"From love to Thee I now lay down my life,

In hope Thy love will raise me up again."

其二百三十一

春心如撚熾秋瞳，蠟炬成灰焰已空。願化飛蛾作燔祭，直投媿嫮熱懷中。

譯箋：唐李商隱《無題》詩："蠟炬成灰淚始乾。"○文理本《舊約・利未記》第一章："如獻牛爲燔祭，當取牡者，純全無疵，獻於會幕門，冀蒙悅納於耶和華。"○戰國楚宋玉《神女賦》："既媿嫮於幽静兮，又婆娑於人間。"○據愛敏《阿拉伯-伊斯蘭文化史》，阿德維婭曾言："我們祈求寬恕本身就需要祈求寬恕；我的主啊，你難道用火來焚燒熱愛你的心嗎？"

The heart, like tapers, takes at beauty's eyes

A flame, and lives by that whereby it dies;

　　And beauty is a flame where hearts, like moths,

Offer themselves a burning sacrifice.

其二百三十二

委身仁義自清高，受躪千般未敢逃。卿問幽冥何處是，世間損友即陰曹。

譯箋：《論語・季氏》："益者三友，損者三友：友直、友諒、友多聞，益矣。友便辟、友善柔、友便佞，損矣。"○英譯原注謂此係哈菲兹所作。

To please the righteous life itself I sell,

And, though they tread me down, never rebel;

 Men say, "Inform us what and where is hell?"

Ill company will make this earth a hell.

其二百三十三

東君神矢射廷簷，瓊液瑩光悅帝瞻。騁騖朝曦已先至，銜樽共飲莫遲淹。

譯箋：東君，屈原《九歌》有《東君》篇，洪興祖《楚辭補注》："《博雅》曰：'朱明、耀靈、東君，日也。'《漢書郊祀志》有東君。"朱熹《楚辭集注》："此日神也。"○唐溫庭筠《蘭塘詞》："東溝繑繑勞回首，欲寄一杯瓊液酒。"帝，英譯原作 Khosrau，疑即波斯薩珊王朝國王霍斯魯一世，五三二至五七九年在位，亦見菲爾多西《列王紀》。《隋書·列傳第四十八西域·波斯》："波斯國，都達曷水之西蘇藺城，即條支之故地也。其王字庫薩和。"○《楚辭·九歌·湘君》："鼂騁騖兮江皋，夕弭節兮北渚。"《文選·班固〈西都賦〉》："連交合眾，騁騖乎其中。"李周翰注："騁騖，猶馳逐。"○莫遲淹，英譯原作 to-day 今日。《後漢書·蔡邕傳》："又二州之士，或復限以歲月，狐疑遲淹，以失事會。"

The sun doth smite the roofs with Orient ray

And, Khosrau like, his wine-red sheen display;

 Arise, and drink! the herald of the dawn

Uplifts his voice, and cries, "Oh, drink to-day!"

其二百三十四

他年聚此憶吾身,清淚何須霑俗塵。但使流觴停舊位,一樽還酹土中人。

譯箋:流觴,英譯原作 the circling wine-cups,輪流的酒杯。晉王羲之《蘭亭集序》:"又有清流激湍,映帶左右,引以爲流觴曲水。"○宋蘇軾《念奴嬌·赤壁懷古》:"一樽還酹江月。"○英譯原注謂此係其二百零五之異譯。參看菲譯其一百零一。

Comrades! when e'er you meet together here,
Recall your friend to mind, and drop a tear;
　　And when the circling wine-cups reach his seat,
Pray turn one upside down his dust to cheer.

其二百三十五

先施恩典未輕訶,喜樂平安賜與多。神旨今教心殄瘁,平波生變卻因何。

譯箋:《詩經·大雅·瞻卬》:"人之云亡,邦國殄瘁。"○英譯原注引《聖經·約伯記》第九章:"彼以暴風折我,無故益我之傷。"

That grace and favor at the first, what meant it?
That lavishing of joy and peace, what meant it?
　　But now thy purpose is to grieve my heart;
What did I do to cause this change? What meant it?

其二百三十六

正衣齊色背儒偷，靈肉胡云本寇讎。白石如能封嗛口，我當覆瓿絕杯甌。

譯箋：《荀子‧非十二子》："正其衣冠，齊其顏色，嗛然而終日不言，是子夏氏之賤儒也。偷儒憚事，無廉恥而耆飲食，必曰君子固不用力，是子游氏之賤儒也。"《爾雅‧釋獸》："寓鼠曰嗛。"郭璞注："頰裡貯食處。寓謂獮猴之類，寄寓木上。"○覆瓿，宋陸游《秋晚寓歎》詩："著書終覆瓿，得句漫投囊。"

These hypocrites who build on saintly show,
Treating the body as the spirit's foe,
　　If they will shut their mouths with lime, like jars,
My jar of grape-juice I will then forego.

其二百三十七

熙熙攘攘疾如梭，名利歡場競若何。狼藉杯盤酣臥去，擁衾託體在山阿。

譯箋：《史記‧貨殖列傳》："天下熙熙，皆爲利來；天下攘攘，皆爲利往。"○清李汝珍《鏡花緣》小說："世上名利場中，原是一座迷魂陣。"○《史記‧滑稽列傳》："日暮酒闌，合尊促坐，男女同席，履舃交錯，杯盤狼藉。"宋蘇軾《赤壁賦》："肴核既盡，杯盤狼藉。相與枕藉乎舟中，不知東方之既白。"○晉陶潛《擬挽歌辭》其三："親戚或餘悲，他人亦已歌。死去何所道，託體同山阿。"

Many have come, and run their eager race,
Striving for pleasures, luxuries, or place,

And quaffed their wine, and now all silent lie,
Enfolded in their parent earth's embrace.

其二百三十八

飽瓜雖熟繫黃昏，臘與飲仙歸一門。倘未倖能排首席，叨陪末座亦懷恩。

譯箋：《論語・陽貨》："吾其匏瓜也哉，焉能繫而不食。"○《新唐書・李白傳》："白自知不爲親近所容，益騖放不自修，與知章、李適之、汝陽王李璡、崔宗之、蘇晉、張旭、焦遂爲酒八仙人。"唐杜甫作有《飲中八仙歌》。

Then, when the good reap fruits of labours past,
My hapless lot with drunkards will be cast;
　　If good, may I be numbered with the first,
If bad, find grace and mercy with the last.

其二百三十九

金樽銀榻毋輕辭，騁慾賞心宜及時。天地不仁芻狗耳，恣歡善惡孰論之。

Of happy turns of fortune take your fill,
Seek pleasure's couch, or wine-cup, as you will;
　　Allah regards not if you sin, or saint it,
So take your pleasure, be it good or ill.

其二百四十

春痕零落吝予歡，上下穹蒼徹痛瘝。來者如知百般苦，豈思再降此牢闌。

譯箋：清丘逢甲《潮州春思》詩："零落春痕五十年。"○《尚書·康誥》："恫瘝乃身，敬哉。"孔傳："恫，痛。瘝，病。"○《玉篇門部》："闌，牢也。"《墨子·天志下》："踰人之欄牢，竊人之牛馬者，與入人之場園，竊人之桃李瓜薑者，數千萬矣。"

Heaven multiplies our sorrows day by day,
And grants no joys it does not take away;
    If those unborn could know the ills we bear,
What think you, would they rather come or stay?

其二百四十一

迷茫命理苦探求，久惑南柯作倦游。富壽夭殤本天定，何曾與汝共籌謀。

譯箋：《孔子家語·賢君》："政之急者，莫大乎使民富且壽也。"《列子·黃帝》："不知樂生，不知惡死，故無夭殤。"《儀禮·喪服傳》："年十九至十六爲長殤，十五至十二爲中殤，十一至八歲爲下殤，不滿八歲以下爲無服之殤。"

Why ponder thus the future to foresee,
And jade thy brain to vain perplexity?
    Cast off thy care, leave Allah's plans to him,
He formed them all without consulting thee.

其二百四十二

渾噩無知失影蹤，寄居奄夐飽蛆蟲。化飛色界微塵去，蜃海雲樓渡劫終。

譯箋：漢揚雄《法言·問神》："虞夏之書渾渾爾，商書灝灝爾，周書噩噩爾。"○《春秋左氏傳·襄公十三年》："若以大夫之靈，獲保首領以歿於地，惟是春秋奄夐之事，所以從先君於禰廟者，請爲靈若厲，大夫擇焉。"杜預注："奄，厚也；夐，夜也。厚夜猶長夜。春秋謂祭祀，長夜謂葬埋。"文理本《舊約·歷代志上》第二十九章："我儕在爾前，爲遠人，爲羈旅，同于列祖，在世之日如影，無永存之希望。"○丁福保《佛學大辭典》："色界，三界之一，謂身體與宮殿國土物質之物，總爲殊妙精好，故云色界。"○《史記·天官書》："海旁蜃氣象樓臺，廣野氣成宮闕然。"唐李白《渡荆門送別》詩："月下飛天鏡，雲生結海樓。"

The tenants of the tombs to dust decay,
Nescient of self, and all beside are they;
　　Their sundered atoms float about the world,
Like mirage clouds, until the judgment day.

其二百四十三

羈魄須抛世事繁，星星嘉卉蔚青原。譬如朝露香難久，一別今宵誰與言。

譯箋：漢張衡《西京賦》："嘉卉灌叢，蔚若鄧林。"○漢曹操《短歌行》："對酒當歌，人生幾何。譬如朝露，去日苦多。"

O soul! lay up all earthly goods in store,

Thy mead with pleasure's flowerets spangled o'er;

　　And know 'tis all as dew, that decks the flowers

For one short night, and then is seen no more!

其二百四十四

聖行神律可高懸，得分即能安享天。盡性全心毋傷毀，可堪命酌可登仙。

譯箋：聖行，英譯原作 Sunna。源於阿拉伯語筍乃台，又譯遜奈。伊斯蘭教中聖行意爲：教訓、告誡、規律、道路，後專指穆聖言行、舉止。〇文理本《舊約‧歷代志下》第三十一章："且命耶路撒冷居民，給祭司與利未人所應得者，俾其專心於耶和華之律。"〇《晉書‧元帝紀》："初鎮江東，頗以酒廢事。王導深以爲言，帝命酌，引觴覆之，於此遂絕。"《世說新語‧任誕》："王子猷居山陰，夜大雪，眠覺，開室，命酌酒，四望皎然。因起彷徨，詠左思《招隱詩》。"〇英譯原注引《古蘭經》第二章第一百七十七節："面向東方、西方，不是問題的真諦，真諦卻在於誠信安拉、末日、天使、經典、先知，並把珍愛的財物錢幣，施捨親戚、孤兒、貧民、漂泊者、乞丐，亦即爭取贖身的奴隸，並且謹守拜功，繳納天課，對盟約謹守信義，對困苦、患難和戰爭能忍耐堅毅。"

Heed not the Sunna, nor the law divine;
If to the poor his portion you assign,
　　And never injure one, nor yet abuse,
I guarantee you heaven, and now some wine!

其二百四十五

法輪何苦弄愚凡,生命載愁馳疾帆。風雨鈴蕾相擁簇,如花斑血印心函。

Vexed by this wheel of things, that pets the base,
My sorrow-laden life drags on apace;
　　Like rosebud, from the storm I wrap me close,
And blood-spots on my heart, like tulip, trace.

其二百四十六

青藤春日挽綢繆,醉倒玉山嘉客稠。浹岸曾經崩滄海,今崩酒海一身休。

譯箋:青藤,指蒲桃藤。綢繆,英譯原作 to pay court to,求好。《詩經·唐風·綢繆》:"綢繆束薪,三星在天。"毛傳:"綢繆,猶纏綿也。"孔穎達疏:"毛以爲綢繆猶纏綿束薪之貌,言薪在田野之中,必纏綿束之,乃得成爲家用。"舊題漢李陵《與蘇武詩》:"獨有盈觴酒,與子結綢繆。"○《世説新語·容止》:"嵇叔夜之爲人也,巖巖若孤松之獨立;其醉也,傀俄若玉山之將崩。"

Youth is the time to pay court to the vine,
To quaff the cup, with revellers to recline;
　　A flood of water once laid waste the earth,
Hence learn to lay you waste with floods of wine.

其二百四十七

富貧一例柱勞形,舉世栖栖爲覓卿。咫尺眼前皆不識,行屍走肉塞聰明。

譯箋:《莊子·漁父》:"苦心勞形,以危其真。"唐劉禹錫《陋室銘》:"無案牘之勞形。"○《詩經・小雅・六月》："六月棲棲，戎車既飭。"朱熹集傳："棲棲，猶皇皇不安之貌。"《論語・憲問》："丘何爲是棲棲者與？無乃爲佞乎？"○英譯原注引哈菲兹《頌詩》云："吾儕之目何能視汝如汝所是。"

The world is baffled in its search for Thee,
Wealth can not find Thee, no, nor poverty;
　　Thou'rt very near us, but our ears are deaf,
Our eyes are blinded that we may not see!

其二百四十八

對斟如遇可心人，盡醉宜消酒百巡。最惡頑賓一夜擾，詰朝謝過下朱輪。

Take care you never hold a drinking bout
With an ill-tempered, ill-conditioned lout;
　　He'll make a vile disturbance all night long,
And vile apologies next day, no doubt.

其二百四十九

浮花浪蕊枉求勞，天道靡常星自高。徒冀咸宜荷天禄，卻將身命一邊拋。

譯箋：宋蘇軾《賀新郎》（乳燕飛華屋）詞："待浮花浪蕊都盡，伴君幽獨。"○秦嘉《贈婦詩》："皇靈無私親，爲善荷天禄。"

The starry aspects are not all benign;
Why toil then after vain desires, and pine

To lade thyself with load of fortune's boons,
Only to drop it with this life of thine?

其二百五十

相約清醑醉德馨,更攜蠻素寄丁寧。殷殷此乃蒲桃血,拼卻一生成赤靈。

譯箋:《春秋左氏傳‧僖公五年》:"黍稷非馨,明德惟馨。"○唐孟棨《本事詩‧事感》:"白尚書姬人樊素善歌,妓人小蠻善舞,嘗為詩曰:櫻桃樊素口,楊柳小蠻腰。"○《文選‧張衡〈南都賦〉》:"松子神陂,赤靈解角。"李善注:"赤靈,赤龍也。"

O comrades! here is filtered wine, come drink!
Pledge all your charming sweethearts as you drink;
　'Tis the grape's blood, and this is what it says,
"To you I dedicate my life-blood! drink!"

其二百五十一

幻藥愁來拈一丸,瓊漿升斗亦增歡。若言高士不當作,豈赴荒原沙石餐。

譯箋:《楞嚴經》卷三:"諸大幻師求太陰精和幻藥。"○升斗,英譯原作 one pint or twain,一二品脫。○高士,原譯作蘇非。○《史記‧五帝本紀》:"而蚩尤最為暴,莫能伐。"張守節正義引《龍魚圖》:"黃帝攝政,有蚩尤兄弟八十一人,並獸身人語,銅頭鐵額,食沙。"

Are you depressed? Then take of *bhang* one grain,

Of rosy grape-juice take one pint or twain;
　　Sufis, you say, must not take this or that,
Then go and eat the pebbles off the plain!

其二百五十二
偶入道旁陶匠廬，和漿搏埴正如荼。忽聞泥喚求輕緩，昨日其猶一肉軀。

譯箋：《説文解字》："埴，黏土也。"《周禮·考工記》："搏埴之工。"○參看菲譯其三十七。

I saw a busy potter by the way
Kneading with might and main a lump of clay;
　　And, lo! the clay cried, "Use me gently, pray;
I was a man myself but yesterday!"

其二百五十三
壺裡乾坤富敵君，佳人美饌掩芳芬。沐曦飲者長吟嘯，廣陵遺曲豈足聞。

譯箋：君，英譯原作 the realm of Jam 賈姆的國度。賈姆，即賈姆什德。○佳人，英譯原作 Miriam。邢秉順譯注謂瑪麗亞姆佳肴，聖餐的象徵，疑非。英譯原注稱參看《古蘭經》第十九章《瑪爾嫣》："樹下有聲音呼喚她説：'妳用不着憂慮，妳的主已在下面辟了一條小溪，妳可以搖撼這棵椰棗樹，成熟的棗就會爲妳紛紛落地。妳喫，妳喝吧！'"。○Bu Sa'id 指 Abū-Sa'īd Abul-Khayr，阿佈·賽義德（967—1049），波斯著名蘇非，一生主要在納霞堡活動，其思想對詩人阿塔爾影響頗深。Bin Adham 即 Ibrahim Bin Adham，艾德海木，卒於七百七十八年,原爲呼羅珊巴里黑王子,後成爲著名蘇非。二者所作詩歌被稱爲聖歌。《晉書・嵇康傳》:"廣陵散於今絕矣!"

Oh! wine is richer that the realm of Jam,
More fragrant than the food of Miriam;
　　Sweeter are sighs that drunkards heave at morn
Than strains of Bu Sa'id and Bin Adham.

其二百五十四

青天碧海拱穹涯,倒覆一杯凡眼遮。人事尋環流水席,酒來遽飲莫咨嗟。

譯箋:唐李商隱《嫦娥》詩:"嫦娥應悔偷靈藥,碧海青天夜夜心。"○參看菲譯其四十三。

Deep in the rondure of the heavenly blue,
There is a cup, concealed from mortals' view,
　　Which all must drink in turn; Oh, sigh not then,
But drink it boldly, when it comes to you!

其二百五十五

菌榮椿壽去何遙,終必同歸逝若潮。帝子乞兒安有別,一抔黃土共魂銷。

譯箋:菌榮椿壽,英譯原作 four, or forty score,八十年或八百年。《莊子・逍遙游》:"朝菌不知晦朔,蟪蛄不知春秋。"晉葛洪《抱朴子・嘉遯》:"無朝菌之榮,望大椿之壽。"○《史記・張釋之列傳》:"假令愚民取長陵一抔土,陛下何以加其法乎？"江淹《別賦》："黯然銷魂者，唯別而已矣。"

Though you should live to four, or forty score,
Go hence you must, as all have gone before;
　　Then, be you king, or beggar of the streets,
They'll rate you all the same, no less, no more.

其二百五十六

別子拋妻覓道山，千絲萬縷斷凡間。枷鐐宜請快刀斬，遠路漫漫誓不還。

譯箋：道山，英譯原作 Him，祂，指神。《後漢書・竇章傳》："是時學者稱東觀爲老氏臧室，道家蓬萊山。"

If you seek Him, abandon child and wife,
Arise, and sever all these ties to life;
　　All these are bonds to check you on your course.
Arise, and cut these bonds, as with a knife.

其二百五十七

古今代謝影幢幢，何事憂心鬱滿腔。俛首惟聽記卿狀，長生墨瀋迸如瀧。

譯箋：唐孟浩然《與諸子登峴山》詩："人事有代謝，往來成古今。"唐元稹《聞樂天授江州司馬》詩："殘燈無焰影幢幢，此夕聞君謫九江。"○《老子・第七章》："天地所以能長且久者，以其不自生，故能長生。"唐杜甫《月》詩："入河蟾不没，擣藥兔長生。"墨瀋，英譯原作 pen，筆。原注謂筆乃指神所以書律令者。宋陸游《雜興》詩："净洗硯池瀦墨瀋，乘涼要答故人書。"○參看菲譯其七十三。

O heart! this world is but a fleeting show,
Why should its empty griefs distress thee so?
　　Bow down, and bear thy fate, the eternal pen
Will not unwrite its roll for thee, I trow!

其二百五十八

逝者如風不可追，誰曾一返說塵霏。花開堪折直須折，一入蓬山安得歸。

譯箋：《論語・微子》："往者不可諫，來者猶可追。"○花開堪折直須折，借杜秋娘句。○唐李商隱《無題》詩："蓬山此去無多路，青鳥殷勤爲探看。"○參看菲譯其六十四。

Whoe'er returned of all that went before,
To tell of that long road they travel o'er?
　　Leave naught undone of what you have to do,
For when you go, you will return no more.

其二百五十九

斷袖安思涸轍喪，黑輪陰毒任輈張。對樽莫戀再生夢，一命嗚呼即永亡。

譯箋：斷袖，英文原譯作 lovers，情人們。Mahmud and Ayaz 瑪赫穆德和埃亞兹。瑪赫穆德乃伽兹尼王朝最顯赫之統治者，公元九九七至一零三零年在位。

埃亞茲爲其寵臣。薩迪《果園》故事之五十四《埃亞茲對瑪赫穆德的忠誠》："一個人開口指責伽茲尼國王，說埃亞茲因何得寵，他並不漂亮。一朵花兒既無芬芳也不鮮豔，不知夜鶯緣何把那花兒貪戀。人把此話回報瑪赫穆德國王，國王聽了不語沉吟半晌。然後他説：'我愛的是他的秉性，不是愛他容顏美好體態輕盈。'"《漢書·佞幸傳》："賢寵愛日甚，爲駙馬都尉侍中，出則參乘，入御左右，旬月間賞賜累巨萬，貴震朝廷。常與上起臥。嘗晝寢，偏藉上袖，上欲起，賢未覺，不欲動賢，乃斷袖而起。"涸轍，見《莊子·外物》。○黑輪，英譯原作 Dark wheel，當喻死亡。輈張，《後漢書·皇后紀下·孝仁董皇后》："后忿恚罵曰：'汝今輈張，怙汝兄耶？當勑票騎斷何進頭來。'"李賢注："輈張猶强梁也。"《詩經·陳風·防有鵲巢》："誰侜予美？"毛傳："侜張，誑也。"《爾雅·釋訓》："侜張，誑也。"《釋文》或作倜，按侜張雙聲連語。《尚書·無逸》："譸張爲幻。"○再生，英文原譯作 two lives 兩個生命。《太平廣記》卷四四《仙傳拾遺田先生》："求其神力，或可再生耳。"

Dark wheel! how many lovers thou hast slain,
Like Mahmud and Ayaz, O inhumane!

　　Come, let us drink, thou grantest not two lives,
When one is spent, we find it not again.

其二百六十

諸王順命聽神卜，酒焰何時如洞燭。七日周而復始中，當教晝夜光盈屋。

譯箋：神卜，英譯原作 Illustrious Prophet，英明先知。應指穆罕默德。

Illustrious Prophet! whom all kings obey,

When is our darkness lightened by wine's ray?
　　On Sunday, Monday, Tuesday, Wednesday, Thursday,
Friday, and Saturday, both night and day!

其二百六十一
何須眉眼戲元元，惹我澂心百慮煩。既命傾杯宜勿視，乃試欹器不教翻。

譯箋：《韓詩外傳》卷二："孔子觀於周廟，有欹器焉。……使子路取水試之，滿則覆，中則正，虛則欹。"○英譯原注謂末句係諺語，意乃無可能也。

O turn away those roguish eyes of thine!
Be still! seek not my peace to undermine!
　　Thou say'st, "Look not" I might as well essay
To slant my goblet, and not spill my wine.

其二百六十二
聖顏難覿禱堂階，何若同筵享饌偕。汝乃太終兼太始，灼吾深內慰吾懷。

譯箋：英譯原注云此章顯係謂真主。○吳經熊譯《新經全集‧默示錄》第一章："吾乃無始之始，無終之終，古今未來永生全能天主也。"又："予乃無始之始，無終之終；永生不變；死於一時，而生於永古；掌握死亡及地獄之管籥者。"○參看菲譯其七十七。

In taverns better far commune with Thee,
Than pray in mosques, and fail Thy face to see!

O first and last of all Thy creatures Thou,
'Tis Thine to burn, and Thine to cherish me!

其二百六十三

君子宜親一世歡，小人宜遠慎盤桓。敢承鴆酒自賢聖，獨拒愚癡解毒丸。

To wise and worthy men your life devote,
But from the worthless keep your walk remote;
　　Dare to take poison from a sage's hand,
But from a fool refuse an antidote.

其二百六十四

化禽振翮出荒榛，策足漫尋要路津。巖穴無人爲庵指，徒由舊徑返雲身。

譯箋：《古詩十九首》其四："何不策高足，先踞要路津。"〇巖穴，英譯原作 higher nest，高巢。《莊子·山木》："夫豐狐文豹，棲於山林，伏於巖穴，靜也。"晉左思《招隱詩二首》其二："巖穴無結構，丘中有鳴琴。"《詩經·魯頌·閟宮》："泰山巖巖，魯邦所詹。"巖巖，高貌。〇參看菲譯其二十七與其二十八。

I flew here, as a bird from the wild, in aim
Up to a higher nest my course to frame;
　　But, finding here no guide who knows the way,
Fly out by the same door where through I came.

其二百六十五

帝降天羅縛眾生，卻教天性絕其萌。相羊進退皆維谷，玉液怎留於覆觥。

譯箋：參看菲譯其七十八。末句覆觥言可與二百六四一章合看。

He binds us in resistless Nature's chain,
And yet bids us our natures to restrain;
  Between these counter rules we stand perplexed,
"Hold the jar slant, but all the wine retain."

其二百六十六

悠悠過客盡無回，彼岸玄論寂夜臺。倘乏切心向慕意，回環吟禱盡飛灰。

譯箋：南朝梁沈約《傷美人賦》："曾未申其巧笑，忽淪軀於夜臺。"○英譯原注謂穆斯林正式禱告多爲頌讚與唱經而非祈願。

They go away, and none is seen returning,
To teach that other world's recondite learning;
  'Twill not be shown for dull mechanic prayers,
For prayer is naught without true heartfelt yearning.

其二百六十七

默默旻天祝豈靈，萬千祈頌付空冥。美人叢裡但沉醉，逝者匆匆誰一停。

譯箋：英譯原注謂此章係覆應前章。

Go to! Cast dust on those deaf skies, who spurn

Thy orisons and bootless prayers, and learn

  To quaff the cup, and hover round the fair;

Of all who go, did ever one return?

其二百六十八

節操珍珠未及穿，心田惡莠掃猶殘。天恩浩蕩何曾惑，獨一真神豈錯看。

譯箋：英譯原注謂神一論係伊斯蘭信仰核心。

Though Khayyam strings no pearls of righteous deeds,

Nor sweeps from off his soul sin's noisome weeds,

  Yet will he not despair of heavenly grace,

Seeing that ONE as two he ne'er misreads.

其二百六十九

吟祈初別黯魂傷，來覓爐邊日月光。每遇玉壺長頸召，便思引頸注瓊漿。

Again to tavern haunts do we repair,

And say "Adieu" to the five hours of prayer;

  Where'er we see a long-necked flask of wine,

We elongate our necks that wine to share.

其二百七十

世事如棋一局中，翻雲覆雨任天公。幾回枰上騰挪罷，終入陰冥韞匵中。

譯箋：唐杜甫《貧交行》："翻手作雲覆手雨，紛紛輕薄何須數。"〇《論語·子罕》："有美玉於斯，韞匵而藏諸，求善賈而沽諸。"何晏集解引馬融："韞，藏也；匵，匱也，謂藏諸匵中。"〇參看菲譯其六十九。

We are but chessmen, destined, it is plain,
That great chess-player, Heaven, to entertain;
　　It moves us on life's chess-board to and fro,
And then in death's dark box shuts up again.

其二百七十一

泡影人生竟乃何，但言此譬證娑婆。湯湯風自虞淵出，復入虞淵浩浩過。

譯箋：《金剛經》："一切有為法，如夢幻泡影。"〇娑婆，丁福保《佛學大辭典》："又作沙訶、娑訶樓陀。新云索訶。堪忍之義，因而譯曰忍土。此界眾生安忍於十界而不肯出離，故名為忍。此為三千大千世界之總名。一佛攝化之境土也。"〇虞淵，英譯原作 the vasty deeps，廣闊深處。英譯原注謂指虛無之海。《淮南子·天文訓》："至於虞淵，是謂黃昏。"《漢書·揚雄傳上》："外則正南極海，邪界虞淵，鴻濛沆茫，碣以崇山。"

You ask what is this life so frail, so vain,
'Tis long to tell, yet will I make it plain;
　　'Tis but a breath blown from the vasty deeps,

And then blown back to those same deeps again!

其二百七十二

更與羣僧醉玉壺，喜狂今日陟仙都。獨來净寺忘形坐，但問吾非汝主乎。

譯箋：羣僧，原譯本作 Maghs，麻葛，即漢譯穆護。○林松譯《古蘭經韻譯》第七章第一百七十二節：" 當時，你的主從阿丹子孫的脊部，把他們的後代生出，並使他們親自承認。（主說）：'難道我不是你們的主？'他們説：'當然，我們已經承認。'"

To-day to heights of rapture have I soared,
Yea, and with drunken Maghs pure wine adored;
    I am become beside myself, and rest
In that pure temple, "Am not I your Lord?"

其二百七十三

宓妃留枕久消磨，翩若驚鴻一日過。羅襪生塵流盼語，但抛玉佩向微波。

譯箋：宓妃，英譯原作 queen，皇后。《感甄記》："植初求甄逸女不遂，後太祖因與五官中郎將，植晝思夜想，廢寢與食。黃初中入朝，帝示植甄后玉鏤金帶枕，植見之，不覺泣下。時已爲郭后讒死。帝仍以枕齎植，植還。度轘轅，息洛水上，因思甄氏，忽若有見，遂述其事，作《感甄賦》。後明帝見之，改爲《洛神賦》。"三國魏曹植《洛神賦》："其形也，翩若驚鴻，婉若游龍。"又："陵波微步，羅襪生塵。"又："執眷眷之款識兮，懼斯靈之我欺。"又："無良媒以接歡兮，託微波而通辭。願誠素之先達兮，解玉佩以要之。"○英譯原注謂毋求愛之回報。

My queen (long may she live to vex her slave!)
To-day a token of affection gave,
　　Darting a kind glance from her eyes, she passed,
And said, "Do good and cast it on the wave!"

其二百七十四
常鼓絳唇詢酒甑，星移日轉若何參。汝提我耳呢喃告，無力回天但醉酣。

譯箋：唐王勃《滕王閣詩》："閑雲潭影日悠悠，日轉星移幾度秋。"〇參看菲譯其三十五。

I put my lips to the cup, for I did yearn
The hidden cause of length of days to learn;
　　He leaned his lip to mine, and whispered low,
"Drink! for, once gone, you never will return."

其二百七十五
一襲魖衣眠冷函，醒向紅塵嚐苦甘。爾命猶疑常不解，何無滴酒出傾罋。

譯箋：魖衣，英譯原作 the cloak of Naught，虛無的風衣、斗篷。《說文解字》："魖，鬼服也。《韓詩傳》曰：'鄭交甫逢二女，魖服。'"

We lay in the cloak of Naught, asleep and still,

Thou said'st, "Awake! taste the world's good and ill";
　　Here we are puzzled by Thy strange command,
From slanted jars no single drop to spill.

其二百七十六

人心幽祕汝能知，危難之中汝輔持。容吾悔過聽吾訟，人訟汝皆聆受之。

譯箋：參看菲譯其八十一。

O Thou! who know'st the secret thoughts of all,
In time of sorest need who aidest all,
　　Grant me repentance, and accept my plea,
O Thou who dost accept the pleas of all!

其二百七十七

古帝骷髏臥枕低，又聞城上夜烏啼，欲知斷續悲號意，應惜煙消息鼓鼙。

譯箋：古帝，英譯原作 Kai Kawus。凱·卡烏斯，波斯薩珊王朝國王卡瓦德一世之長子。《莊子·至樂》："莊子之楚，見空髑髏，髐然有形，撽以馬捶因而問之，曰：'夫子貪生失理，而爲此乎？將子有亡國之事，斧鉞之誅，而爲此乎？將子有不善之行，愧遺父母妻子之醜，而爲此乎？將子有凍餒之患，而爲此乎？將子之春秋故及此乎？'於是語卒，援髑髏，枕而臥。"〇城，英譯原作 Tus。圖斯，古波斯呼羅珊省城市，近納霞堡。曾被亞歷山大大帝佔領，後毀於成吉思汗之手。

I saw a bird perched on the walls of Tus,

Before him lay the skull of Kai Kawus,

  And thus he made his moan, "Alas, poor king!

Thy drums are hushed, thy 'larums have rung truce."

其二百七十八

勸君莫信再生緣，往事還如一縷煙。惟有真銀爲現利，昔時來歲肯誰憐。

Ask not the chances of the time to be,

And for the past, 'tis vanished, as you see;

  This ready-money breath set down as gain,

Future and past concern not you or me.

其二百七十九

誰教日月共經天，盈縮卷舒誰引牽。蠡測疇人安有術，略無一子定逡躔。

譯箋：《淮南子・俶真訓》：「是故至道無爲，一龍一蛇，盈縮卷舒，與時變化。」《史記・曆書》：「幽、厲之後，周室微，陪臣執政，史不記時，君不告朔，故疇人子弟分散。」裴駰集解引如淳曰：「家業世世相傳爲疇。」《方言》：「躔，歷行也。日運爲躔，月運爲逡。」

What launched that golden orb his course to run,

What wrecks his firm foundations, when 'tis done,

  No man of science ever weighed with scales,

Nor made assay with touchstone, no, not one!

其二百八十

請君傾耳受芹茆，踵事增華須盡拋。來世今生皆一瞬，長生安可換塵勞。

譯箋：芹茆，《禮記·祭統》："水草之菹，陸產之醢。"鄭玄注："水草之菹，芹茆之屬。"○南朝梁蕭統《文選序》："蓋踵其事而增華，變其本而加厲。物既有之，文亦宜然。"

I pray thee to my counsel lend thine ear,
Cast off this false hypocrisy's veneer;
　　This life a moment is, the next all time,
Sell not eternity for earthly gear!

其二百八十一

心中愁惑結千千，徒把愚痴辯汝前。混跡袄方竟何故，穆民潦倒愧誰憐。

Ofttimes I plead my foolishness to Thee,
My heart contracted with perplexity;
　　I gird me with the Magian zone, and why?
For shame so poor a Mussulman to be.

其二百八十二

行樂及時飛羽觴，情迷嬌靨鬱金香。人生幾日會良讌，莫待別離空惋傷。

譯箋：《古詩十九首》其四："今日良宴會，歡樂難具陳。"○參看菲譯其四十二。

Khayyam! rejoice that wine you still can pour,
And still the charms of tulip cheeks adore;
　　You'll soon not be, rejoice then that you are,
Think how 'twould be in case you were no more!

其二百八十三
一日陶坊牖下窺，杯盤列座塵談庵。洶洶一物高聲問，瓦缶誰摶復鬻誰。

譯箋：《名苑》："麈大者曰麈，羣鹿隨之，視麈尾所轉而往，古之談者揮焉。"○參看菲譯其八十二、其八十三與其八十七。

Once, in a potter's shop, a company
Of cups in converse did I chance to see,
　　And lo! one lifted up his voice, and cried,
"Who made, who sells, who buys this crockery?"

其二百八十四
蹣跚弄影夜歸酣，邂逅賢人抱酒罎。但說天恩無盡藏，玉山頹倒不須慚。

譯箋：宋蘇軾《赤壁賦》："是造物者之無盡藏也。"○玉山，參見其百四十六。○參看菲譯其五十八。

Last night, as I reeled from the tavern door,
I saw a sage, who a great wine-jug bore;
　　I said, "O Shaikh, have you no shame?" Said he,

"Allah hath boundless mercy in his store."

其二百八十五

命泉即酒地仙藏，我乃靈媒覓八方。真宰親言人可益，心魂宜享此豐糧。

譯箋：地仙，英譯原作 Khizir，與穆薩同時。林松譯《古蘭經韻譯》第十八章："他倆便發現我的僕人之一，我曾把發自我的仁慈賞賜他，並以除自我的智慧對他教育。"注云："此人名叫黑滋爾，據傳是一個放棄皇位繼承權而潛蹤於江湖海島的太子，知識淵博，亦屬先知之列。"○靈媒，英譯原作 Elias，易勒雅斯，一譯伊洛押司，爲猶太先知，即《舊約》之以利亞。林松譯《古蘭經韻譯》第六章："宰凱里雅、葉哈亞、爾薩和易勒雅斯，個個樂善好義。"○林松譯《古蘭經韻譯》第二章："他們問你關於飲酒和賭博的問題，你說：'這兩件事中包含著大罪，對詩人雖然有某些利益，但他倆的危害超過了利益。'"第十六章："從椰棗和蒲桃的果實中，你們釀醇酒，制美食，此中對通曉事理者確實含有徵跡。"

Life's fount is wine, Khizir its guardian,
I, like Elias, find it where I can;
　'Tis sustenance for heart and spirit too,
Allah himself calls wine "a boon to man."

其二百八十六

絃歌日夜杯光浸，飲復飲兮安可禁。秉燭金尊處處逢，但麼一滴餘皆飲。

Though wine is banned, yet drink, forever drink!

By day and night, with strains of music drink!

    Where'er thou lightest on a cup of wine,

Spill just one drop, and take the rest and drink!

其二百八十七

信經可列七三篇，執一惟中乃敬天。順逆忠姦非旨要，衆生有汝即完全。

譯箋：七三篇，參看温譯其一百九十四譯箋。○《古蘭經》第二十九章："你們不要跟有經典的人爭議，除非方式態度適宜，對背義者不循此例。你們應該説：'我們相信對我們和對你們的降諭，我們的主和你們的主都是一個，我們都只對他順從皈依。'"《尚書‧大禹謨》："人心惟危，道心惟微。惟精惟一，允執厥中。"○英譯原注謂信仰形式乃無關宏旨。

Although the creeds number some seventy-three,

I hold with none but that of loving Thee；

    What matter faith, unfaith, obedience, sin？

Thou'rt all we need, the rest is vanity.

其二百八十八

德行屈指數寥寥，身罪盼將功抵消。過忒休教犯天怒，聖陵再望赦恩遙。

譯箋：聖陵，英譯原作 Mohammed's tomb 穆罕默德之墓，即穆聖墓，在麥地那。○英譯原注謂此章亦非莪默所作。

Tell one by one my scanty virtues o'er；

As for my sins, forgive them by the score;
　　Let not my faults kindle Thy wrath to flame;
By blest Mohammed's tomb, forgive once more!

其二百八十九

難敵病愁休懼來，遠謀無計獨登臺。莫欺定命且歡醉，那管人間一世哀。

譯箋：中聖，參見其十一譯箋。

Grieve not at coming ill, you can't defeat it,
And what far-sighted person goes to meet it?
　　Cheer up! bear not about a world of grief,
Your fate is fixed, and grieving will not cheat it.

其二百九十

惟憑聖睿造金甌，實乃化工之冕旒。何故匠人捶碎盡，一汪覆水已難收。

譯箋：英譯原注引《聖經·約伯記》第十章："爾手所造，則虐待之，輕視之。惡人之謀，則焜耀之，爾豈以是為善乎。"

There is a chalice made with wit profound,
With tokens of the Maker's favour crowned;
　　Yet the world's Potter takes his masterpiece,
And dashes it to pieces on the ground!

其二百九十一

玉醴精靈淡若煙，瓦甖藏魄澈纏綿。往來未遇濁公子，惟此濁杯奇可憐。

譯箋：《周禮・春官・鬯人》："凡祭祀，社壝用大罍。"鄭玄注："大罍，瓦罍。"

In truth wine is a spirit thin as air,
A limpid soul in the cup's earthen ware;
  No dull, dense person shall be friend of mine
Save wine-cups, which are dense and also rare.

其二百九十二

無渴無飢自無縛，鈞輪虐我如甌鱷。其仁心未勝塼輪，機女猶能持紡絡。

譯箋：三國魏曹植《光禄大夫荀侯誄》："機女投杼，農夫輟耕。"鈞輪，見菲譯其二十五譯箋。

O wheel of heaven! no ties of bread you feel,
No ties of salt, you flay me like an eel!
  A woman's wheel spins clothes for man and wife,
It does more good than you, O heavenly wheel!

其二百九十三

薔薇不復綴怡園，荆棘一由蕪冷喧。煩惱青絲難遽斷，何妨椎髻入仙門。

譯箋：怡園，英譯原作 Paradise，樂園。《尔雅・釋詁》："怡，乐也。"○《漢書·李陵傳》:"兩人皆胡服椎結。"顏師古注:"結讀曰髻,一撮之髻,其形如椎。"唐玄奘《大唐西域·記婆羅疤斯國》:"或斷髮,或椎髻,露形無服,塗身以灰,精勤苦行,求出生死。"末二句本言若無拜氈、念珠和賢哲,彼基督教之鈴鼓、聖帶吾亦不蔑棄。蘇非詩人魯米有詩云:"我頭戴伊斯蘭教的纏頭,腰繫瑣羅亞斯德教的腰帶,我戴著基督教的標誌,我帶著光明。不要離開我,不要離開我。我是一個穆斯林,但也是基督徒,是婆羅門教徒,是瑣羅亞斯德教徒。至高無上的主啊,我信賴你。不要離開我,不要離開我。"與此章意相類。

Did no fair rose my paradise adorn,
I would make shift to deck it with a thorn;
　And if I lacked my prayer-mats, beads, and Shaikh,
Those Christian bells and stoles I would not scorn.

其二百九十四

玉帛榮華天未應,干戈玷辱自須領。誰辭美酒夜光杯,舉石吾將碎其頸。

"If heaven deny me peace and fame," I said,
"Let it be open war and shame instead;
　The man who scorns bright wine had best beware,
I'll arm me with a stone, and break his head!"

其二百九十五

熹微侵曉破穹蒼,對飲晨軒亦不妨。待得愁消天大白,不知吾輩在何鄉。

See! the dawn breaks, and rends night's canopy;

Arise! and drain a morning draught with me!
 Away with gloom! full many a dawn will break
Looking for us, and we not here to see!

其二百九十六
刀山火海勇登臨，濯足黃泉勿變心。但逐陰風歇薪焰，濁囊化土散駸駸。

譯箋：戴逵《流火賦》："火憑薪以傳焰，人資氣以享年。苟薪氣之有歇，何年焰之恒延。"〇英譯原注謂此章或係某虔誠讀者對莪默譏嘲之回覆。參見其二百二十三首譯箋。

O you who tremble not at fires of hell,
Nor wash in water of remorse's well,
 When winds of death shall quench your vital torch,
Beware lest earth your guilty dust expel.

其二百九十七
人間遊戲亦堂皇，造化神工誰識量。但得延歌更呼酒，邯鄲驚破幾黃粱。

譯箋：黃粱，見唐沈既濟《枕中記》傳奇。

This world a hollow pageant you should deem;
All wise men know things are not what they seem;
 Be of good cheer, and drink, and so shake off
This vain illusion of a baseless dream.

其二百九十八

娉婷柳態艷薔容,彩袖殷勤捧玉鍾。一霎陰風碎衣帶,便飛花葉落重重。

譯箋:借宋晏幾道《鷓鴣天》詞:"彩袖殷勤捧玉鍾,當年拚卻醉顏紅。"

With maids stately as cypresses, and fair
As roses newly plucked, your wine-cups share,
  Or e'er Death's blasts shall rend your robe of flesh
Like yonder rose leaves, lying scattered there!

其二百九十九

孤棲何必坐愁慵,宜得蒲桃愛女從。養在深閨人未識,麗姿殊勝母儀容。

譯箋:唐白居易《長恨歌》:"楊家有女初長成,養在深閨人未識。"○蒲桃愛女,英譯原注謂指酒。

Cast off dull care, O melancholy brother!
Woo the sweet daughter of the grape, no other;
  The daughter is forbidden, it is true,
But she is nicer than her lawful mother!

其三百

心隨朗月阻溪湍,欲訴衷情期艾難。夸父臨川終渴死,古來烈士最奇觀。

譯箋:《史記·張丞相列傳》:"昌為人口吃,又盛怒,曰:'臣口不能言,然臣期期知其不可。'"又南朝宋劉義慶《世説新語・言語》:"鄧艾口吃,語稱艾艾。"○《山海經・海外北經》:"夸父與日逐走,入日。渴,欲得飲,飲於河、渭,河、渭不足,北飲大澤。未至,道渴而死。棄其杖,化爲鄧林。"

My love shone forth, and I was overcome,
My heart was speaking, but my tongue was dumb;
　　Beside the water-brooks I died of thirst.
Was ever known so strange a martyrdom?

其三百零一

隔葉黄鸝深樹鳴,賓筵鼓瑟復吹笙。壺泉奔瀉淙淙響,對酌豈能無此聲。

譯箋:唐杜甫《蜀相》詩:"隔葉黄鸝空好音。"唐韋應物《滁州西澗》詩:"上有黄鸝深樹鳴。"○《詩經・小雅・鹿鳴》:"我有嘉賓,鼓瑟吹笙。"

Give me my cup in hand, and sing a glee
In concert with the bulbul's symphony;
　　Wine would not gurgle as it leaves the flask,
If drinking mute were right for thee and me!

其三百零二

真道安能予佞輩,千金買骨實虛聞。倘延遐壽知天命,玄化或能臻幾分。

譯箋:《戰國策・燕策》:"古之君人,有以千金求千里馬者,三年不能得。涓人言於君曰:'請求之。'君遣之,三月得千里馬。馬已死,買其骨五百金,反以報君。君大怒曰:'所求者生馬,安事死馬而捐五百金?'涓人對曰:'死馬且買之五百金,況生馬乎?天下必以王爲能市馬,馬今至矣。'"○《論語・爲政》:"子曰:'吾十有五而志於學,三十而立,四十而不惑,五十而知天命。'"○英譯原注謂第三行字面意謂"除非汝深掘汝之靈魂,復飲血五十年"。結歡"真理"之"狀態",或即指玄秘之神。

The "Truth" will not be shown to lofty thought,
Nor yet with lavished gold may it be bought;
 But, if you yield your life for fifty years,
From words to "states" you may perchance be brought.

其三百零三
迢迢星漢降斯身,脫縛超乎三界塵。絲網已開千萬結,獨餘死結瘅心神。

譯箋:星漢,英譯原作 Saturn's wreath,土星光環。古波斯人以土星爲天之最高處。參見菲譯第五版其三十一首。○三界,指衆生所居之欲界、色界、無色界。○參看菲譯其三十一。

I solved all problems, down from Saturn's wreath
Unto this lowly sphere of earth beneath,
 And leapt out free from bonds of fraud and lies,
Yea, every knot was loosed, save that of death!

其三百零四

滄海桑田久未諳，知行有術亦難探。人生得意莫如醉，日月壺中可盡參。

譯箋：晉葛洪《神仙傳·麻姑》："麻姑自說云：'接待以來，已見東海三爲桑田。'"○《尚書說命中》："非知之艱，行之惟艱。"○唐李白《將進酒》詩："人生得意須盡歡，莫使金樽空對月。"○晉葛洪《神仙傳·壺公》："公語長房曰：'卿見我跳入壺中時，卿便隨我跳，自當得入。'長房承公言爲試，展足不覺已入。既入之後，不復見壺，但見樓觀五色，重門閣道，見公左右侍者數十人。公語長房曰：'我仙人也，忝天曹職，所統供事不勤，以此見謫，暫還人間耳，卿可教，故得見我。'"○參看菲譯其五十四。

Peace! the eternal "Has been" and "To be"
Pass man's experience, and man's theory;
    In joyful seasons naught can vie with wine,
To all these riddles wine supplies the key!

其三百零五

慈恩信可琢瑕身，公義昭昭在上真。皮蛻縱然隨罪滅，他年天亦惜微塵。

Allah, our Lord, is merciful, though just;
Sinner! despair not, but His mercy trust!
    For though to-day you perish in your sins,
To-morrow He'll absolve your crumbling dust.

其三百零六

可惱天行健轉輪，重枷莫使瘝吾身。倘惟愚者荷君寵，吾甯不爲明哲人。

譯箋：《周易·乾卦》："天行健。"○《詩經·大雅·烝民》："既明且哲，以保其身。"

Your course annoys me, O ye wheeling skies!
Unloose me from your chain of tyrannies!
　　If none but fools your favours may enjoy,
Then favour me, — I am not very wise!

其三百零七

避地高陽多誤身，歧迷猶勝說經人。我雖渴飲蒲桃血，何忍如卿吞魄神。

譯箋：《史記·酈生陸賈列傳》："走！復入言沛公，吾高陽酒徒也，非儒人也。"○解經人，英譯原作 Mufti 穆夫提，阿拉伯語音譯，意爲教法解說人。○英譯原注謂暗指穆夫提背義。案亦諷教法派之意。

O City Mufti, you go more astray
Than I do, though to wine I do give way;
　　I drink the blood of grapes, you that of men:
Which of us is the more bloodthirsty, pray?

其三百零八

悠悠來日莫心焦，昨日煩憂事可銷。倘借囚龍一日醉，揚鱗脫鎖去逍遙。

'Tis well to drink, and leave anxiety
For what is past, and what is yet to be;
　　Our prisoned spirits, lent us for a day,
A while from season's bondage shall go free!

其三百零九

司命一勾前債銷，弊囊脫似葉飛飄。欣欣拋卻紅塵去，留得粃糠入火燒。

譯箋：《史記·天官書》："北魁戴匡六星……四曰司命。"清王夫之《楚辭通釋》："大司命統司人之生死，而少司命則司人子嗣之有無。以其所司者嬰稚，故曰少；大，則統攝之辭也。"金文《齊侯壺》："辭誓於大辭（司）命，用兩璧、兩壺、八鼎。"○吳經熊譯《福音馬寶傳》第三章第十二節："其手執箕，簸淨厥場，斂麥入倉，以不滅之火而燒其糠。"○參看菲譯其八。

When Khayyam quittance at Death's hand receives,
And sheds his outworn life, as trees their leaves,
　　Full gladly will he sift this world away,
Ere dustmen sift his ashes in their sieves.

其三百一十

羣生惶恐仰穹隆，身影飛馳類轉蓬。日燭塵寰形萬象，幢幢走馬一燈中。

譯箋：唐李商隱《無題》詩："走馬蘭台類轉蓬。"○英譯原注謂指中國燈籠或走馬燈。參看菲譯其六十八首。

This wheel of heaven, which makes us all afraid,
I liken to a lamp's revolving shade,
　　The sun the candlestick, the earth the shade,
And men the trembling forms thereon portrayed.

其三百一十一

泥骸一具任誰搏，誰爲縫裘誰補氈。冠飾墨幪眉上覆，咸非由己實堪憐。

譯箋：《尚書大傳》："唐、虞象刑，而民不敢犯。苗民用刑，而民興相漸。唐、虞之象刑：上刑，赭衣不純；中刑，雜屨；下刑、墨幪。以居州里，而民恥之。"鄭玄注："時人尚德義，犯刑者但易之衣服，自爲大恥。幪，巾也。使不得冠飾，以恥之也。"《荀子·正論》："世俗之類說者曰：治古無肉刑而有象刑：墨黥。"楊倞注："墨黥當爲墨幪，但以墨巾幪其頭而已。"

Who was it that did mix my clay? Not I.
Who spun my web of silk and wool? Not I.
　　Who wrote upon my forehead all my good,
And all my evil deeds? In truth not I.

其三百一十二

客驛莫憂明日身，相歡今日即良辰。詰朝亦出此門去，同作悠悠萬古人。

譯箋：萬古，原作七十年。英譯原注謂印度-波斯歷史學家拜達歐尼言自阿丹全其時代有七千年。○參看菲譯其二十一。

O let us not forecast to-morrow's fears,
But count to-day as gain, my brave compeers!
　　To-morrow we shall quit this inn, and march
With comrades who have marched seven thousand years.

其三百一十三

安忍金樽一日捐，但教心性發狂顛。天魔倘得餘沾飲，斷羨凡塵不羨仙。

譯箋：天魔，英譯原作 Iblis 易卜劣廝，阿拉伯語"魔鬼"。又英譯 Adam 亞當，《古蘭經》譯作阿丹。林松譯《古蘭經韻譯》卷一第二章："當時，我對天使們下令：'你們應該向阿丹行叩頭禮！'他們當即叩頭行禮，只有易卜劣廝抗拒，他狂妄驕縱，他本來是叛逆者之一。"

Ne'er for one moment leave your cup unused!
Wine keeps heart, faith, and reason too, amused;
　　Had Iblis swallowed but a single drop,
To worship Adam he had ne'er refused!

其三百一十四

倦眸粉靨帶花黃，樓月舞低人斷腸。三盞五杯何足道，千鍾不憶蜀雲鄉。

譯箋：倦眸，英譯原作 sweet Narcissus eyes，甜美水仙花之目。水仙花在西方文學乃自戀象徵，然未知是否為我默之意。英譯原注謂乃疲倦之意。○宋晏幾道《鷓鴣天》:"舞低楊柳樓心月,歌盡桃花扇底風。"

Come, dance! while we applaud thee, and adore
Thy sweet Narcissus eyes, and grape-juice pour;
  A score of cups is no such great affair,
But 'tis enchanting when we reach three score!

其三百一十五
已休塵想掩柴扉,貴賤不通遊遠陲。天意憐幽獨知我,浮沉身世一何悲。

譯箋:英譯原注謂自哀其境遇。

I close the door of hope in my own face,
Nor sue for favours from good men, or base;
  I have but ONE to lend a helping hand,
He knows, as well as I, my sorry case.

其三百一十六
九重圜轉棄離人,六慾卑污毀賤身。無計全拋凡俗念,繁華一任誘紅塵。

Ah! by these heavens, that ever circling run,
And by my own base lusts I am undone,
  Without the wit to abandon worldly hopes,
And wanting sense the world's allures to shun!

其三百一十七

茸茸茵碧衆皆眠，安識泥中別有天。來者古人荒漠去，烏鄉按堵俗依然。

譯箋：《漢書·高帝紀上》："吏民皆按堵如故。"顏師古注："應劭曰：'按，按次第。堵，牆堵也。'師古曰：'言不遷動也。'"〇英譯原注謂眠於泥中者指沉迷邪教與愚闇之人。

On earth's green carpet many sleepers lie,
And hid beneath it others I descry;
　　And others, not yet come, or passed away,
People the desert of Non-entity!

其三百一十八

莫憂朝聖罪猶存，慎勿趑趄近主尊。昨夜梅邊降恩雪，脫胎換骨鑄新魂。

Sure of Thy grace, for sins why need I fear?
How can the pilgrim faint whilst Thou art near?
　　On the last day Thy grace will wash me white,
And make my "black record" to disappear.

其三百一十九

憑虛遺世未驚呼，羽化神馳影若無。寂滅安能使生畏，惶惶憂死衹塵軀。

譯箋：宋蘇軾《赤壁賦》："浩浩乎如馮虛禦風，而不知其所止；飄飄乎如遺世獨立，羽化而登仙。"

Think not I dread from out the world to hie,
And see my disembodied spirit fly;
　　I tremble not at death, for death is true,
'Tis my ill life that makes me fear to die!

其三百二十

鈍智宜除夢勿耽，何須再學老僧談。陶人先奉一罌飲，再碎吾身作酒罌。

Let us shake off dull reason's incubus,
Our tale of days or years cease to discuss,
　　And take our jugs, and plenish them with wine,
Or e'er grim potters make their jugs of us!

其三百二十一

醉柳眠花喜冶遊，正人指斥語難休。檀珠鶴氅歸君有，醇婦何妨我自留。

譯箋：《史記·魏公子列傳》："飲醇酒，多近婦女。"

How much more wilt thou chide, O raw divine,
For that I drink, and am a libertine?
　　Thou hast thy weary beads, and saintly show,
Leave me my cheerful sweetheart, and my wine!

其三百二十二

迷魂陣裡戰猶酣，力屈難支愧那堪。甲帳雖聞傳赦令，將軍仍抱一腔慙。

譯箋：清李汝珍小說《鏡花緣》第十六回："世上名利場中，原是一座迷魂陣。"

Against my lusts I ever war, in vain,
I think on my ill deeds with shame and pain;
    I trust Thou wilt assoil me of my sins,
But even so, my shame must still remain.

其三百二十三

卿卿與我若圓規，一體二元形影隨。環步同心天地畫，終相聚首不睽離。

譯箋：菲氏曾在所譯其五十六註釋中引此首詩：You and I are the image of a pair of compasses; though we have two heads we have one body; when we have fixed the centre for our circle, we bring our heads together at the end.

In these twin compasses, O Love, you see
One body with two heads, like you and me,
    Which wander round one centre, circlewise,
But at the last in one same point agree.

其三百二十四

匆匆駒隙寄浮生，當挈佳人載酒行。莫問須彌久與暫，一朝鶴逝底干卿。

譯箋：唐杜牧《遣懷》詩："落魄江湖載酒行。"

We shall not stay here long, but while we do,
'Tis folly wine and sweethearts to eschew;
　　Why ask if earth etern or transient be?
Since you must go, it matters not to you.

其三百二十五

濟濟蹌蹌入淨祠，不因祈頌料神知。禱氈竊得一枚返，再赴當須破弊時。

譯箋：《詩經·小雅·楚茨》："濟濟蹌蹌，絜爾牛羊。"毛傳："濟濟蹌蹌，言有容也。"鄭玄箋："言威儀敬慎也。"○英譯原注謂"竊一禱氈"指大庭廣衆下禱告。對某些虛僞者之諷刺，或即就自己而言。

In reverent sort to mosque I wend my way,
But, by great Allah, it is not to pray;
　　No! but to steal a prayer-mat! When 'tis worn,
I go again, another to purvey.

其三百二十六

莫愁舛命毁安詳，瓊液但教傾夜光。造化戕人釀其血，他年我亦啖其漿。

No more let fate's annoys our peace consume,
But let us rather rosy wine consume;
　　The world our murderer is, and wine its blood,
Shall we not then that murderer's blood consume?

其三百二十七

水竭陵無不轉消，誓將清譽爲卿抛。蒼天縱使作芻狗，甘忍終期化劫燒。

譯箋：漢樂府《上邪》："我欲與君相知，長命無絶衰。山無陵，江水爲竭，冬雷陣陣，夏雨雪，天地和，乃敢與君絶。"○《老子・第五章》："天地不仁，以萬物爲芻狗；聖人不仁，以百姓爲芻狗。"○《法華經》："假令劫燒，擔負乾草入中不燒。"《維摩經・佛道品》："或現劫盡燒，天地皆洞然。"

For Thee I vow to cast repute away,
And, if I shrink, the penalty to pay;
  Though life might satisfy Thy cruelty,
'Twere naught, I'll bear it till the judgment-day!

其三百二十八

歧路彷徨仰宇穹，凡夫桀驁轉謙恭。紅塵憂樂已多倦，何日長離逝若風。

In Being's rondure do we stray belated,
Our pride of manhood humbled and abated;
  Would we were gone! long since have we been wearied
With this world's griefs, and with its pleasures sated.

其三百二十九

青燈照酒樂其中，色界本空身亦空。休寄諄諄勸降表，揭竿我已抗天公。

譯箋：漢賈誼《過秦論上》："斬木爲兵，揭竿爲旗。"

The world is false, so I'll be false as well,
And with bright wine, and gladness ever dwell!
　　They say, "May Allah grant thee penitence!"
He grants it not, and, did he, I'd rebel!

其三百三十

相與北邙泉下塗，紛紛毛血灑平蕪。但搏骸骨成樽缶，一得歆香命可蘇。

譯箋：晉陶潛《擬古》其四："一旦百歲後，相與還北邙。"○唐杜甫《畫鷹》詩："何當擊凡鳥，毛血灑平蕪。"○參看菲譯其八十九。

When Death shall tread me down upon the plain,
And pluck my feathers, and my life-blood drain,
　　Then mould me to a cup, and fill with wine;
Haply its scent will make me breathe again.

其三百三十一

人間運數枉探求，陰錯陽差足可羞。祝福無緣亦無分，罪因懷璧禍誰收。

譯箋：《春秋左氏傳・桓公十年》："周諺有之：'匹夫無罪，懷璧其罪。'"

So far as this world's dealings I have traced,
I find its favours shamefully misplaced;
　　Allah be praised! I see myself debarred
From all its boons, and wrongfully disgraced.

其三百三十二

清聞拋如碎玉卮,倦心頓復飲霞曦。百年夙願捐棄已,聽琴且倚鬋雲垂。

譯箋:五代和凝《春光好》詞:"紗窗暖,畫屏閑。鬋雲鬟。"○參看菲譯其四十一。

'Tis dawn! my heart with wine I will recruit,
And dash to bits the glass of good repute;
　　My long-extending hopes I will renounce,
And grasp long tresses, and the charming lute.

其三百三十三

萬罪一身何穢污,知君恩恕信能涂。窮途當哭君皆顧,潦倒窮途誰若吾。

譯箋:《晉書‧阮籍傳》:"時率意獨駕,不由徑路,車跡所窮,輒慟哭而反。"

Though I had sinned the sins of all mankind,
I know Thou would'st to mercy be inclined;
　　Thou sayest, "I will help in time of need."
One needier than I where wilt Thou find?

其三百三十四

漫誣食菜事邪魔,醉臥壺天何錯訛。那管諸宗誤相認,自由自在任風過。

譯箋:宋莊季裕《雞肋編》卷上:"事魔食菜,法禁甚嚴。有犯者,家人雖不知情,亦流于遠方,以財產半給告人,餘皆没官。"英譯 Gueber or infidel,指袄教徒與不信宗教者或其他異教徒。

Am I a wine-bibber? What if I am?
Gueber or infidel? Suppose I am?
　　Each sect miscalls me, but I heed them not,
I am my own, and, what I am, I am.

其三百三十五
糟丘擬臥一生終,元夕傾觴作善功。拋臂來牽玉壺頸,絳唇亂點坐懷中。

譯箋:《韓詩外傳》卷四:"桀爲酒池,可以運舟,糟丘足以望十里,而牛飲者三千人。"○元夕,英譯 Kadr 指蓋德爾夜,意爲珍貴之夜,爲穆斯林一隆重節日,在伊斯蘭曆齋月(九月)中,真主於此夜賜降《古蘭經》。故伊斯蘭教鼓勵穆斯林在此夜多行善功,以圖真主萬倍厚賞。林松譯《古蘭經韻譯》第九十七章:"的確,我在珍貴之夜把它下降。你可知道,珍貴之夜怎麼樣?珍貴之夜,比一千一個月價值更高昂。"

All my life long from drink I have not ceased.
And drink I will to-night on Kadr's feast;
　　And throw my arms about the wine-jar's neck,
And kiss its lip, and clasp it to my breast!

其三百三十六

仰觀俛察可通玄，存否是非能曉全。倘有真知勝壺境，樂拋所學拜其前。

譯箋：唐陸德明《經典釋文》："宓犧氏之王天下，仰則觀於天文，俛則察於地理。"〇參看菲譯其五十六。

I know what is, and what is not, I know
The lore of things above, and things below;
　　But all this lore will cheerfully renounce,
If one a higher grade than drink can show.

其三百三十七

本非浪子蕩游婪，除卻春醪未敢貪。自戀如君安敢效，折腰惟拜酒盈甔。

譯箋：英譯原注謂斥自負貪婪之學者。亦歸安瓦里所作。

Though I drink wine, I am no libertine,
Nor am I grasping, save of cups of wine;
　　I scruple to adore myself, like you;
For this cause to wine-worship I incline.

其三百三十八

夜窗剪燭話元元，乃是陶泥混莽搏。百載煩憂一骸集，炎涼淺啖赴黃泉。

譯箋：《戰國策・秦策一》："制海內，子元元，臣諸侯，非兵不可。"高誘注：

"元,善也,民之類善故稱元。"唐陳子昂《感遇》其十九:"聖人不利己,憂濟在元元。"○參看菲譯其四十八。

To confidants like you I dare to say
What mankind really are — moulded of clay,
　　Affliction's clay, and kneaded in distress,
They taste the world awhile, then pass away.

其三百三十九
酒缶宜爲佈道場,數升膽氣可開張。神祠歲月如能易,寧可蹉跎滯醉鄉。

譯箋:英譯原注謂此章或闡玄義。

We make the wine-jar's lip our place of prayer,
And drink in lessons of true manhood there,
　　And pass our lives in taverns, if perchance
The time mis-spent in mosques we may repair.

其三百四十
萬物芸芸人至靈,還如慧眼有瞳明。茫茫大塊指環繞,上鐫羣生作印銘。

譯箋:英譯原注謂人乃一微觀宇宙。

Man is the whole creation's summary,
The precious apple of great wisdom's eye;

The circle of existence is a ring,
Whereof the signet is humanity.

其三百四十一

掙離珊網絳雲排，境入太虛惟酒偕。蛻卻皮囊今始悟，土中來罷土中埋。

譯箋：珊網，英譯原作 earth's low trammels，地上束縛。trammel 有"漁網"義。《新唐書·西域傳下·拂菻》："海中有珊瑚洲，海人乘大舶，墮鐵網水底。珊瑚初生磐石上，白如菌，一歲而黃，三歲赤，枝格交錯，高三四尺。鐵發其根，繫網舶上，絞而出之，失時不取即腐。"○太虛，英譯原作 heaven，天。晉孫綽《遊天台山賦》："太虛遼廓而無閡，運自然之妙有。"李善注："太虛，謂天也。"○皮囊，英譯原作 fleshly clog，肉體之負累。清曹雪芹小說《紅樓夢》第五六回："空有皮囊，真性不知往那裡去了。"

With fancies, as with wine, our heads we turn,
Aspire to heaven, and earth's low trammels spurn；
　　But, when we drop this fleshly clog, 'tis seen
From dust we came, and back to dust return.

其三百四十二

倦夜無眠憎命乖，殊非蓄意破清齋。守期更漏錯聽盡，納福盤飱早入懷。

譯箋：齋月，按伊斯蘭教義乃穆斯林精神昇華之期。其間白天飲食、房事均當禁止。開齋則指日落後進食。據穆罕默德云，開齋乃齋月每日持齋終了之時真主所賜福祉。馬堅譯《古蘭經》第二章第一百八十五節："賴買丹月中，開始降示《古蘭經》，指導世人，昭示明證，以便遵循正道，分別真僞。故在此月中，你們應當齋戒，害病或旅行的人，當依所缺的日數補齋。真主要你們便利，不要你們困難，以便你們補足所缺的日數，以便你們讚頌真主引導你們的恩德，以便你們感謝他。"

If so it be that I did break the fast,

Think not I meant it; no! I thought 'twas past; ——

　　That day more weary than a sleepless night, ——

And blessed breakfast-time had come at last!

其三百四十三

甜醪至美未能嘗，毒手黃連已浸觴。食匱鹽梅不成味，但教和淚痛肝腸。

譯箋：黃連，英譯原作 a drop of gall 一滴膽汁。〇英譯原注謂第四行字面義爲"吃一片自己的烤肝"。

I never drank of joy's sweet cordial,

But grief's fell hand infused a drop of gall;

　　Nor dipped my bread in pleasure's piquant salt,

But briny sorrow made me smart withal!

其三百四十四

拂曙登途趨酒壚，狂僧坐共日西偏。幽明垂象誰能示，惟盼承恩禱昊天。

譯箋：拂曙，英譯原作 At dawn，黎明。《初學記》卷四引隋蕭愨《奉和元日》

詩:"帝宫通夕燎,天門拂曙開。"○幽明,英譯原作 things secret, and things known,默示與明示。《周易‧繫辭上》:"仰以觀於天文,俯以察於地理,是故知幽明之故。"韓康伯注:"幽明者,有形無形之象。"《尚書‧舜典》:"三載考績,三考黜陟幽明。"孔傳:"黜退其幽者,升進其明者。"《周易‧繫辭上》:"天垂象,見吉凶,圣人像之"漢許慎《説文解字》:"示,天垂象,見吉凶,所以示人也。"

At dawn to tavern-haunts I wend my way,
And with distraught Kalendars pass the day;
　O Thou! who know'st things secret, and things known,
Grant me Thy grace, that I may learn to pray!

其三百四十五

煩惱堪同芥子觀,日嗜一粒那須歎。庖廚塵世無滋味,莫乞人間腐鼠餐。

譯箋:芥子,英譯原作 one grain,一粒穀。《維摩經‧不可思議品》:"若菩薩住是解脱者,以須彌之高廣,内芥子中,無所增減,須彌山王本相如故。"○《莊子‧秋水》:"惠子相梁,莊子往見之。或謂惠子曰:'莊子來,欲代子相。'於是惠子恐,搜於國中三日三夜。莊子往見之,曰:'南方有鳥,其名爲鵷鶵,子知之乎?夫鵷鶵發於南海而飛於北海,非梧桐不止,非練實不食,非醴泉不飲。於是鴟得腐鼠,鵷鶵過之,仰而視之曰:嚇!今子欲以子之梁國而嚇我邪?'"

The world's annoys I rate not at one grain,
So I eat once a day I don't complain;

And, since earth's kitchen yields no solid food,
I pester no man with petitions vain.

其三百四十六
塵勞命薄縛重重，片暇歡愉亦未逢。雖侍王良學調馭，終無一技入亨通。

譯箋：王良，英譯原作 fate，命運。《淮南子·覽冥訓》："昔者，王良、造父之御也，上車攝轡，馬爲整齊而斂諧，投足調均，勞逸若一，心怡氣和，體便輕畢，安勞樂進，馳騖若滅，左右若鞭，周旋若環，世皆以爲巧，然未見其貴者也。"高誘注："王良，晉大夫郵無恤子良也。所謂御良也。"

Never from worldly toils have I been free,
Never for one short moment glad to be!
　　I served a long apprenticeship to fate,
But yet of fortune gained no mastery.

其三百四十七
右持杯爵左翻經，時正時邪半夢醒。湛湛青天顧憐我，清真不染異端形。

譯箋：清真，英譯原作 Muslim，穆斯林。清真一語漢語中指伊斯蘭教。明朱元璋《御制至聖百字贊》："降邪歸一，教名清真，穆罕默德，至貴聖人。"

One hand with Koran, one with wine-cup dight,
I half incline to wrong, and half to right;
　　The azure-marbled sky looks down on me

A sorry Moslem, yet not heathen quite.

其三百四十八

吾於穆聖敬如神，悃款將持一問陳。既許生民飲酸湩，何推天下禁清醇。

譯箋：穆聖，英譯原作 Mustafa，即 Mohammed 穆罕默德。〇悃款，英譯原作 with due reverence，以應有之崇敬。《楚辭·卜居》："吾寧悃悃款款樸以忠乎？將送往勞來斯無窮乎？"〇酸湩，英譯原作 acid whey，酸乳清。《説文解字》："湩，乳汁也。"《穆天子傳》："至于巨蒐氏，巨蒐之人□奴，乃獻白鵠之血，以飲天子，且具牛馬之湩，以洗天子之足，及二乘之人。"郭璞注："湩，乳也。"

Khayyam's respects to Mustafa convey,
And with due reverence ask him to say,
　　Why it has pleased him to forbid pure wine,
When he allows his people acid whey?

其三百四十九

莪默解經休曲違，清規簡約最宜歸。酣觴誰道概爲錯，賢者無傷不肖非。

Tell Khayyam, for a master of the schools,
He strangely misinterprets my plain rules:
　　Where have I said that wine is wrong for all?
'Tis lawful for the wise, but not for fools.

其三百五十

月旦評吾明哲人，惟天知曉實非真。今生何在亦何故，降此紅塵寄一身。

譯箋：月旦，英譯原作 My critics，我的批評者們。《後漢書·許劭傳》："初，劭與靖俱有高名，好共核論鄉黨人物，每月輒更其品題，故汝南俗有月旦評焉。"明哲人，英譯原作 philosopher，哲學家，相對神學家言。《尚書·說命》："知之曰明哲，明哲實作則。"○參看菲譯其五十七。

My critics call me a philosopher,
But Allah knows full well they greatly err;
　　I know not even what I am, much less
Why on this earth I am a sojourner!

其三百五十一

愈投死地愈逢生，愈處卑宮愈駿升。大道絪縕化醇一，愈能醉飽愈明澂。

譯箋：《孫子·九地》："投之亡地而後存，陷之死地然後生。"○《論語·泰伯》："禹，吾無間然矣。菲飲食，而致孝乎鬼神。惡衣服，而致美乎黻冕。卑宮室，而盡力乎溝洫。"○《周易·繫辭下》："天地絪縕，萬物化醇；男女構精，萬物化生。"孔穎達疏："萬物感之，變化而精醇也。"○《詩經·大雅·既醉》："既醉以酒，既飽以德。君子萬年，介爾景福。"

The more I die to self, I live the more,
The more abase myself, the higher soar;
　　And, strange! the more I drink of Being's wine,

More sane I grow and sober than before.

其三百五十二
樊口絳唇金玉鑲，薔薇美艷勝檀郎。行人若問何憑信，脫贈斑斑帶血裳。

譯箋：檀郎，英譯原作 Yusuf，尤素福，即《舊約》中之約瑟，傳爲美少年。李煜《一斛珠》："爛嚼紅茸，笑向檀郎唾。"檀郎，潘安小字。○《舊約》記諸兄因嫉約瑟得父寵而鬻其於以實瑪利人。文理本《舊約·創世紀》第三十七章："流便至井，窺約瑟不在，遂裂己衣。返見諸弟曰：'孺子不在，我將焉往。'昆弟宰牡山羊，濡約瑟衣於血，遣人攜之詣父曰：'我儕得此，試觀爲爾子之衣否。'雅各識之，曰：'是吾子之衣也。彼爲惡獸所食，約瑟破裂無疑矣。'"林松譯《古蘭經韻譯》第十二章："他們還帶來了假血染紅的襯衣。"

Quoth rose, "I am the Yusuf flower, I swear,
For in my mouth rich golden gems I bear":
　　I said, "Show me another proof." Quoth she,
"Behold this blood-stained vesture that I wear!"

其三百五十三
程門立雪十年中，丘壑煙霞盡在胸。欲問於今何所獲，來隨黃土去隨風。

譯箋：唐厲霆《大有詩堂》詩："胸中元自有丘壑，盞裡何妨對聖賢。"宋黃庭堅《題子瞻枯木》詩："胸中元自有丘壑，故作老木蟠風霜。"○英譯原注謂菲氏比之於莫爾克臨終之呼："吾將逝於風之手中。"參看菲譯其二十七與其二十八。

I studied with the masters long ago,
And long ago did master all they know;
　　Here now the end and issue of it all,
From earth I came, and like the wind I go!

其三百五十四
來時歡笑去愁啼，降世冰清死墮泥。怒火焚身淚洗面，終隨風散壞中棲。

Death finds us soiled, though we were pure at birth,
With grief we go, although we came with mirth;
　　Watered with tears, and burned with fires of woe,
And, casting life to winds, we rest in earth!

其三百五十五
神杯照世徹須彌，海陸能覘擬試之。哲士賢人暗相告，吾身靈肉即斯卮。

譯箋：照世杯，喻人即一小宇宙。參看菲譯其五。

To find great Jamshid's world-reflecting bowl
I compassed sea and land, and viewed the whole;
　　But, when I asked the wary sage, I learned
That bowl was my own body, and my soul!

其三百五十六

橘中皇后何陰毒，遁甲奇門馬換卒。更召千軍倒海來，奪吾車乘贏終局。

譯箋：唐牛僧孺《玄怪錄》卷三《巴邛人》："有巴邛人，不知姓。家有桔園，因霜後，諸桔盡收。餘有二大桔，如三四斗盎。巴人異之，即令攀摘，輕重亦如常桔，剖開，每桔有二老叟，鬚眉皤然，肌體紅潤，皆相對象戲，身僅尺餘，談笑自若，剖開後，亦不驚怖，但與決賭。"○亦興寄象棋，參看菲譯其六十九及溫譯其二百七十。

Me, cruel Queen! you love to captivate,
And from a knight to a poor pawn translate;
  You marshal all your force to tire me out,
You take my rooks with yours, and then checkmate!

其三百五十七

此身未得正心加，我思豈能无一邪。自是百行難掩錯，獨惟真宰絕疵瑕。

譯箋：《詩經·魯頌·駉》："思無邪。"《論語·為政》引之。○是章乃論神定、原罪及自由意志之矛盾。人之罪瑕何來，自由意志何起，皆一神教神學議題。○前亦譯作："天既定餘難正心，縱思誠意枉勞心。諸行自是萬般錯，除彼誰能正一心。"

If Allah wills me not to will aright,
How can I frame my will to will aright?
  Each single act I will must needs be wrong,

Since none but He has power to will aright.

其三百五十八
千紅萬紫鬧春臺,破戒縱心惟此回。姹女童男花頰豔,曠原照眼錦茵開。

"For once, while roses are in bloom," I said,
"I'll break the law, and please myself instead,
　　With blooming youths, and maidens' tulip cheeks
The plain shall blossom like a tulip-bed."

其三百五十九
血雨腥風豈由我,我之所在何關我。我身我有自祂生,何在何來何是我。

譯箋:英譯原注謂意即人之真實存在非由自身,乃由真道即宇宙本體所定。

Think not I am existent of myself,
Or walk this blood-stained pathway of myself;
　　This being is not I, it is of Him.
Pray what, and where, and whence is this "myself"?

其三百六十
無邊苦海氣雲蒸,美酒稍嗜岸可登。吾已罍身壺國去,舉杯再飲恐無能。

Endure this world without my wine I cannot!
Drag on life's load without my cups I cannot!

I am the slave of that sweet moment, when
They say, "Take one more goblet," and I can not!

其三百六十一

塵寰日夜枉逡巡，何處能安末劫身。待得他年命終日，光陰一例視同仁。

You, who both day and night the world pursue,
And thoughts of that dread day of doom eschew,
　　Bethink you of your latter end; be sure
As time has treated others, so 'twill you!

其三百六十二

造化鍾神人盡收，浮生碌碌總煩憂。滄桑且飲麻姑酒，與爾同銷萬古愁。

譯箋：唐杜甫《望嶽》詩："造化鍾神秀，陰陽割昏曉。"○晉葛洪《神仙傳·麻姑》："麻姑自說云：'接侍以來，已見東海三爲桑田。向到蓬萊，水又淺於往者。會時略半也，豈將復還爲陵陸乎？'方平笑曰：'聖人皆言海中復揚塵也。'"麻姑，原譯指薩吉。○唐李白《將進酒》詩："與爾同銷萬古愁。"○英譯原注引華茲華斯詩句"這塵世拖累我們可真夠厲害"（楊德豫譯），並云蘇非派不求現世與來世，但求對真主無私之虔敬。

O man, who are creation's summary,
Getting and spending too much trouble thee!
　　Arise, and quaff the Etern Cupbearer's wine,
And so from troubles of both worlds be free!

其三百六十三

二宗獨顯幸能聞，往復斯間若轉輪。彼學紅塵辨善惡，斯門遺世復忘身。

譯箋：英譯原注謂二宗分指實用主義與神秘主義之信徒。案疑即教法派與蘇非派。

In this eternally revolving zone,
Two lucky species of men are known;
　　One knows all good and ill that are on earth,
One neither earth's affairs, nor yet his own.

其三百六十四

莫教零落羣芳妒，蟬翼安能卸重露。今日但求心所安，來年俱託天恩恕。

譯箋：宋陸游《卜算子·詠梅》詞："無意苦爭春，一任羣芳妒。零落成泥輾作塵，只有香如故。"唐駱賓王《在獄詠蟬》詩："露重飛難進，風多響易沉。"

Make light to me the world's oppressive weight,
And hide my failings from the people's hate,
　　And grant me peace to-day, and on the morrow
Deal with me as Thy mercy may dictate!

其三百六十五

幽心早把世情諳，禍福相依騁兩驂。禍有終兮福有盡，並迎其降並同儋。

譯箋：《老子·第五十八章》："禍兮福之所倚，福兮禍之所伏。"

Souls that are well informed of this world's state,

Its weal and woe with equal mind await;

    For, be it weal we meet, or be it woe,

The weal doth pass, and woe too hath its date.

其三百六十六

好景難常毋哭謳，及時行樂趁春留。既知福運他方去，休望其能再轉頭。

譯箋：參看菲譯其二十三。

Lament not fortune's want of constancy,

But up! and seize her favours ere they flee;

    If fortune always cleaved to other men,

How could a turn of luck have come to thee?

其三百六十七

至交深契近吾前，莫爲乾圜百慮煎。但且安身處卑下，觀其嬉逐樂周旋。

譯箋：《周易·說卦》："乾爲天，爲圜。"

Chief of old friends! harken to what I say,

Let not heaven's treacherous wheel your heart dismay;

    But rest contented in your humble nook,

And watch the games that wheel is wont to play.

其三百六十八

慢遊荒宴責何庸，我默之言或可從。吟禱封齋須盡破，恣歡饕餮且優容。

譯箋：《尚書·皋陶謨》："無若丹朱傲，惟慢遊是好，傲虐是作。"南朝宋顏延之《五君詠·劉參軍》："韜精日沉飲，誰知非荒宴。"○英譯原注此乃慈憫勝於獻祭論之猛烈延展。

Hear now Khayyam's advice, and bear in mind,
Consort with revellers, though they be maligned,
　　Cast down the gates of abstinence and prayer,
Yea, drink, and even rob, but, oh! be kind!

其三百六十九

靈乃乾元體即坤，雲仙妙意制身魂。蟲魚草木化其毓，太一獨安天地根。

譯箋：妙意，英譯原作 senses，理性、感覺。丁福保《佛學大辭典》："思量事物曰意。《唯識論》五曰：'薄伽梵，處處經中說心、意、識。三種別義，集起名心，思量名意，了別名識。是三別義。'《俱舍論》四曰：'集起故名心，思量故名意，了別故名識。心意識三名，所詮義雖異，而體是一如。'"明高啟《青丘子歌》："妙意俄同鬼神會，佳景每與江山爭。"○《禮記·禮運》："必本於太一，分而為天地，轉而為陰陽，變而為四時。"疏："太一者，謂天地未分混沌之元氣也。"《淮南子·詮言訓》："洞同天地混沌為樸，未造而成物，謂之太一。"《老子·第六章》："谷神不死，是謂玄牝。玄牝之門，是謂天地根。"○英譯原注引蒲伯云："一切皆部分。"

This world a body is, and God its soul,

And angels are its senses, who control

    Its limbs — the creatures, elements, and spheres;

The ONE is the sole basis of the whole.

其三百七十

泥像夤宵誘我心，熊熊慾焰利熏侵。謂予萬事一杯足，救藥須從此處尋。

Last night that idol who enchants my heart,

With true desire to elevate my heart,

    Gave me his cup to drink; when I refused,

He said, "Oh, drink to gratify my heart!"

其三百七十一

何倖能親玉頸溫，但思歡醉徹神魂。執吾所執信吾信，難罄悲涼祇罄樽。

譯箋：英譯原注引《舊約・傳導書》第二章："人式食式飲，享福於操作，無善於此。依我觀之，亦由上帝手也。"

Would'st thou have fortune bow her neck to thee,

Make it thy care to feed thy soul with glee;

    And hold a creed like mine, which is to drain

The cup of wine, not that of misery.

其三百七十二

淩虛求索問吾友，上下漫漫何所有。三月人間美景多，誰如花靨同春酒。

Though you survey, O my enlightened friend,
This world of vanity from end to end,
　　You will discover there no other good
Than wine and rosy cheeks, you may depend!

其三百七十三

河湄臥賞夜波平，窈窕相隨蚌蜃盈。火齊生光閽者起，誤登譙閣報天明。

譯箋：火齊，玫瑰珠也。齊，音濟。

Last night upon the river bank we lay,
I with my wine-cup, and a maiden gay,
　　So bright it shone, like pearl within its shell,
The watchman cried, "Behold the break of day!"

其三百七十四

生涯回首罪滔滔，愧怍盈懷作苦熬。雖擁江山終一棄，誰能有力負之逃。

譯箋：《莊子·大宗師》："夫藏舟於壑，藏山於澤，謂之固矣。然而夜半有力者負之而走，昧者不知也。"

Have you no shame for all the sins you do,

Sins of omission and commission too?
　　Suppose you gain the world, you can but leave it,
You can not carry it away with you!

其三百七十五
非邪非正若流離，荒野壟逢薄倖兒。神律天條渾不怕，世間捲勇孰如斯。

譯箋：英譯原注謂指蘇非律法廢棄論者。

In a lone waste I saw a debauchee,
He had no home, no faith, no heresy,
　　No God, no truth, no law, no certitude;
Where in this world is man so bold as he?

其三百七十六
正道或求於節文，或研經卷信疑分。有聲帷外斥愚妄，茅塞二塗焉得聞。

譯箋：英譯原注謂真理惟向神祕主義者啓示而向神學家與哲學家隱沒。〇基督教亦尚聖靈之啓示而斥儀文之墨守。吳經熊譯《新經全集・聖保祿致羅馬人書》第七章云："宜以自由自在之精神，昭事天主，不當再拘泥於文字之陳跡矣。"《聖保祿致格林多人書二》第三章云："蓋文字乃肅殺之具，而聖神則生命之源也。"〇參看菲譯其二十五。

Some look for truth in creeds, and forms, and rules;
Some grope for doubts or dogmas in the schools;

But from behind the veil a voice proclaims,
"Your road lies neither here nor there, O fools."

其三百七十七
但看天極一龍蟠，不察潛龍伏土寒。慧眼中間何所察，羣空凡駑正蹣跚。

譯箋：龍，英譯原作 bull，公牛。借指金牛座 Taurus。○《周易·乾卦》："潛龍勿用。"波斯傳說大地由一牛以角支撐，而牛立於一魚背，魚游於海中。○唐韓愈《送溫處士赴河陽軍序》："伯樂一過冀北之野而馬羣遂空。夫冀北馬多天下，伯樂雖善知馬，安能空其羣耶？解之者曰：'吾所謂空，非無馬也，無良馬也。伯樂知馬，遇其良，輒取之，羣無留良焉。苟無良，雖謂無馬，不爲虛語矣。'"

In heaven is seen the bull we name Parwin,
Beneath the earth another lurks unseen;
　　And thus to wisdom's eyes mankind appear
A drove of asses, two great bulls between!

其三百七十八
感君良語謝諄諄，怎惜悲秋病酒身。若問緣由自須認，難消晨渴與佳人。

譯箋：宋李清照《鳳凰臺上憶吹簫》詞："新來瘦，非干病酒，不是悲秋。"○《西京雜記》卷二："長卿素有消渴疾，及還成都悅文君之色，遂以發痼疾。乃作《美人賦》。欲以自刺而終不能改。卒以此疾至死。"唐李商隱《病中早訪招國李十將軍遇挈家遊曲江》詩："相如未是真消渴，猶放沱江過錦城。"

The people say, "Why not drink somewhat less?
What reasons have you for such great excess?"
　　First, my Love's face, second, my morning draught;
Can there be clearer reasons, now confess?

其三百七十九

倘能與帝共商量，席捲乾坤掃八荒。重建自由新世界，清魂飛舞若鷹揚。

譯箋：漢賈誼《過秦論上》："有席捲天下，包舉宇內，囊括四海之意，併吞八荒之心。"○《詩經·大雅·大明》："維師尚父，時維鷹揚。"毛傳："鷹揚，如鷹之飛揚也。"○參看菲譯其九十九。

Had I the power great Allah to advise,
I'd bid him sweep away this earth and skies,
　　And build a better, where, unclogged and free,
The clear soul might achieve her high emprise.

其三百八十

疊疊愁山心上橫，漸寬衣帶為傾城。侍兒頻酌相思酒，卻是吾心血釀成。

譯箋：宋柳永《鳳棲梧》詞："衣帶漸寬終不悔 為伊消得人憔悴。"○侍兒，英譯原作 Cupbearer，當即薩吉。○英譯原注云意謂神創造時於一切造物中所注入之生命之酒，即存在。

This silly sorrow-laden heart of mine

Is ever pining for that love of mine;
    When the Cupbearer poured the wine of love,
With my heart's blood he filled this cup of mine!

其三百八十一

遊冶章臺醉舞塵,虛文假飾豈吾倫。眠花狨酒倘成錯,苦煞幾多天上人。

To drain the cup, to hover round the fair,
Can hypocritic arts with these compare?
    If all who love and drink are going wrong,
There's many a wight of heaven may well despair!

其三百八十二

英雄意氣總消磨,秉燭何須泣汨羅。天地悠悠竟何是,美人醇酒一娑婆。

譯箋:唐陳子昂《登幽州臺歌》:"念天地之悠悠,獨愴然而涕下。"○娑婆,參見溫譯其二百七十一譯箋。

'Tis wrong with gloomy thoughts your mirth to drown, —
To let grief's millstone weigh your spirits down;
    Since none can tell what is to be, 'tis best
With wine and love your heart's desires to crown.

其三百八十三

安名享譽固應宜，怨物尤天怍自知。蹈步倘教逋客笑，何如欹帽醉難支。

譯箋：《周書・獨孤信傳》：" 在秦州，嘗因獵，日暮，馳馬入城，其帽微側，詰旦，而吏人有戴帽者，咸慕信而側帽焉。" 宋陸游《早春出遊》詩：" 欹帽捫髯常半醉，逢人誰與話無憀。" ○逋客，英譯原作 Pharisaic，法利賽人，指《新約》中拘守律法之虛僞者。孔稚珪《北山移文》：" 請迴俗士駕，爲君謝逋客。"

'Tis well in reputation to abide,

'Tis shameful against heaven to rail and chide;

　　Still, head had better ache with over drink,

Than be puffed up with Pharisaic pride!

其三百八十四

迷途失足酒壚間，摻手空擒玉甕端。塊壘胸中叠孿負，幽心安拯繫南冠。

譯箋：《春秋左氏傳・成公九年》：" 晉侯觀於軍府，見鍾儀，問之曰：'南冠而縶者誰也？' 有司對曰：'鄭人所獻楚囚也。'" 杜預注：" 南冠，楚冠也。"

O Lord! pity this prisoned heart, I pray,

Pity this bosom stricken with dismay!

　　Pardon these hands that ever grasp the cup,

These feet that to the tavern ever stray!

其三百八十五

我執宜蠲向主求，去私即與爾同儔。歡天喜地逍遙去，不作人間善惡囚。

譯箋：英譯原注謂此章乃神祕主義之祈禱。

O Lord! from self-conceit deliver me.
Sever from self, and occupy with Thee!
　　This self is captive to earth's good and ill,
Make me beside myself, and set me free!

其三百八十六

造化弄人謀算聰，知交零落剩煢煢。勿哀去日祈來日，一醉但求今日中。

Behold the tricks this wheeling dome doth play,
And earth laid bare of old friends torn away!
　　O live this present moment, which is thine,
Seek not a morrow, mourn not yesterday!

其三百八十七

栖栖一世畔牢愁，無奈常懷千歲憂。不降於斯豈非倖，既生宜毋久羈留。

譯箋：《漢書·揚雄傳上》："又旁《惜誦》以下至《懷沙》一卷，名曰《畔牢愁》。"顏師古注引李奇："畔，離也。牢，聊也。與君相離，愁而無聊也。"〇《古詩十九首》其十五："生年不滿百，常懷千歲憂。"

Since all man's business in this world of woe
Is sorrow's pangs to feel, and grief to know,
　　Happy are they that never come at all,
And they that, having come, the soonest go!

其三百八十八

順天立命理誠真，昧性不知安竇身。司命還如執鞭士，但凴夏楚導迷津。

譯箋：《論語・述而》："富而可求也，雖執鞭之士，吾亦爲之。"○《禮記・學記》："夏楚二物，收其威也。"

By reason's dictates it is right to live,
But of ourselves we know not how to live,
　　So Fortune, like a master, rod in hand,
Raps our pates well to teach us how to live!

其三百八十九

天命幽玄誰可猜，金縢無籥豈能開。緇帷聞語卿吾事，帷啓卿吾安在哉。

譯箋：《尚書・金縢》："啓籥見書，乃並是吉。公曰：'體！王其罔害。予小子新命于三王，惟永終是圖；茲攸俟，能念予一人。'公歸，乃納册于金縢之匱中。"王肅曰："籥，藏占兆書管也。"孔安國傳："藏之於匱，緘之以金，不欲人開也。"○緇帷，參看菲譯其三十二譯箋。○英譯原注云意即吾儕皆現象帷幕之部分，並隱於神之本體中。倘象盡掃，吾儕安在。○參看菲譯其三十二。

Nor you nor I can read the etern decree,
To that enigma we can find no key;
　　They talk of you and me *behind* the veil,
But, if that veil be lifted, where are *we*?

其三百九十

我我卿卿百載身，卻教天妒化爲塵。曾經相與蒿萊坐，轉瞬已成蒿里人。

譯箋：首句英譯原作 thy precious life, and mine，卿我寶貴之生命。《世説新語·惑溺》："親卿愛卿，是以卿卿，我不卿卿，誰當卿卿?"○《韓詩外傳》卷一："原憲居魯，環堵之室，茨以蒿萊。"三國魏阮籍《詠懷》其三一："戰士食糟糠，賢者處蒿萊。"○《漢書·武帝紀》："高里。"伏儼曰："山名，在泰山下。"師古曰："此高字自作高下之高，而死人之里，謂之蒿里，或呼爲下里者也，字則爲蓬蒿之蒿。或者見泰山神靈之府，高里山又在其旁，即誤以高里爲蒿里。"古樂府《蒿里》："蒿里誰家地? 聚斂魂魄無賢愚。鬼伯一何相催促? 人命不得少踟蹰。"○參看菲譯其二十三。

O Love, forever doth heaven's wheel design
To take away thy precious life, and mine;
　　Sit we upon this turf, 'twill not be long
Ere turf shall grow upon my dust, and thine!

其三百九十一

魂歸后土下河汾，一對埤銘鐫誌文。旋化塵灰塑埤去，轉賣鄰鬼砌新墳。

譯箋：漢元鼎四年，漢武至河東郡汾陽縣祭祀后土，泛舟汾河，作《秋風辭》。

When life has fled, and we rest in the tomb,
They'll place a pair of bricks to mark our tomb;
　　And, a while after, mould our dust to bricks,
To furnish forth some other person's tomb!

其三百九十二
宫阙崔嵬指绛霄，列王匍匐拜朝朝。而今我向桥楼望，但立鹪鸪悲寂寥。

譯箋：絳霄，英譯原作 the welkin blue，藍色蒼穹、天宮。南朝梁元帝《玄覽賦》："鬱如蓬萊之臨滄海，憬如崑崙之出絳霄。"○鹪鸪，英譯原作 ringdove，斑鳩。鹪鸪鳴似行不得也哥哥。元梁棟《四禽言》詩："行不得也哥哥，湖南湖北秋水多。九疑山前叫虞舜，奈此乾坤無路何。行不得也哥哥。"○菲氏曾言此作鐫於波斯波利斯廢墟上。英譯原注謂：Coo（Ku）意爲"他們在哪裡"。

Yon palace, towering to the welkin blue,
Where kings did bow them down, and homage do,
　　I saw a ringdove on its arches perched,
And thus she made complaint, "Coo, Coo, Coo, Coo!"

其三百九十三
攘攘熙熙獲幾多，迴文織錦已停梭。禪身焚卻化塵去，碧宇遺痕煙若何。

譯箋：《晉書·列女傳·竇滔妻蘇氏》："竇滔妻蘇氏，始平人也，名蕙，字若蘭。善屬文。滔，苻堅時爲秦州刺史，被徙流沙，蘇氏思之，織錦爲回文旋圖詩以贈滔。宛轉回圈以讀之，詞甚淒惋，凡八百四十字。"○唐賈島《哭僧》詩："寫留行道影,焚卻坐禪身。"○英譯原注引《聖經·傳道書》第二章:"智者愚者,永不見憶。蓋至來日,皆必遺忘,噫,智者之死,曷同於愚者哉。"煙,即痕跡。

We come and go, but for the gain, where is it?
And spin life's woof, but for the warp, where is it?
　　And many a righteous man has burned to dust
In heaven's blue rondure, but their smoke, where is it?

其三百九十四

活水生源隱絳脣,勿教杯扣挹泉珍。倘吾不吮杯中血,唧爾樊櫻誰氏人。

譯箋:唐孟棨《本事詩》:"白居易有姬人樊素和小蠻,樊素善歌,小嘴長得豔若櫻桃;小蠻善舞,細腰則纖纖似柳。樂天公至愛此二美眉,詩曰:'櫻桃樊素口,楊柳小蠻腰。'"○英譯原注謂致一情人。

Life's well-spring lurks within that lip of thine!
Let not the cup's lip touch that lip of thine!
　　Beshrew me, if I fail to drink his blood,
For who is he, to touch that lip of thine?

其三百九十五

百載持身帝力欽,憫心助護至於今。悠悠終歲常求索,迷罪慈恩孰更深。

譯箋:文理本《舊約·撒母耳記上》:"撒母耳取一石,立于米斯巴與善間,名之曰以便以謝。曰:'延及此時,耶和華助我儕。'"○吳經熊譯《聖保祿致羅馬人書》第三章:"舉世莫非罪人,固未有能懷天主之明德者也。故人之稱義,惟憑耶穌基督之救贖;此實天主之慈恩,不勞而獲者也。"第五章:"雖然,恩寵之效,固非罪惡之累所得同日而語矣。夫因一人之罪,致衆受其死,則因一人之功,不更能使衆沾其恩耶?"

Such as I am, Thy power created me,
Thy care hath kept me for a century!
　　Through all these years I make experiment,
If my sins or Thy mercy greater be.

其三百九十六

攜羔提壺步水湄,潺湲遠望草披靡。天光慌忽旋鈎影,飛入金樽化碧漪。

譯箋:《楚辭·九歌·湘夫人》:"慌忽兮遠望,觀流水兮潺湲。"

"Take up thy cup and goblet, Love," I said,
"Haunt purling river bank, and grassy glade;
　　Full many a moon-like form has heaven's wheel
Oft into cup, oft into goblet, made!"

其三百九十七

莫問新陳但滿卮,人間美惡醉中遺。三生石上精魂去,煙棹茫茫任所之。

譯箋:遺,英譯原作 sell for two grains,意謂賤售。《詩經·小雅·谷風》:"棄予如遺。"鄭箋:"如遺者,如人行道遺忘物,忽然不省存也。"○唐袁郊《甘澤謠·圓觀》有歌云："三生石上舊精魂，賞月吟風不要論，慚愧情人遠相訪，此身雖異性常存。""身前身後事茫茫，欲話因緣恐斷腸，吳越江山尋已遍，欲回煙棹上瞿塘。"

We buy new wine and old, our cups to fill,
And sell for two grains this world's good and ill;
　　Know you where you will go to after death?
Set wine before me, and go where you will!

其三百九十八

人非賢聖孰無疵，凡俗亡羊因道歧。圭玷難磨當毋罪，以邪報惡豈卿爲。

譯箋：《老子·第十章》："滌除玄覽，能無疵乎。"○《列子·説符》："大道以多歧亡羊，學者以多方喪生。"○《詩經·大雅·抑》："白圭之玷，尚可磨也。斯言之玷，不可爲也。"○卿，指真主。

Was e'er man born who never went astray?
Did ever mortal pass a sinless day?
　　If I do ill, do not requite with ill!
Evil for evil how can'st Thou repay?

其三百九十九

赤瓊屬國獻奇珍，更慰盈樽突厥春。篤信如須絶旨酒，世間安覓敬虔人。

譯箋：屬國，英譯原作Badakhshan，《清史稿》譯作巴達克山。明譯八達黑商、把丹沙，地即今阿富汗、塔吉克所屬之巴達赫尚。馮承鈞譯《馬可波羅行紀》："巴達哈傷（Badakchan）一州之地，人民崇拜摩訶末，自有其語言，是爲一大國。君位世襲，王族皆是亞歷山大與波斯大國君主大留士女之後裔。"又云："此州出產巴剌思紅寶石（rabis balais），此寶石甚美，而價甚貴。"○《戰國策·魏策二》："昔者，帝女令儀狄作酒而美，進之禹，禹飲而甘之，遂疏儀狄而絕旨酒。"

Bring forth that ruby gem of Badakhshan,
That heart's delight, that balm of Turkestan;
　　They say 'tis wrong for Musulmen to drink,
But ah! where can we find a Musulman?

其四百

兹體從天受骨骸，神機更遣寄靈臺。人天合一乘其化，性本乎天歸去來。

譯箋：神機，英譯原作 spirit，精神、神靈。《黃帝内經素問·五常政大論》："根於中者，命曰神機，神去則機息。"靈臺，英譯原作 soul，靈魂、心靈。《莊子·庚桑楚》："不可内於靈臺。"郭象注："靈臺者，心也。"《文選·劉孝標〈廣絕交論〉》："寄通靈臺之下，遺跡江湖之上。"李善注："寄通神於心府之下，遺跡相忘於江湖之上也。"魯迅《自題小像》："靈臺無計逃神矢，風雨如磐闇故園。"○晉陶淵明《歸去來辭》："聊乘化以歸盡，樂夫天命復奚疑。"○《禮記·中庸》："天命之謂性。"○哈拉智立人主渾化之説，此章似闡此論。○英譯原注謂吾儕生、動皆在其中，故有我在。

My body's life and strength proceed from Thee!

My soul within and spirit are of Thee!
My being is of Thee, and Thou art mine,
And I am Thine, since I am lost in Thee!

其四百零一

人如蹴鞠往來飞，效命馳驅未敢違。何事教吾苦鏖戰，彀中原委乃天機。

譯箋：參看菲譯其七十。

Man, like a ball, hither and thither goes,
As fate's resistless bat directs the blows;
But He, who gives thee up to this rude sport,
He knows what drives thee, yea, He knows, He knows!

其四百零二

青蠅肢弱力能擎，螻蟻雖微視甚明。萬物芸芸賴汝德，鄙行賤質豈關卿。

O Thou who givest sight to emmet's eyes,
And strength to puny limbs of feeble flies,
To Thee we will ascribe Almighty power,
And not base, unbecoming qualities.

其四百零三

何推私慾役心扉，壯志空教梵網圍。不作塵沙任風逐，甯爲霆火瀑流飛。

Let not base avarice enslave thy mind,

Nor vain ambition in its trammels bind;
 Be sharp as fire, as running water swift,
Not, like earth's dust, the sport of every wind!

其四百零四
殷勤胡女侍樽前，百福人間盡可捐。極樂無垠充萬物，上窮碧落下黃泉。

譯箋：○英譯原注謂 Kalendars 指嗜酒之蘇非。傳聞大地安於魚背之上。○參看菲譯其五十一譯箋。

'Tis best all other blessings to forego
For wine, that charming Turki maids bestow;
 Kalendars' raptures pass all things that are,
From moon on high down into fish below!

其四百零五
身世浮沉莫恐惶，杞憂徒惱最宜忘。皮囊終碾微塵碎，小德踰閑亦不妨。

譯箋：《論語・子張》："子夏曰：'大德不踰閑，小德出入可也。'"

Friend! trouble not yourself about your lot,
Let futile care and sorrow be forgot;
 Since this life's vesture crumbles into dust,
What matters stain of word or deed, or blot?

其四百零六

所歷一身惟罪辜，休思金殿宥恩殊。未修善德誰能祐，既作惡行安避誅。

譯箋：英譯原注謂此首係阿佈・賽義德所作，爲覆傳爲阿維森納所作之第四百二十首。

O thou who hast done ill, and ill alone,
And thinkest to find mercy at the throne,
　　Hope not for mercy! for good left undone
Can not be done, nor evil done undone!

其四百零七

人生甲子夢原賒，但賞長安滿路花。莫望骷髏化榼榼，且耽永夜醉無涯。

譯箋：榼榼，參看温譯其一百七十九譯箋。

Count not to live beyond your sixtieth year,
To walk in jovial courses persevere;
　　And ere your skull be turned into a cup,
Let wine-cups ever to your hand adhere!

其四百零八

漠漠層霄若覆瓢，羣賢翹首仰天遙。玉瓶欲舐瓢中血，佯戀紅唇故折腰。

譯箋：參看菲譯其七十二。

These heavens resemble an inverted cup,

Whereto the wise with awe keep gazing up;

　　So stoops the bottle o'er his love, the cup,

Feigning to kiss, and gives her blood to sup!

其四百零九

散髮旗亭曳闠塵，今生來世那堪云。二端乘轂如同至，醉裡吾惟售一文。

譯箋：旗亭，英譯原作 tavern（酒館）。唐薛用弱《集異記》："開元中，詩人王昌齡、高適、王之渙齊名，時風塵未偶，而遊處略同。一日天寒微雪，三詩人共詣旗亭，貰酒小飲。"

I sweep the tavern threshold with my hair,

For both world's good and ill I take no care;

　　Should the two worlds roll to my house, like balls,

When drunk, for one small coin I'd sell the pair!

其四百一十

滴水悲號別海淵，滄波卻笑體仍全。大千即理外無物，一轂回闠萬輻旋。

The drop wept for his severance from the sea,

But the sea smiled, for "I am all," said he,

　　"The Truth is all, nothing exists beside,

That one point circling apes plurality."

其四百一十一

得失平常豈足欺，樂夫天命亦何難。安知元氣幾時絕，但請盈樽至夜闌。

Shall I still sigh for what I have not got,
Or try with cheerfulness to bear my lot?
　　Fill up my cup! I know not if the breath
I now am drawing is my last, or not!

其四百一十二

豈因薄命坐生憂，莫爲良朋起別愁。但付春心絳唇醉，風塵莫擲歲華休。

Yield not to grief, though fortune prove unkind,
Nor call sad thoughts of parted friends to mind;
　　Devote thy heart to sugary lips, and wine,
Cast not thy precious life unto the wind!

其四百一十三

禱祝持齋莫絮煩，憐吾尚許飲高軒。醉歸但入塵中去，製缶搏壺不復言。

Of mosque and prayer and fast preach not to me,
Rather go drink, were it on charity!
　　Yea, drink, Khayyam, your dust will soon be made
A jug, or pitcher, or a cup, may be!

其四百一十四
總是怨鶯嗔紫薇,春風薄倖碎紅衣。灼灼滿園今幾度,出泥榮發入泥歸。

譯箋:參看菲譯其九。

Bulbuls, doting on roses, oft complain
How froward breezes rend their veils in twain;
　　Sit we beneath this rose, which many a time
Has sunk to earth, and sprung from earth again.

其四百一十五
生如書卷一翻過,得意春風馳急梭。縱享悠悠百年福,百年之後又如何。

Suppose the world goes well with you, what then?
When life's last page is read and turned, what then?
　　Suppose you live a hundred years of bliss,
Yea, and a hundred years besides, what then?

其四百一十六
誰是自由蔥鬱身,青松百合鬭清魂。縱生百手不爭賄,雖有千喉亦默存。

譯箋:青松,英譯原作 Cypress,柏樹。○英譯原注引薩迪《薔薇園》第八部:"舌如花蕊,手如棗枝。"

How is it that of all the leafy tribe,

Cypress and lily men as "free" describe?

　　This has a dozen tongues, yet holds her peace,

That has a hundred hands which take no bribe

其四百一十七
美酒金樽侍女妍，珍饈玉饌不辭筵。賢愚同入歡情縠，吾亦安能不縶牽。

Cupbearer, bring my wine-cup, let me grasp it!
Bring that delicious darling, let me grasp it!
　　That pleasing chain which tangles in its coils
Wise men and fools together, let me grasp it!

其四百一十八
韶華虛擲散形骸，湛樂禁臠休已哉。畔道離經成底事，黯然慚怍面如灰。

Alas! my wasted life has gone to wrack!
What with forbidden meats, and lusts, alack!
　　And leaving undone what 'twas right to do,
And doing wrong, my face is very black!

其四百一十九
往事悠悠悔萬般，最難訣別醉鄉關。縱成清教一高士，不捨仙漿塵世間。

譯箋：仙漿，英譯原作 Magian wine 穆護之酒，穆護，袄教祭司。詳參其二百零五譯箋。

I could repent of all, but of wine, never!

I could dispense with all, but with wine, never!

  If so be I became a Musulman,

Could I abjure my Magian wine? no, never!

其四百二十

惟當獨仰上天恩，抵罪以功安可論。惡善雖行當未作，慈懷由己否減存。

譯箋：文理本《舊約·出埃及記》第三十三章："我必顯我諸德，宣耶和華名於爾前，我所欲矜恤者矜恤之，欲憐憫者憐憫之。"○英譯原注謂此章亦屬阿維森納作。

We rest our hopes on Thy free grace alone,

Nor seek by merits for our sins to atone;

  Mercy drops where it lists, and estimates

Ill done as undone, good undone as done.

其四百二十一

大塊體成真宰靈，觀身奇妙運冥冥。自脩可否臻佳善，復變初生大範形。

譯箋：其二百二十一異文。

This is the form Thou gavest me of old,

Wherein Thou workest marvels manifold;

  Can I aspire to be a better man,

Or other than I issued from Thy mould?

其四百二十二
芸芸萬物伏君階，貴賤無論祝禱偕。君賜福兮或降禍，我之福禍任安排。

O Lord! to Thee all creatures worship pay,
To Thee both small and great for ever pray,
    Thou takest woe away, and givest weal,
Give then, or, if it please Thee, take away!

其四百二十三
谷風悲響尚遲淹，老至聲名漸已潛。胼胝漸成馬蹄足，空將驢尾擬疏髥。

With going to and fro in this sad vale
Thou art grown double, and thy credit stale,
    Thy nails are thickened like a horse's hoof,
Thy beard is ragged as an ass's tail.

其四百二十四
誰鼓虛無橐籥風，未開草昧即鴻蒙。觀無馳運深淵面，身後乃空前亦空。

譯箋：橐籥，參看菲譯其二十九譯箋。

O unenlightened race of humankind,
Ye are a nothing, built on empty wind!

Yea, a mere nothing, hovering in the abyss,

A void before you, and a void behind!

其四百二十五

晨言罷飲自今宵,柳七從茲遠酒寮。忽遇薔薇春日灼,前衷舊誓擲雲霄。

譯箋:柳七,宋詞人柳永。○參見菲譯其七與其九十四。

Each morn I say, "To-night I will repent

Of wine, and tavern haunts no more frequent";

  But while 'tis spring, and roses are in bloom,

To loose me from my promise, O consent!

其四百二十六

何若美鬢流賞中,凡論哲理已成空。毋教司命饗君血,舉盞漫傾缶血紅。

譯箋:參看菲譯其四十一。

Vain study of philosophy eschew!

Rather let tangled curls attract your view;

  And shed the bottle's life-blood in your cup,

Or e'er death shed your blood, and feast on you.

其四百二十七

幽心玄祕費思量，智者搔頭恨斷腸。天上人間安可得，人間天上醉中嚐。

譯箋：參看菲譯其六十二。

O heart! can'st thou the darksome riddle read,
Where wisest men have failed, wilt thou succeed?
　　Quaff wine, and make thy heaven here below,
Who knows if heaven above will be thy meed?

其四百二十八

往聖前賢何處覯，紛埋幽幻土中寒。玄談妙諦風中散，真物但從杯底看。

譯箋：英譯原注引《聖經・傳導書》第一章："我復專心以明智慧，而知狂妄愚蒙，乃覺亦屬捕風。"○參看菲譯其二十六。

They that have passed away, and gone before,
Sleep in delusion's dust for evermore;
　　Go, boy, and fetch some wine, this is the truth,
Their dogmas were but air, and wind their lore!

其四百二十九

美饌心期降至尊，失而復得我終存。他年一飲迎賓酒，即可逃離生死門。

譯箋：英譯原注謂真我乃己中死、神中生。

O heart! when on the Loved One's sweets you feed,
You lose yourself, but find your Self indeed;
　　And, when you drink of His entrancing cup,
You hasten your escape from quick and dead!

其四百三十

生涯雖慣酒沉淪，凡輩何須責我身。諸惡如皆醉翁作，世間安有一醒人。

Though I am wont a wine-bibber to be,
Why should the people rail and chide at me?
　　Would that all evil actions made men drunk,
For then no sober people should I see!

其四百三十一

地造天生氣若萠，一朝飲罷去斯間。千言萬語應須記，入地上天皆不還。

譯箋：參看菲譯其三十五。

Child of four elements and sevenfold heaven,
Who fume and sweat because of these eleven,
　　Drink! I have told you seventy times and seven,
Once gone, nor hell will send you back, nor heaven.

其四百三十二

機穽天教佈滿途，戰兢憂墜怕遭屠。率濱帝力無窮已，順命亦難逃罪辜。

譯箋：英譯原注謂蘇非派視安拉爲唯一真實之動因。○參看菲譯其八十。

With many a snare Thou dost beset my way,
And threatenest, if I fall therein, to slay;
　　Thy rule resistless sways the world, yet Thou
Imputest sin, when I do but obey!

其四百三十三

一思天髓費躊躇，何視正邪同若無。孽海沉迷恩可悟，但求免我一生辜。

To Thee, whose essence baffles human thought,
Our sins and righteous deeds alike seem naught;
　　May Thy grace sober me, though drunk with sins,
And pardon all the ill that I have wrought!

其四百三十四

人生果若戲臺空，日日笙歌樂亦同。萬事當能制所慾，報償何懼百年終。

譯箋：英譯原注稱尼古拉斯以 taklid 爲 authority（權力、授權）之義，溫氏不以爲然，謂當暗指《古蘭經》第二十九章："這種今世的生活，不過是娛樂遊戲，後世的歸宿，才具有蓬勃生機，如果他們知悉。"則溫譯 'lid 乃 taklid 之略。塔格利德，或作 taqlid, taqleed，源自阿拉伯語 taqlld，係伊斯蘭教法術語，字面義爲因襲，意謂因襲傳統或對權威之無條件服從。友人或以爲 'ld 即 Eid，此詞用於伊斯蘭開齋節與宰牲節，恐未必然。

If this life were indeed an empty play,
Each day would be an *'lid* of festal day,
    And men might conquer all their hearts' desire,
Fearless of after penalties to pay!

其四百三十五
圜轉穹蒼挫慾心，寡歡破碎裂衣襟。飲漿恨遇泥沙下，運息偏逢毒焰侵。

O wheel of heaven, you thwart my heart's desire,
And rend to shreds my scanty joy's attire,
    The water that I drink you foul with earth,
And turn the very air I breathe to fire!

其四百三十六
清魂倘得棄皮囊，須化飛天繞玉皇。降此凡塵爲異客，能無愧怍去銀潢。

譯箋：參看菲譯其四十四。

O soul! could you but doff this flesh and bone,
You'd soar a sprite about the heavenly throne;
    Had you no shame to leave your starry home,
And dwell an alien on this earthly zone?

其四百三十七

擬請陶人暫息工，莫將屍骨恣搏攻。忍看圜轉陶輪上，盡碎侯王血肉紅。

譯箋：侯王，英譯原指 Faridun, Kai Khosrau，法里東、凱·霍斯魯。法里東，乃俾什達迪王朝國王，曾三分伊朗國土予三子。凱·霍斯魯，凱揚王朝之國王，凱·卡烏斯之孫。英譯原注謂多認爲即居魯士。

Ah, potter, stay thine hand! with ruthless art
Put not to such base use man's mortal part!
　　See, thou art mangling on thy cruel wheel
Faridun's fingers, and Kai Khosrau's heart!

其四百三十八

人間最美是薔薇，如酒勝於珠蚌暉。時運春風舊曾識，此番何故又相違。

O rose! all beauties' charms thou dost excel,
As wine excels the pearl within its shell;
　　O fortune! thou dost ever show thyself
More strange, although I seem to know thee well!

其四百三十九

庖廚塵世逐腥中，雜列佳餚實乃空。饕餮吞身至喪實，持身不失一何豐。

譯箋：《呂氏春秋·先識》："周鼎著饕餮，有首無身，食人未咽，害及其身，以言報更也。"

From this world's kitchen crave not to obtain

Those dainties, seeming real, but really vain,

    Which greedy worldlings gorge to their own loss;

Renounce that loss, so loss shall prove thy gain!

其四百四十

宵吟恐破侶儔寧，夜寤噦天不忍聽。富貴榮華莫矜得，藏舟盜去有誰醒。

譯箋：藏舟，參看其三百七十四譯箋。

Plot not of nights, thy fellows' peace to blight,

So that they cry to God the live-long night;

    Nor plume thee on thy wealth and might, which thieves

May steal by night, or death, or fortune's might.

其四百四十一

清魂曾爲金屋嬌，長門何事對寒寥。秦樓已失良歡會，莫向凡塵寄玉簫。

譯箋：舊題漢劉向《列仙傳·蕭史》："蕭史者，秦穆公時人也。善吹簫，能致孔雀、白鶴於庭。穆公有女，字弄玉，好之，公遂以女妻焉。日教弄玉作鳳鳴。居數年，吹似鳳聲。鳳凰來止其屋，公爲作鳳台，夫婦止其上。不下數年，一旦皆隨鳳凰飛去。故秦人爲作鳳女祠于雍宮中，時有簫聲而已。"

This soul of mine was once Thy cherished bride,

What caused Thee to divorce her from Thy side?

Thou didst not use to treat her thus of yore,
Why then now doom her in the world to abide?

其四百四十二
人間何處可療傷，天路漫漫終至鄉。待得萬年冬日盡，如花復艷綻芬芳。

譯箋：參看菲譯其九十七。

Ah! would there were a place of rest from pain,
Which we, poor pilgrims, might at last attain,
　　And after many thousand wintry years,
Renew our life, like flowers, and bloom again!

其四百四十三
漫尋征跡豔詞篇，至樂心聲出少年。倘伴嬋娟美如月，願將剎那換長年。

While in love's book I sought an augury;
An ardent youth cried out in ecstasy,
　　"Who owns a sweetheart beauteous as the moon,
Might wish his moments long as years to be!"

其四百四十四
行狀漸書至卷腳，寒冬已逝春潮作。人生誠若毒砒霜，除卻酒漿難救藥。

譯箋：參看菲譯其九。

Winter is past, and spring-tide has begun,

Soon will the pages of life's book be done!

  Well saith the sage, "Life is a poison rank,

And antidote, save grape-juice, there is none."

其四百四十五

倘得榮歸高士行，宜收矯節卸嚴裝。先嘗一盞杜康酒，再與美人嬉蔭涼。

譯箋：杜康酒，原譯作穆爾塔扎所供之酒，穆爾塔扎，伊斯蘭教中意乃主喜者，具體指何人未詳。

Beloved, if thou a reverend Molla be,

Quit saintly show, and feigned austerity,

  And quaff the wine that Murtaza purveys,

And sport with Houris 'neath some shady tree!

其四百四十六

狂醉前宵禮盡愆，舉杯恨擲石拳拳。忽聞杯躍怒相叱，卿必隨吾同覆顛。

Last night I dashed my cup against a stone,

In a mad drunken freak, as I must own,

  And lo! the cup cries out in agony,

"You too, like me, shall soon be overthrown."

其四百四十七

假節虛文心倦加，殷勤彩袖勸杯叉。拜氈纏帕換新酒，贏得安然自在誇。

My heart is weary of hypocrisy,

Cupbearer, bring some wine, I beg of thee!

  This hooded cowl and prayer-mat pawn for wine,

Then will I boast me in security

其四百四十八

檢點平生債有終，一來一去盡空空。停杯惜命君休勸，飲否皆歸抔土中。

Audit yourself, your truce account to frame,

See! you go empty, as you empty came；

  You say, "I will not drink and peril life,"

But, drink or no, you must die all the same!

其四百四十九

眾妙之門汝最真，何從何去啓吾門。凡人所指皆爲妄，獨汝真言可永存。

Open the door！O entrance who procurest,

And guide the way, O Thou of guides the surest!

  Directors born of men shall not direct me,

Their counsel comes to naught, but Thou endurest!

其四百五十

瀆神枉道罪難逃，謠諑嫉余尤善謠。諸過纏身縱坦認，譏人能否轉清高。

In slandering and reviling you persist,
Calling me infidel and atheist:
　　My errors I will not deny, but yet
Does foul abuse become a moralist?

其四百五十一

承瘝忍苦爲療傷，處禍不驚瘳有方。窮困猶存感恩意，斯途必可得豐穰。

To find a remedy, put up with pain,
Chafe not at woe, and healing thou wilt gain;
　　Though poor, be ever of a thankful mind,
'Tis the sure method riches to obtain.

其四百五十二

一片乾餱酒一囊，散銀常匱富詩章。陋居常與佳人伴，不換千年帝祚長。

譯箋：參看菲譯其十二。

Give me a skin of wine, a crust of bread,
A pittance bare, a book of verse to read;
　　With thee, O love, to share my lowly roof,
I would not take the Sultan's realm instead!

其四百五十三

五覺四元難究窮，幽玄乃一抑多宗。終將閒笛隨塵去，小酌即乘風入空。

譯箋：原譯 the four 疑即四元 four elements，指構成世界的四種元素地水火風。the five 疑即五覺 Five senses，指五種感覺色、聲、香、味、觸。見溫譯第一百二十首。四元、五覺，見該首譯箋。

Reason not of the five, nor of the four,
Be their dark problems one, or many score;
    We are but earth, go, minstrel, bring the lute,
We are but air, bring wine, I ask no more!

其四百五十四

經義何須爭訟之，但書一紙謫杯詩。倦身當日酒中沒，恰若真神赦宥時。

譯箋：原文 Yasin 指《古蘭經》第三十六章《雅欣》。Barat 指《古蘭經》第九章《懺悔（討白）》。仝道章譯《古蘭經》第九章《懺悔（討白）》第一至第三節："安拉和他的使者（已宣佈）廢除（豁免）那些與你們簽約的拜偶像者之間的條約義務。你們隨意在地上旅行四個月吧，（你們）就會知道你們不能逃避安拉，而安拉卻會使得不信者受辱了。（這是）安拉和他的使者在漢志（巡禮）日向全人類的一項宣佈。安拉和他的使者解除了（他們）跟拜偶像者之間的（條約）義務。如果你們懺悔，那將對你們是最好的；如果你們避開，（你們）要知道你們是不能逃避安拉的。你（穆聖）向那些不信的人宣佈嚴刑的消息吧。"仝云："本章章名《懺悔》，取自第 104 節；本章又名《豁免（巴拉特）》，取自首節第一句。"第三十六章《雅欣》第一至第七節："雅欣。憑這充滿了智慧的古蘭，你的確是使者之一，（並且是）在正道上的（一位使者）。這（古蘭）是由大能的、大慈的主降下的天啓。以便你警告他們的祖先們不曾獲得警告的人們。所以他們是不留意的。這話（安拉的話）已證實了他們當中大多數人（如此），所以他們不信。"沙班月（伊曆第八個月）的第十五晚，稱爲巴拉特之夜。巴拉特一詞含獲得赦免之意，聖訓稱此夜真主將特赦懺悔僕人，故是夜被稱爲懺悔夜或者特赦夜。

Why argue on Yasin and on Barat?
Write me the draft for wine they call Barat!
    The day my weariness is drowned in wine
Will seem to me as the great night Barat!

其四百五十五

濁囊一旦戴閑閑，便落閻君掌馭間。賁育來圍惟自禦，休期魏忌卻師還。

譯箋：賁育，原譯 Rustums 魯斯塔姆之複數，魯斯塔姆，《列王紀》所載之勇士，見前箋。魏忌，即信陵君魏公子無忌，英譯原作 Hatim Tai 哈蒂姆台，以慷慨著稱之阿拉伯貴族。參看菲譯其十。

Whilst thou dost wear this fleshy livery,
Step not beyond the bounds of destiny;
    Bear up, though very Rustums be thy foes,
And crave no boon from friends like Hatim Tai!

其四百五十六

絳脣歌酒與孌童，琴瑟玩珍諸物充。塵世歡愉皆泡影，倘君不捨一身空。

These ruby lips, and wine, and minstrel boys,
And lute, and harp, your dearly cherished toys,
　　Are mere redundancies, and you are naught,
Till you renounce the world's delusive joys.

其四百五十七

天禍全將付一樽，忍安舛世伏乾坤。此身終始皆於土，惟獨今時土上存。

Bow down, heaven's tyranny to undergo,
Quaff wine to face the world, and all its woe;
　　Your origin and end are both in earth,
But now you are *above* earth, not *below*!

其四百五十八

俗世玄機已識真，何教惶懼噬其身。莫期萬事屈君意，但向眼前歡樂陳。

譯箋：參看菲譯其四十九與其五十。

You know all secrets of this earthly sphere,
Why then remain a prey to empty fear?
　　You can not bend things to your will, but yet
Cheer up for the few moments you are here!

其四百五十九
無限風光醉眼中，瑤池泉沸碧蔥蘢。愁消荒野成仙界，天女行行樂不窮。

譯箋：瑤池泉，英譯原作 Kausars，考賽爾。參看其一百三十二譯箋。

Behold, where'er we turn our ravished eyes,
Sweet verdure springs, and crystal Kausars rise;
    And plains, once bare as hell, now smile as heaven:
Enjoy this heaven with maids of Paradise!

其四百六十
紅塵譎詐友難依，暗贈一言君勿疑。忍痛休尋解毒葯，煩愁莫使路人知。

Never in this false world on friends rely,
(I give this counsel confidentially),
    Put up with pain, and seek no antidote,
Endure your grief, and ask no sympathy!

其四百六十一
慧心獨運體羣經，殊美惟看二義明。禁食持齋勝饗餮，幽居強若聚朋行。

Of wisdom's dictates two are principal,
Surpassing all your lore traditional;
    Better to fast than eat of every meat,
Better to live alone than mate with all!

其四百六十二

青澀蒲桃熟轉甘，釀成味烈一杯啣。良材既斲湘靈瑟，白琯何能再削劋。

譯箋：《說文解字》："舜之時，西王母來獻其白琯。"

Why unripe grapes are sharp, prithee explain,
And then grow sweet, while wine is sharp again?
　　When one has carved a block into a lute,
Can he from that same block a pipe obtain?

其四百六十三

挑曙玄天銀練移，驚鴉淒切起哀思。忽看光染琉璃界，一夜浮生逝未知。

譯箋：英譯原注引《聖經・約伯記》第三十七章："爾能偕上帝展布穹蒼，堅如鑄鑒乎。"

When dawn doth silver the dark firmament,
Why shrills the bird of dawning his lament?
　　It is to show in dawn's bright looking-glass
How of thy careless life a night is spent.

其四百六十四

赤醪血艷溢深罌，世嫉能療請盡傾。何處得朋如此物，醇真不雜慰平生。

Cupbearer, come! from thy full-throated ewer

Pour blood-red wine, the world's despite to cure!
　　Where can I find another friend like wine,
So genuine, so solacing, so pure?

其四百六十五
常共聖賢相見歡，一麾或把指金鑾。但傾照世杯中酒，后羿終從墓草看。

譯箋：聖賢，原譯作 Aristo 厄辣斯托，當係指古希臘斯多噶派哲學家。照世杯，原譯作 Jemshid's goblet 賈姆什德之杯，后羿，原譯作 Bahram 巴赫拉姆，皆見前箋。

Though you should sit in sage Aristo's room,
Or rival Cæsar on his throne of Rūm,
　　Drain Jemshid's goblet, for your end's the tomb,
Yea, were you Bahram's self, your end's the tomb!

其四百六十六
偶入陶坊恍惚行，旋鈞但覩走營營。丐足君顱雜然沒，娉婷泥甍宛然生。

譯箋：《漢書・揚雄傳上》："羽騎營營，昈分殊事。"顏師古注："營營，周旋貌也。"○此譯折腰。○參看菲譯其三十八。

It chanced into a potter's shop I strayed,
He turned his wheel and deftly plied his trade,
　　And out of monarchs' heads, and beggars' feet,

Fair heads and handles for his pitchers made!

其四百六十七

真樸無知是有知，壚前但飲永生卮。除斯安得歸真樸，天下愚夫難悟之。

譯箋：《老子·第三章》："常使民無知、無欲，使夫智者不敢爲也。"又《老子·第十九章》："見素抱樸，少私寡欲，絶學無憂。"又《老子·第二十八章》："爲天下谷，常德乃足，復歸於樸。"又《老子·第三十七章》："化而欲作，吾將鎮之以無名之樸。"○英譯原注云意即玄幽真樸。

If you have sense, true senselessness attain,
And the Etern Cupbearer's goblet drain;
　　If not, true senselessness is not for you,
Not every fool true senselessness can gain!

其四百六十八

對酌圍罍消困酲，杯樽頻滿錯籌觥。攜卿他日鄧都去，同被陶人作酒罌。

譯箋：困酲，英譯原作 headache，頭痛。英譯原注謂頭痛暗指樂園之酒。林松譯《古蘭經韻譯》第五十六章："青春永葆的童僕仔伺候周旋，傳盞遞壺，滿杯醴泉，他們不會因它而頭痛，也不會爛醉暈眩。"

O Love! before you pass death's portal through,
And potters make their jugs of me and you,
　　Pour from this jug some wine, of headache void,

And fill your cup, and fill my goblet too!

其四百六十九
柔情似水蕩愁山，趁此良辰暫賦閑。但恐淵恩未能久，稍淋甘露即離還。

O Love! while yet you can, with tender art,
Lift sorrow's burden from your lover's heart;
　　Your wealth of graces will not always last,
But slip from your possession, and depart!

其四百七十
司命無情終一逢，但拼心力享塵中。信知彼岸無何有，去日惟攜雙手空。

Bestir thee, ere death's cup for thee shall flow,
And blows of ruthless fortune lay thee low;
　　Acquire some substance *here*, there is none *there*,
For those who thither empty-handed go!

其四百七十一
蟲沙猿鶴帝君搏，憎命洪鈞獨自旋。戴罪身由爾遷謫，不知造我竟何緣。

譯箋：《太平御覽》卷九六一引《抱朴子》：「周穆王南征，一軍盡化，君子爲猿爲鶴，小人爲蟲爲沙。」○洪鈞，參見溫譯其二十五譯箋。○參看菲譯其八十一。

Who framed the lots of quick and dead but Thou?
Who turns the troublous wheel of heaven but Thou?
　　Though we are sinful slaves, is it for Thee
To blame us? Who created us but Thou?

其四百七十二

汩汩瓊漿澆病骸，晶瑩幻若玉新裁。行人誤認儀狄降，敬問我從何處來。

譯箋：《呂氏春秋・勿躬》："儀狄作酒。"

O wine, most limpid, pure, and crystalline,
Would I could drench this silly frame of mine
　　With thee, that passers by might think 'twas thou,
And cry, "Whence comest thou, fair master wine?"

其四百七十三

上師恨與館娃逢，直詰荒淫似罪傭。女曰吾誠浪形跡，爾心豈若貌雍容。

譯箋：上師，原譯作 Shaikh，阿拉伯語尊稱，通譯謝赫，意即教長、族長或智者。

A Shaikh beheld a harlot, and quoth he,
"You seem a slave to drink and lechery";
　　And she made answer, "What I seem I am,
But, Master, are you all you seem to be?"

其四百七十四

須彌轉轂陋廬間，醉裡還同一芥看。欲質微軀換佳釀，酒家哂棄如泥丸。

譯箋：《維摩詰經》："若菩薩住是解脱者，以須彌之高廣内芥子中無所增減，須彌山王本相如故，而四天王、忉利諸天，不覺不知己之所入，唯應度者乃見須彌入芥子中，是名：不可思議解脱法門。"唐淨覺《楞伽師資記》："芥子入須彌，須彌入芥子也。"

If, like a ball, earth to my house were borne,
When drunk, I'd rate it at a barley-corn;
　　Last night they offered me in pawn for wine,
But the rude vintner laughed that pledge to scorn.

其四百七十五

聖容時隱白雲深，或現旻天萬國臨。獨造獨覩如獨戲，榮光獨賞至而今。

譯箋：參看菲譯其五十二。

Now in thick clouds Thy face Thou dost immerse,
And now display it in this universe;
　　Thou the spectator, Thou the spectacle,
Sole to Thyself Thy glories dost rehearse.

其四百七十六

抖擻精神共樂天，安居莫向大荒遷。慾繮情鎖安能戴，何若幽囚釋萬千。

Better to make one soul rejoice with glee,

Than plant a desert with a colony;

    Rather one freeman bind with chains of love,

Than set a thousand prisoned captives free!

其四百七十七

卿何但爲己歡愉，忍把憂瘝寄友于。卓智澄靈毀堪泣，咸將屠滅一何愚。

O thou who for thy pleasure dost impart

A pang of sorrow to thy fellow's heart,

    Go! mourn thy perished wit, and peace of mind,

Thyself hast slain them, like the fool thou art!

其四百七十八

倘有殷勤斗酒緣，不妨大噯暫成仙。吾抛悽愴君離肅，頓遣身魂縱九天。

Wherever you can get two maunds of wine,

Set to, and drink it like a libertine;

    Whoso acts thus will set his spirit free

From saintly airs like yours, and grief like mine.

其四百七十九
乾饟更有異香聞，斗酒羊肩誰與分。花罎茅廬相對坐，直堪糞土萬邦君。

譯箋：參看菲譯其十二。

So long as I possess two maunds of wine,
Bread of the flower of wheat, and mutton chine,
　　And you, O Tulip cheek, to share my hut,
Not every Sultan's lot can vie with mine.

其四百八十
幽居獨處競猜疑，鵲起聲名更毀訾。賢若由巢亦須記，人間不必覓相知。

譯箋：由巢，許由、巢父。英譯原作黑滋爾與易勒雅斯。詳參其二百八十五譯箋。

They call you wicked, if to fame you're known,
And an intriguer, if you live alone;
　　Trust me, though you were Khizr or Elias,
'Tis best to know none, and of none be known.

其四百八十一
呼朋攜酒樂花間，雖悔迷津難自還。洚水警予休絮説，但傾淥酒蕩身瘝。

譯箋：《孟子‧滕文公下》："《書》曰：'洚水警予。'洚水者，洪水也。"英譯作諾亞與洪水，典出《舊約》。

Yes! here am I with wine and feres again!
I did repent, but, ah! 'twas all in vain;
 Preach not to me of Noah and his flood,
But pour a flood of wine to drown my pain!

其四百八十二
同心擬結但空歎，孑立煢煢不自安。愁緒無憑與誰說，歡情苦痛恨奇難。

For union with my love I sigh in vain,
The pangs of absence I can scarce sustain,
 My grief I dare not tell to any friend;
O trouble strange, sweet passion, bitter pain!

其四百八十三
忽聽呼召集神宮，猶臥爐前曦始紅。肅穆虔祈時即至，莫相接耳貌宜恭。

譯箋：參看菲譯其三。

'Tis dawn! I hear the loud Muezzin's call,
And here am I before the vintner's hall;
 This is no time of piety. Be still!
And drop your talk and airs devotional!

其四百八十四

翼仙拂曙御風臨，奉爵擬邀同嘯吟。且唱雄王化塵土，年輪月轂碾駸駸。

譯箋：雄王，原文作 Jemshids and Khosraus 賈姆什德與霍斯勞之複數。○年輪月轂，原譯作從四月至十二月。○參看菲譯其九。

Angel of joyful foot! the dawn is nigh;
Pour wine, and lift your tuneful voice on high,
　　Sing how Jemshids and Khosraus bit the dust,
Whelmed by the rolling months, from Tir to Dai!

其四百八十五

饕餮安須蹙額顰，理須持正視同然。醉醒無別但長飲，入地永難重見天。

譯箋：林松譯《古蘭經韻譯》十六章："他們中有的人接受安拉的指引，有的人卻是頑固執迷，你們應該在大地上遊歷，去考察頑抗者是怎樣的結局。"

Frown not at revellers, I beg of thee,
For all thou keepest righteous company;
　　But drink, for, drink or no, 'tis all the same,
If doomed to hell, no heaven thou'lt ever see.

其四百八十六

願神重慮定坤乾，萬物一新呈目前。除我名於生死簿，直教跳脫奈何天。

譯箋：參看菲譯其九十八。

I wish that Allah would rebuild these skies,
And earth, and that at once, before my eyes,
　　And either 'rase my name from off his roll,
Or else relieve my dire necessities!

其四百八十七
願主一傾慷慨杯，更充豐廩粟成堆。仙漿令我狂歡醉，疾首渾然忘禍災。

Lord! make thy bounty's cup for me to flow,
And bread unbegged for day by day bestow;
　　Yea, with thy wine make me beside myself,
No more to feel the headache of my woe!

其四百八十八
或付熾心幽府焚，終須坐待焰雲熏。休教慈憫予真宰，誰學誰教有定分。

譯箋：英譯原注謂波斯文前言云，莪默死後曾向母託夢，並向她吟詠此章。

Omar! of burning heart, perchance to burn
In hell, and feed its bale-fires in thy turn,
　　Presume not to teach Allah clemency,
For who art thou to teach, or He to learn?

其四百八十九

運繫冥冥且莫愁，焉勞口舌與行修。明朝萬事皆前定，恩允何曾向爾求。

譯箋：英譯原注謂此章旨述預定論。〇參看菲譯其七十四。

Cheer up! your lot was settled yesterday!
Heedless of all that you might do or say,
　　Without so much as "By your leave" they fixed
Your lot for all the morrows yesterday!

其四百九十

去不由衷枉見招，來非所願亦無聊。一言可蔽君知否，生住去來宜毀銷。

譯箋：文理本《舊約·傳道書》第二章："我遂惡生，因於日下經營，乃爲煩惱，悉屬虛空，莫非捕風。"〇參看菲譯其三十。

I never would have come, had I been asked,
I would as lief not go, if I were asked,
　　And, to be short, I would annihilate
All coming, being, going, were I asked!

其四百九十一

魄化酒漿身化罍，靈爲鳴籟體爲笙。依君測度人何若，走馬幻燈心獨明。

Man is a cup, his soul the wine therein,

Flesh is a pipe, spirit the voice within;

    O Khayyam, have you fathomed what man is?

A magic lantern with a light therein!

其四百九十二
块圠無垠賤者全，良人質物易糧錢。炱炱微若優曇鉢，猶勝如斯湛湛天。

譯箋：块圠無垠，漢賈誼《鵩鳥賦》："大鈞播物兮，块圠無垠。"參看溫譯其二十五譯箋。○優曇鉢，梵語，無花果也。

O skyey wheel, all base men you supply

With baths, mills, and canals that run not dry,

    While good men have to pawn their goods for bread：

Pray, who would give a fig for such a sky?

其四百九十三
曾睹陶工妙手旋，澄泥零落出瑚璉。驀然回首凝眸處，初祖塵軀恣意搏。

譯箋：初祖，英譯原作 Adam，阿丹。○參看菲譯其三十八。

A potter at his work I chanced to see,

Pounding some earth and shreds of pottery;

    I looked with eyes of insight, and methought

'Twas Adam's dust with which he made so free!

其四百九十四

禍種俱教鎖篋中,侍兒諳曉我情衷。尋常一樣愁鄉月,才有杯觴便不同。

譯箋:宋杜耒《寒夜》詩:"尋常一樣窗前月,才有梅花便不同。"

The Saki knows my *genus properly*,
To all woe's *species* he holds a key;
    Whene'er my *mood* is sad he brings me wine,
And that makes all the *difference* to me!

其四百九十五

早知司命性乖張,毒螫相追無處藏。不愛良人愛浪子,豈因昏憒抑愚狂。

譯箋:《詩經‧大雅‧桑柔》:"維此良人,作爲式穀。"

Dame Fortune! all your acts and deeds confess
That you are foul oppression's votaress;
    You cherish bad men, and annoy the good;
Is this from dotage, or sheer foolishness?

其四百九十六

慾海沉淪何處邊,愴神銷骨度華年。心頭鎮壓千般事,終碎精魂化碧煙。

You, who in carnal lusts your time employ,
Wearing your precious spirit with annoy,

Know that these things you set your heart upon
Sooner or later must the soul destroy!

其四百九十七
曾從靈界受玄聞，萬類甄陶在一身。人獸仙魔此軀竝，含元體物幻耶真。

譯箋：英譯原注謂人即一小宇宙。○《後漢書・郅惲傳》載惲上書王莽曰："臣聞天地重其人，惜其物，故運機衡，垂日月，含元包一，甄陶品類，顯表紀世，圖錄豫設。"案荄默此章其萬物皆備於我之謂歟？

Hear from the spirit world this mystery;
Creation is summed up, O man, in thee;
　　Angel and demon, man and beast art thou,
Yea, thou *art* all thou dost *appear* to be!

其四百九十八
諾諾阿唯三教門，自能左右盡逢源。爾躬既得賢愚敬，縱有微瑕誰敢言。

譯箋：三教，按原譯指伊斯蘭教、基督教和猶太教三教中人。○刺鄉愿也。

If popularity you would ensue,
Speak well of Moslem, Christian, and Jew;
　　So shall you be esteemed of great and small,
And none will venture to speak ill of you.

其四百九十九

何事洪鈞轉九霄,萬般苦我未輕饒。壺漿須待奴顏乞,斗米教人竟折腰。

譯箋:洪鈞,見溫譯其二十五譯箋。○《晉書‧陶潛傳》:"吾不能爲五斗米折腰,拳拳事鄉里小人邪。"

O wheel of heaven, what have I done to you,
That you should thus annoy me? Tell me true;
   To get a drink I have to cringe and stoop,
And for my bread you make me beg and sue.

其五百

休沉苦海滯悲情,濁世脩姱自潔清。人物蕭條終代謝,宜拋塵慮一身輕。

譯箋:人,主觀之我。物,客觀之物。物我終泯於世間,而渾化於真宰,是爲蘇非之真境。○唐王勃《山中》詩:"長江悲已滯,萬里念將歸。"○戰國楚屈原《離騷》:"余雖好脩姱以鞿羈兮,謇朝誶而夕替。"洪興祖《楚辭補注》:"脩姱……謂脩潔而姱美也。"○唐孟浩然《與諸子登峴山》詩:"人事有代謝,往來成古今。"

No longer hug your grief and vain despair,
But in this unjust world be just and fair;
   And since the issue of the world is naught,
Think you are naught, and so shake off dull care!

圖書在版編目（CIP）數據

莪默絕句集譯箋/（古波斯）莪默・伽亞謨著；眭謙
譯箋. —上海：華東師範大學出版社，2016.3
ISBN 978-7-5675-5000-1

Ⅰ.①莪… Ⅱ.①莪… ②眭… Ⅲ.①詩集-波斯帝
國-中世紀 Ⅳ.①I373.22

中國版本圖書館 CIP 資料核字（2016）第 062891 號

莪默絕句集譯箋

原著者	［古波斯］莪默・伽亞謨
英譯者一	［英］愛德華・菲茨傑拉德
英譯者二	［英］愛德華・亨利・温菲爾德
漢譯及箋	眭　謙
責任編輯	龐　堅
封面題簽	章燕紫
裝幀設計	崔　楚

出版發行	華東師範大學出版社
社　　址	上海市中山北路 3663 號　郵編 200062
網　　址	www.ecnupress.com.cn
電　　話	021-60821666　行政傳真 021-62572105
客服電話	021-62865537　門市（郵購）電話 021-62869887
地　　址	上海市中山北路 3663 號華東師範大學校內先鋒路口
網　　店	http://hdsdcbs.tmall.com/
印刷者	浙江臨安市曙光印務有限公司
開　　本	890×1240　32 開
印　　張	10.25
插　　頁	4
字　　數	283 千字
版　　次	2016 年 7 月第 1 版
印　　次	2016 年 7 月第 1 次
書　　號	ISBN 978-7-5675-5000-1/I・1504
定　　價	36.00 元

出版人　王　焰

（如發現本版圖書有印訂質量問題，請寄回本社客服中心調換或電話 021-62865537 聯繫）